MADNESS

AN ALEX WATTS THRILLER

WESLEY CROSS

JOIN THE STORY

To receive free books, get behind-the-scenes stories, and be the first to hear about new releases—sign up for the newsletter.

See the back of the book for details.

PUBLISHER INFORMATION

This is a work of fiction. Names, characters, businesses, places, events, and incidents are either the product of the author's imagination or used in a fictitious manner. Any resemblance to actual persons, living or dead, or actual events is purely coincidental.

Published by
Cerberus Prints
New York

ONE

"Would you like to take a look at the dessert menu?" She flashed the group at the party table a wide smile and held out her hand with a stack of laminated cards.

"No, sweet Caroline from Carolina," the man at the top of the table said, giving her a wink and patting his flat stomach over a crisp white shirt. "I'm stuffed. We'll take the check."

The shift was going like gangbusters, one party after the next, all tipping well. But this was certainly going to be the crown jewel of the night. There were twelve of them, eight men and four women. All in their early thirties. All finance bros, judging by the way they talked and hollered, even the ladies. She was certain that nobody even glanced at the prices on the menu before placing orders.

The man in charge, Italian or Greek, judging by his olive complexion and jet-black hair stylishly slicked back with a touch of gel, seemed to take a liking to her. She flirted right back. He was too short for her taste, but his face was handsome—strong chin and prominent cheekbones. A pair of intense dark-brown eyes. The brooding type. She was young and single, and she was new to the city. And flirting was good for business.

"Right away, sir." She headed back to the computer station, putting an extra swing to her hips as she weaved between clients, waiters taking orders, and busboys cleaning a table for the next party.

"You're on fire today." Linda, her friend and a fellow waitress, gave her shoulder a friendly smack with a leather-bound check presenter. "Twenty bucks says he'll give you his number before he leaves."

"I don't know." She sneaked a peek at the man at the party table as she printed the check. He caught her eye and gave her yet another wink. "He's probably out of my league."

"Cluck, cluck, cluck." Linda jabbed her hands into her sides and flapped her elbows. Then she pulled a twenty-dollar bill out of her apron and slapped it on the shelf next to the register. "Don't be a chicken."

"Fine." Caroline pulled out a stack of bills and separated a twenty. She put it on top of Linda's and pressed it down with a sugar caddy. "You're on."

She grabbed the check and returned to the table, placing it beside the man's right hand. "Thank you."

"No, thank you, sweet Caroline, from Carolina." The man pulled out his credit card and stuck it into the presenter without looking at the bill. "Which Carolina are you from again?"

"South."

"South," he said, imitating her Southern drawl. "I love it. And only a month in the city?"

"Yes, sir. Five weeks."

"Look at you. Landed on your feet already. I like people with drive." He pulled out a business card and jotted a number on its back. "This is my cell. What do you say if I show you around the city sometime, Caroline?"

"I'll think about it," she said, taking the card and giving him a shy smile.

"Don't think too long."

Her cheeks grew hot, and she hurried back to the register station to run his credit card.

"Told ya," Linda said as the two twenty-dollar bills disappeared in her pocket. "You should give him yours, too."

"That's okay," she said. "I haven't decided if I'm going to go out with him yet."

"Let me tell you something." Linda put her hand on Caroline's shoulder. "This isn't a small town where you're the hottest dish on the menu. A guy like this... He's cute. He's got a lot of money. Girls are throwing themselves at men like him. It's cool to play hard to get. Gives you value. Just don't overdo it."

"I said I'll think about it."

"Sure thing. O'Reilly's tonight?" Linda asked, referring to the bar next door. She glanced at her wristwatch. "We'll be closing soon, anyway."

"Why not? It's Friday."

It was, indeed, Friday, and O'Reilly's, busy even on regular nights, was packed to the gills. It was a typical Irish pub. A hole in the wall with a circular bar in the middle of the darkly lit room tended by two women in black tank tops and leggings. Another two women shuttled the drinks from the bar to the row of two-seater tables by the back wall. A jukebox in the corner was blasting "Gimme Shelter" by the Rolling Stones.

Caroline and Linda pushed their way through the crowd and landed themselves at the sticky counter, squeezed between a man with a bright-yellow jacket of a city worker and a rambunctious group of twenty-somethings watching a game on a large flat-screen TV.

"Two margaritas. And start the tab, please," Linda shouted to the bartender over the music. She patted her hand on Caroline's shoulder. "She's paying."

"I am?"

"Sure you are. Your boyfriend's tip alone was two fifty. You killed it today."

"Fine." Caroline pulled a card from her wallet and handed it to the bartender. "Let's celebrate."

"Come on," Linda said, pushing the drink to her. "In one go. Bottoms up."

They clinked their glasses and downed the margaritas.

"Keep 'em coming," Caroline shouted to the bartender.

"So." Her friend leaned on the counter and tilted her head. "What's the big plan?"

"The big plan?"

"You know." Linda drew a wet circle on the bar with her empty glass. "After this. You're not planning to wait tables forever, are you?"

"No." Caroline thought about it for a moment. "I am not."

"What is it, then?"

"Fashion." She was already slightly buzzed, and she was enjoying herself. It was the first time she'd ever admitted her plan to anyone. It felt good. Liberating.

"Fashion? Like modeling and stuff? You sure your momma's gonna be all right with you swinging your hips, half-naked in front of strangers?"

She frowned as the images of a woman with sunken cheeks, drool running down her chin, flashed in her head. That's how she found her mother the night she decided to move out—sleeping in a muddy puddle in front of the trailer, her head on the first step of the porch.

"I'm just joking," Linda yelled.

"Not modeling." Caroline willed the images away. "High-fashion photography. I want to take pictures for a living."

"Oh." Her friend pulled away and studied her face, as if seeing it for the first time. "I like it. You should take some pictures of me then. I'll sell them when you're rich and famous."

"Deal. What about you?"

"I don't know yet." Her friend shrugged. "I'll figure it out. I always do."

A new round of drinks arrived, and Caroline was about to take her glass when a cold shiver ran down her spine. A touch of primal fear. She spun, looking around the bar, but saw nothing but a sea of faces. Smiling. Shouting. Drinking.

She scanned the crowd. There was something else. She could feel it. Her gaze stopped on a man, sitting at one of the two-seaters, his back to the bar. He was huge, his broad shoulders barely fitting between the closely spaced tables. He wore a gray hoodie wrapped around his muscular back like a cloak. She couldn't see his face. All she could see was the back of his head. Shoulder-length, platinum-blond hair. Caroline watched a waitress make her way to his table and take a credit card. She smiled and leaned over, as if trying to hear what the man had to say. Then the woman laughed, her head thrown back, her teeth gleaming in the light of overhead lamps.

"You okay?" Linda placed a hand on her arm, breaking the spell.

"Yeah." She picked up her glass and touched it to her friend's. "Not sure what came over me."

They left the bar when it was past two o'clock. Caroline looked around as she headed for the door, but the large man was gone, replaced by a pair of women.

"Taking a train?" her friend asked.

"Nah," she said, looking up and down the empty street. "At this hour, I'd walk home faster. I'll take a cab. Want to share?"

"You're going to Queens, and I'm going to Brooklyn. How's that going to work?"

"We'll go to Queens first, and then you'll go down to Brooklyn."

"I sometimes forget that you're not from around here." Linda patted her on the shoulder. "Good luck finding a driver willing to do that at this hour. They'll tell you they are going back to the base and kick you out."

"We won't tell him then." She smiled. "When we get to Queens, you'll say you changed your mind and need to go to Brooklyn."

"Evil." Her friend returned the smile. "I like it, but no. I'm off tomorrow. I'll stick with the subway. Save some money."

They hugged, and she watched Linda go down to the station at the corner of the street and disappear below the surface.

Caroline walked down a block and headed east. If she were to catch a taxi at this hour, she had to go with the flow. A few cars passed until she saw the brightly lit roof lights on top of the yellow cab swimming toward her two blocks away.

She stepped closer to the curb, ready to lift her hand, when somebody grabbed her from behind. A powerful arm wrapped around her chest, squeezing her in a vise-like grip as a hand shoved a wet, sweet-smelling rag into her face. She opened her mouth for a yell, but it never came. Her knees buckled, and then the darkness consumed her.

The sounds came back first. There was a ticking of a clock somewhere behind her, and an almost imperceptible hissing in long, well-defined intervals. Then there was a sensation of a light draft on her body. Every time she heard a hiss, she felt a gentle touch of cool air a moment later. Her skin was raised in goose bumps. *Why am I naked?* she thought with little interest.

Her head was heavy, the base of her skull hot and tender. She must have had one too many margaritas, she thought, trying to stay still. It'd go away as long as she didn't sit up too quickly. Not the first time.

She stirred, trying to turn, but couldn't. Her ankles hurt, and her wrists were tight. That was odd. She blinked and opened her eyes, craning her head and trying to look at her feet. The room remained pitch black, her eyelashes scratching against something soft.

She panicked, trying to reach for her face, as the last remnants of the fog cleared her mind, and that's when it dawned on her—she was bound, her body suspended upside down by her ankles, her wrists anchored to something below her. A wave of nausea washed over her as the images of the night flashed through her head. The dark corner of the street. The glowing lights of a cab two blocks away. And then the rapid drumbeat of footsteps behind her and the overwhelming panic as a wet, sweet-smelling rag was shoved into her face.

She screamed and thrashed, trying to break free, but her body barely moved, taut between two opposing forces. One pulling her up, another pulling her down.

"And now she awakens." The voice was low, purring like a big cat. Deliberate. "Don't struggle."

"Help!" she screamed, pulling on the restraints. "Somebody, help!"

"No one can hear you here." The purring voice returned, accompanied by a gentle touch to the skin of her thigh. The finger ran down her side until it stopped at her armpit. "Your skin is flawless. Perfect."

"Help! Somebody!" She bucked wildly. "Please!"

"I can't let you hurt yourself," the voice said.

She heard a few clicks, and the bonds pulled on her. Hard. She stopped moving, stretched like a string of a longbow. Straining for breath.

"Much better."

"Why can't I see?" she managed.

"I taped your eyes," the voice said. "Where you're going, you don't need to see anything. I want you to concentrate on how you feel. It's important that you pay attention to what you feel. Otherwise, you won't create a bridge. I want you to stay still now."

She felt a prick in the crook of her left elbow and cried out. A pitiful yelp of a frightened animal.

"This is just an adrenaline drip. To help you stay awake while I work."

A lightning bolt struck her arm, live heat running through her body in an instant, like a shock wave. She arched, gasping for air. Her heart raced so hard, she thought it was about to explode. Her skin, cold just a moment ago, was now damp and electrifyingly hot. Even the slightest movement of cool air was overwhelming.

"Good," the voice purred. "It's working."

"Stop," she begged. "Please. I've never seen your face. I won't tell anyone. Just let me go. You don't have to do this."

"But I do."

A cold, sharp object touched her stomach, just above her pubic bone. A blade.

That was all it was—the slightest of touches, and yet she could almost see the pain radiating from where the hard metal met her flesh. Pulsating. Like the circles from a stone thrown into the lake.

Caroline froze, unable to move a muscle.

"I'm sorry," the voice said. "It will hurt. But I won't become Him unless I collect them all."

She felt a push, and then there was nothing but pain.

TWO

"Alex, Alex, Alex, what the hell are you doing?" I heard him yell as I moved through the house at lightning speed, shoving his clothes, books, and stupid ship models into a laundry hamper.

"Please, can we talk about it?"

"Talk about what?" I stopped for a moment, looking at him in disbelief. His face was flushed, his cheeks glowing hot pink, but his boyish good looks weren't working on me today. "What do you want us to talk about?"

"I fucked up—"

"You think?" I cut him off before he could say anything else. "We have nothing to talk about."

"Honey." He reached out and grabbed my arm, trying to turn me around.

That was a mistake. My mind went blank, and before I could stop myself, my right fist connected with his nose.

Something cracked.

"What the fuck?" he wailed, awkwardly landing on his ass, holding his hands up. Blood was already running down his face, dripping on his white business shirt and skinny silver tie. "You're fucking crazy, you know that?"

I marched through the living room, dragging the hamper behind. Then, in one fluid motion, I opened the front door and flung the basket out. It rolled to the top of the stairs and balanced there for a split second, swaying under the bright April sun. But then, it slowly tipped over, model ships falling out of it and bumping down the granite steps toward the sidewalk, their delicate masts breaking on impact. An older couple looked up at me as they stepped around a banged-up replica of HMS *Victory* and continued down the street. I gave them a cheerful wave and turned to face my soon-to-be ex-boyfriend.

He slowly got up and walked to the door, wiping the blood off his face with the back of his hand. "You won't get away with this," he said as he stopped next to me, his index finger stabbing the air in front of my face. "I'll file charges."

I faked a jab, and he jerked back, slamming his head into the wall.

"Coward," I said. "Get out."

"She's ten times better than you in bed," he shouted as he walked out. "And at least she has tits!"

I slammed the door without bothering to answer, then went to the kitchen, poured a large glass of water, and downed it in one go. My hands were trembling.

There was some blood on my knuckles. I put my hand under the running water to wash it off. It stung, but the pain felt good.

"Asshole," I said out loud.

The truth was, the split was long overdue, and it probably wasn't his first infidelity either.

We had nothing in common. We met when I had to leave the NYPD two years ago. Since then, I worked as a PI, keeping the most unpredictable schedule and barely making enough money to pay the bills. He was a well-off banker, working long but otherwise normal hours. A classic fast-talking, hard-charging, adrenaline-chasing bad boy I fancied I could tame with some patience and time. The joke was on me, I guess.

I had to be honest with myself. Money had been a part of the equation, the reason I never tried to snoop around. I didn't pick him for his money, of course; I'm not that shallow. He was charming and smart and easy to look at. But who am I kidding? The Black American Express that popped out of his wallet like some magical jack-in-the-box every time I needed to pay for something surely didn't hurt.

There were moments when, deep in my gut, there was a nudge to ask him a question. Or ten. But I didn't. It was my version of the "don't ask, don't tell" policy.

However, it all changed when I came home after a shitty, two-week-long trip to Chester County in Pennsylvania. The trip was supposed to last three weeks, but I had to cut it short, which meant no bonus and smaller daily pay. The client, a wealthy Upper East Side woman, hired me to spy on her husband, who she claimed went to his farm in PA to visit his mistress.

"I'm sure he's doing all kinds of kinky stuff with her out there," she told me then. "He's a pervert, that's what he is, and I can't stand him. Goes there almost every month. And it's never a day or two. It's always at least a week."

I suppressed the urge to say, "And I can't stand him," in the squeakiest, most annoying voice I could muster, and simply nodded along.

"Just checking on my farm, darling," she said in a mocking baritone, presumably imitating her husband. "Yeah, right. Like I'm one of his gullible whores from the country. I know what he's doing. He's trying to get away from me."

She wanted a divorce, but with a prenup, she could only take him to the cleaners if he cheated, and that's where I came in. In my experience, the jealous types were usually the cheaters themselves, but what did I care? I'm here for the money, not to pass judgment.

I negotiated a generous three-week pay, two weeks in advance, and a sizable bonus when I returned with the goods. Unfortunately, being a PI, you quickly learn that bonuses are like slimy eels in the muddy pond—you rarely see them, and catching them is harder still.

I spent the next two weeks trudging through dirt, jumping electric fences, and freezing my behind in the woods. But the only possible mistress candidates for the man I could find were his cows, pigs, and his neighbor Gary. Together, the two men smoked cigars almost every other day, drank Scotch, and commiserated about baseball. The guy was trying to get away from his wife, all right, just not for the reasons she told me.

I could, of course, stick around for another week to collect the rest of the money, but I was too cold, tired, and dirty, and all I could think of was a hot shower and my own mattress. Besides, considering the mission was a fiasco, I wasn't sure that last week's pay would materialize. In retrospect, freezing for another week in the woods might have been healthier for my psyche than going home.

The house was a mess. I owned a two-story townhouse in a historic neighborhood of Bay Ridge in Brooklyn, and no, I didn't buy it with the fortune I've earned in my PI business. There are some perks of being a third-generation Brooklynite. When my grandfather bought it, he paid a cool thirty grand for it, and it stayed in the family ever since. Tina, my older sister, should have gotten the house, but Tina, well... Let's just say there were people who did well in life, and there was Tina. But I won't be looking a gift horse in the mouth, or in my case, a gift house with a crumbling pink stucco, no parking space, and tiny windows that hadn't been changed since the 1950s.

Don't get me wrong, I'm not a neat freak. Whatever genes are responsible for that trait were taken up by my sister. Anything left over is usually enough to keep the place organized, but it's not a museum. So, when I say the house was a mess, I don't mean his shoes were by the door rather than in the closet. I mean two weeks' worth of dirty dishes in the kitchen sink and clutter all over the first floor. Empty bottles and paper plates. I didn't need to be a detective to figure out someone had a few wild parties while I was freezing my ass in the woods.

I'm not sure what came over me at that point. But instead of taking a hot shower and staking a place on the couch in front of the TV, I put my travel bag down and started to clean. The kitchen was first, and after that, I was on autopilot—dust, vacuum, mop, and move on to the next room. Dust, vacuum, mop. I did the living room first, then the dining, and then moved on to the master bedroom.

That's where things went off the rails. As I moved the chair to vacuum, there it was—a crotchless pink thong that rendered any logical calculus meaningless. I'm not a prude. You can find some fun things in my closet, and if you know me really well, I might even show you a small box I keep at the bottom of my dresser. But that particular article of clothing wasn't mine. It was one thing to turn a blind eye to something that may or may not have happened elsewhere. But there wouldn't be any hanky-panky in my own place, in my own bed, that didn't include me.

I heard the door open just as I picked up the panties with a hanger hook, holding them like a venomous snake as far away from my body as possible.

"Honey? Are you already home?" There was fear in his voice even before he made it to the bedroom.

"Fuck you," I said in return and walked past him to the kitchen to dispose of the evidence of his crime. Then I kicked him out of the house.

I took a long shower afterward, getting the jitters out. After that, I threw on a robe and tried some daytime television, but there was nothing worth watching. I flipped through some channels and stayed on the news station for a minute. A tall, handsome weatherman was talking about a possible cold front coming down from the north in the next few weeks. A pity. The weather had been gorgeous for the past few days. Then commercials took over, and I switched the TV off, went to my desk, and started the laptop.

I could use a good case. Something to take my mind off things. Something that paid well and lasted for some time, like a surveillance operation.

Suspicious spouses were good, but attorneys were the best. My greatest payday ever came from a case where I'd been hired by a law firm to spy on somebody suspected of wire fraud. Easy money.

The laptop chimed as it turned on, and I perked up, looking at a new email in the inbox. There was one message from an email address with a last name and ESQ at the end. An attorney. It seemed that the gods did occasionally smile on me, after all.

I scanned the text. It seemed straightforward. There was a bank robbery a couple of weeks back. It was an embarrassing case that was all over the news. A local bank recently opened to much fanfare, lost power on a Friday night, and stayed that way for two days. Their backup generator never kicked in, and the alarm never went off. A small-time gang from the neighborhood took notice and broke in, but to their apparent dismay, there was almost no cash at the branch. They took twenty-three safe deposit boxes, but the press speculated they might have also been empty. The lack of vigor in the police response seemed to confirm that, too.

But it looked like at least one of the boxes must have contained something valuable. Somebody went to the trouble of hiring Ezekiel Morton, Esq., and tasked him to find a PI to track down and return the box to him. Or her. But probably him. In my experience, safe deposit owners were almost exclusively men. I scrolled down to the signature line and punched the number into my phone.

"Mr. Morton's office."

"This is Alex Watts," I said. "He'd be expecting me."

"One moment, please."

There was a brief silence, and then a male voice answered. "This is Morton."

He sounded confident and fat. I could picture him sitting in a huge tufted brown leather chair, his thick fingers squeezing the plastic of the phone. Multiple chins rolled over the collar of his shirt, jiggling every time he uttered a syllable.

"Alex Watts," I said for the second time. "You sent me an email."

"Prompt," he said. "I like it."

"Gotta make hay when the sun is shining."

"I assume you'll be taking the case?"

"Maybe," I said. "Can you tell me who the client is and what's in the box?"

He chuckled. I pictured the rolling fat on his belly as he did, like a giant wave going under the surface of his bulging shirt. "I'm afraid not. Attorney-client privilege. You know how it is."

"I've heard. But I doubt the guys who picked them up have. Or that they're planning to keep those boxes intact. Let's just get clear about what I'm looking for, and it's not going to be the boxes. They opened them the same day they took them from the bank."

He stayed silent for some time, mulling it over, my imagination painting a picture of stubby fingers pinching the jiggly flesh under his chin.

"Give me some solid leads," he finally said. "If you have something concrete, I'll bring it to my client, and we'll take it from there."

"Fine. As for my ongoing rate—"

"My client will pay you a ten-thousand-dollar deposit plus two fifty per day for expenses for the first two weeks," he said, cutting me off. "Another twenty-five thousand when you return the contents of the box. Would that be sufficient?"

"That sounds reasonable," I said, playing it cool. That wasn't reasonable. That was way higher than my usual rates.

"Great." There was a smacking sound in the background, as if he clapped his meaty hand on the table. "I'll have my assistant send you the docs. Everything's electronic. Sign it, and we'll wire you the deposit."

"Lawyers," I said after the line disconnected. "Easy money."

THREE

The tunnel was quiet. John Levy stepped past the yellow line and balanced at the platform's edge, dangerously leaning into the void as he peered into the darkness. Standing like that, he could see the dim lights of the Cortland Street subway station. There was no train in sight, and he stepped back, fixing the strap of his backpack over his shoulder.

"You've missed it. Just left," a woman's voice said behind him. "It's probably going to be a while at this hour."

"Lucky us." He turned around and politely smiled. He hadn't noticed her when he arrived at the platform, but there she was, standing by the wall between a bench and a vandalized poster of a rom-com movie hanging there since Valentine's Day. She was in her early forties, if he had to guess, a professional type. A nice, off-the-rack suit. Sensible shoes. A beige satin blouse with a V cut deep enough to intrigue without being too provocative. She smiled back at him when he met her eyes. Her cheeks had slight dimples that gave her a mischievous look. "I thought I heard it leaving as I was walking over, but wasn't sure if it was this line."

"Didn't realize it was already past eight," she said, glancing at her watch as if apologizing. "Tax season. At least it's Friday. But I'll probably have to work over the weekend anyway."

"An accountant?"

"Guilty." She took a few steps forward until she stood before him and offered a hand. "The name's Lilly."

"John." Her hand was small, but her handshake was warm and strong. Standing this close, he could smell her perfume. A light, elegant blend. Spring notes with a touch of lilac and jasmine. Before he could stop himself, his eyes drifted along the contour of her blouse, but she didn't seem to mind.

"What about you?"

"Pardon me?"

"What do you do for a living?"

"Oh. I'm a writer, um—" He caught himself and chuckled. "At least when I'm off the clock. I work at a call center during the day."

"Pays the bills while you're paving the road to fame and riches?" Her words teased, but in a non-threatening, good-natured way, and he smiled in response.

"Something like that. I think I can hear the train. Shocking."

They stood quietly for a moment, listening as the low, rumbling noise grew louder. A draft of stale, warm air pushed out of the tunnel, spinning candy wrappers and loose newspapers on the platform. A few seconds later, the screeching hit a crescendo, and John covered his ears as the train rolled into the station. After what seemed an eternity, it stopped, the doors hissing as they opened.

"I guess we are lucky," she said.

"Pardon?"

"You said we were lucky for missing the train."

"Oh yes, I did." He looked around the empty car and took a seat at the end of a long three-seater bench.

"Do you mind?" She gestured at the spot beside him.

"Not at all." He watched her in surprise as she took the seat. He'd planned to write on his trip home, his old laptop perched on top of a worn-out Eddie Bauer backpack. Most of the writing he had done so far was during his commute. More in the morning while his mind was still fresh. Some nights were productive, too, but his heart wasn't in it tonight.

"Tell me," she said. "What do you write? Any books that I'd know?"

"No, this is my first. Though sometimes I like to fantasize how I'd be on a subway and somebody would be sitting across, reading my book, and they'd have no idea I was there." He was suddenly embarrassed. "Not quite sure why I'm telling you this."

"That's quite all right. It sounds like a worthy dream."

"Thanks. I have this interesting story in my head, and I haven't read anything similar, but of course, every writer thinks that way."

"Do tell," she said. "If you don't mind giving away the plot."

For a moment, there seemed to be a halo around her head. A glow, a weird play of light. John tilted his head slightly and blinked. It disappeared.

"Well," he said, "it's a mystery novel. I've outlined most of the story already. About three-quarters, maybe more. I also wrote a bunch of scenes that I think will be useful in the book. And now I'm starting to write the whole thing down. Got a few chapters so far. There's this guy, Luca. A very elusive serial killer. He's on a rampage, but he's smart, and the police are struggling to catch up. There's also a PI who has a connection to the killer. Initially, the cops even suspected the PI could be the murderer, but he's able to clear his name. Eventually, it turns out he was the key to catching the killer."

"Sounds interesting," she said. "Scary."

"Thanks."

"Why is he doing it?"

"Who? The private eye?"

"No. The killer. Why is he killing his victims? You said the story is unique. So far, you haven't told me what makes it unlike any other serial killer mystery. I'm not trying to be a critic." She gave him a reassuring smile. "I'm just curious. Do you know how, in *The Silence of the Lambs*, the killer wants to transform into a woman? That was his motivation. What's Luca's?"

John pondered the question for a moment. Part of him wanted to tell her the story. What excited him about the twists and turns of the plot he'd worked on for the last two years. How he was planning to trap his main character into a seemingly inescapable position before letting him concoct a brilliant way out. Another part of him, he suddenly realized, couldn't care about any of that. All he wanted to do was to bring this woman home. It was a strange feeling. It was raw and primal, but also there was this connection. An unexplainable invisible bridge between them that he wanted to walk across.

"He's found an ancient book," he said, trying to shake off the feeling. "At first, he thinks nothing of it. A curiosity. A cool thing to show to his friends. Like an old-school collectible car. But as time passes, he feels this pull by the book, which eventually consumes him and drives him mad."

"What's the book about?"

"The first part of the book describes the princes of demons. Four higher princes and eight lower princes. The book's second part is a manual on acquiring them all."

"What does that mean?" she asked. "Summoning demons and turning them into his servants?"

"No, not turning them into slaves. Possessing them. Absorbing their powers. The book claims that those spirits use certain people as vessels for travel. Without them even being aware of their presence. And it teaches the reader how to find those people and trap the demons."

"And Luca learns that skill, I take it?"

"Yes," he said. "Luca's skeptical at first, but eventually, he comes to believe that the book is real and that by finding a vessel person and ritualistically killing them, he can open a portal. And once it opens, he can collect the demon's spirit. Absorb the demon into his soul. He needs to collect the spirits of the lower princes first and then consume the four higher demons."

"Sounds like he's got issues," she said, laughing. Her eyes were a deep brown, almost black.

Looking at her closely now, John realized she was much more beautiful than he'd first thought. Her symmetrical features made her face look like an exquisite work of art, an ancient statue.

"It might sound like a dumb question, but do demons have spirits?"

"It's more complicated than that," John said. "I've done a lot of research on this, but I'm still not an authority on the subject. From what I understand, however, demons are spirits."

"Interesting. But why does he want to collect them?"

"Luca believes that when God cast Lucifer to Hell, the rebellious archangel didn't survive the fall and shattered into pieces. And those pieces eventually became spirits of their own. An antithesis to the Holy Trinity. The unholy dozen, if you will. And Luca thinks that if he collected all twelve spirits, he would become Lucifer, the highest of angels, as he was before he was cast to Hell. And in his new form, he will be even stronger than the original incarnation. Perhaps even powerful enough to challenge God himself."

"Not your regular serial killer book, then? I do like the paranormal angle. Wait." She reached out and touched his forearm. "Is there a paranormal angle, or is he just crazy?"

"I'd say you'd have to read the book to find out," he said, laughing.

"You are a tease," she said, smiling back, looking him up and down. "I just might. What are you going to call your book?"

"I haven't decided yet. But the working title is *Madness*. Makes you wonder. Is it the killer who is mad, or is the world going to descend into madness if the killer is not crazy and manages to become Lucifer himself?"

"I like it." She took her hand back, but the warmth of her touch lingered.

"To be frank," he said, "I haven't decided if there will be a paranormal element. Or how it ends."

"That's why you've only outlined three-quarters of the story?"

"Right." He sighed. "It needs a satisfying resolution to make the readers happy. That much is obvious. I just need to figure out if it's more dramatic when the killer is caught at the end of the book or if, against all odds, he outsmarts everybody and gets away with murder? I went back and forth and decided that if I just start writing the chapters, when I get to that point, the story will tell me which way to go."

"I love it," she said. "I'd definitely read it."

"Tell me if I'm out of line," John said before he could stop himself, "but would you like to have a drink with me?"

"It is Friday, I guess." She paused, a mischievous look on her face. "But before I say yes, I gotta ask."

"What?"

"I'm not going to wake up on an altar, surrounded with demonic symbols, while you're standing there with a ceremonial knife, ready to sacrifice me to Lucifer?"

John laughed as he admired her profile, the way the smile wrinkled her nose. She was way out of his league. "I'm not writing an autobiography. I promise I'll be a perfect gentleman."

Her stop was just before his, and they ended up in a German bar they both frequented. It was natural. The conversation flowed on its own, and before their third round had arrived, their lips were locked, their tongues dancing.

He dropped a few bills on the table, and they left the bar before the next round of drinks arrived. The cool night air took things down a notch. For a moment, they shared an awkward silence as they strolled down Third Avenue heading to his place, looking at the lights of the Verrazzano Bridge looming over the buildings. But then her hand found his, and they were kissing again, and the rest of the world became blurry.

"Come on in," John said as he unlocked the door. His apartment was on the second floor of the building, its windows facing a small courtyard with a large magnolia tree and two benches under it, usually occupied during the day by a group of older ladies. At this hour, the area was empty, and the blossoming tree, lit by four blue spotlights, made the yard look majestic. Otherworldly.

But then Lilly was on him, and he forgot about the view. He first took her in the foyer before they even had a chance to remove their shoes. Then, leaving a trail of articles of clothing, they made their way to the kitchen table.

He panicked for a brief moment, as he thought he'd left a pack of antidepressants out, but the bright-orange box was nowhere to be seen, and then another moment later, it didn't matter anymore.

They were finally naked when they made it to the bedroom, and, this time, he took it slow, exploring her body inch by inch until neither of them had any strength left.

They laid on the bed for a long time afterward, her head on his shoulder, her hand playing with his chest hair and tracing elaborate shapes on his skin. Neither talked, but it was a comfortable silence of life-long partners who didn't have to say things to fill the air with sounds.

"It was nice," she finally said. "But I should probably get going. Mornings tend to be harsh fellows after nights of passion."

"Stay," he asked, caressing the back of her head. "I'll make us eggs with bacon and brew the best coffee you've ever had."

"Those are some pretty big promises." She sounded tired. Sleepy. "You sure you won't regret this in the morning?"

"I am sure," he said. "Don't go. You're safe here."

As he held her, John watched her drift to sleep. He stayed motionless, listening to her soft breathing, soaking up the warmth radiating from her body. He wanted to stay like this forever, holding her tight, basking in her smell. Finally, as his eyelids grew heavy, he closed his eyes and let himself go.

FOUR

I slowed the car down to a crawl, prompting an angry honk from a Mercedes van behind me. I ignored it, rolled over the curb to climb on a cobblestone patch separating Third Avenue and a service road, and parked.

Technically, you're not supposed to park between the support beams holding up the Belt Parkway over the road. However, people still do, and the cops won't bother you as long as nothing is happening in the area. Since I was planning to stay in the car the entire time, the worst thing that could happen to me would be somebody telling me to move. I liked those odds.

Morton paid me, just as he'd promised. The moment I got off the call with the lawyer, my cell phone pinged with a new message. There was an electronic questionnaire, and once I signed the disclosure, my phone pinged again. It was the same sound, but I could've sworn it sounded happier than the first as it announced that my bank account got fatter by thirteen and a half thousand dollars. The money didn't come from Morton's office but rather from a numbered account with no name attached to it. While unusual, it wasn't particularly surprising. I've seen lawyers jump through all kinds of hoops to keep their clients' identities secret.

Since Morton kept his side of the bargain, I was trying to uphold mine.

I was in Sunset Park, a blue-collar neighborhood and home to a large Mexican diaspora, squeezed between pretending-to-be posh Bay Ridge and snooty Prospect Park. It was just after eight in the morning, and it was already bright and hot, even in the shadow of the overpass. Whatever cold front the handsome weatherman had predicted didn't seem to be materializing. I envied his job. He could promise a fifty percent chance of rain and still collect one hundred percent of his salary. I lowered the seat, cracked the passenger window open, letting some breeze in, and relaxed, watching the intersection before me.

As I started digging for the traces of safe deposit boxes, I began spending Morton's money. Working as a PI is not that much different from being an undercover cop. You make every effort to blend in. You develop a network of informants. You try to make friends with local movers and shakers.

Pretty much like in the old days when I ran around in an unmarked police car with a detective's badge on my belt. Except now, I don't get medical, pension, overtime, or paid leave. I also can't call for backup if things get hairy. You get the idea. At least, as a former cop, I get to carry a gun. Otherwise, it'd be easier to become a mayor while openly working as a call girl than to get a license to carry in this city.

On the plus side, I'm free to waste my time and money as I see fit, pursuing the leads without the approvals of senior commanders and budget considerations, and that's exactly what I was doing. Last night, I paid a visit to one of my informants. Pete was a skinny thirty-something with a penchant for bursts of violence. He always dressed in a pair of worn-out jeans and a leather jacket regardless of the season. Pete was a permanent fixture on a few corners in Sunset Park as he dealt in ecstasy and other happy pills and occasionally ran courier jobs for Diablitos. Little Devils had been founded in the early 2000s by some runaway elements of the infamous Los Zetas, who eventually made their way into the land of the free and settled on the East Coast.

Diablitos was nothing but a shadow of the fearsome cartel its founders had come from. But nobody in their right mind would want to mess with them. Unless, of course, you were a PI with an urgent need to pay the bills.

Pete told me he'd heard about the bank run, though he wasn't sure about the details. Usually, I take such declarations from him with a pound of salt, as Pete was never sure about any details until you lubricated his cognitive abilities with a few dollar bills. But this time, he was genuinely hazy on specifics. The only bit of useful information I could extract from him was that Rico and Lopez, two low-level gang members, were at the scene. They were roommates and worked a night shift at a body shop off Third Avenue in Sunset Park.

Unbeknownst to Pete, this was as good of a lead as any. I'd never heard of Rico or Lopez before this. Still, after some digging, I learned that they were often tasked with unloading stolen merchandise that didn't have much value. If the safe deposit boxes were as much of a dud as everyone was describing, there was a good chance the two were in possession of at least some of them. I had no idea what hole they called home, but all I needed to do was wait for them to get out of the shop and follow them.

Contrary to what you see in the movies when two grizzly policemen exchange zingers as they sit in a firehouse-red Mustang, puff Cubans, and watch a smoking-hot blonde changing through the half-drawn curtains of her Malibu house, stakeout is usually an incredibly dull affair. Not to mention challenging for a single operator like myself. As a cop, you get a partner where you can take turns watching the scene, taking naps, or answering nature's calls. When by yourself, there's no one to watch your back. And don't even start me on bathroom breaks.

And, of course, no detective would ever be caught dead in a

flashy car while on the job. I drive a gray two-year-old Toyota Corolla, one of America's most popular cars. That makes me practically invisible.

While I hate them, stakeouts are invaluable in any detective's work. Finding guys like Rico and Lopez isn't as straightforward as finding John Smith, who has a regular job, pays taxes, and owns some property. These days, you can trace most people with or without a heartbeat within minutes as long as they've got a Social Security number. But not people like these two. Guys like that work for cash, own no tangibles, crossed into the country on foot, and aren't registered in any database. They use fake IDs and Social Security numbers; for all I know, their real names might not even be Rico and Lopez. So, there I was, watching the one-way street coming out of the cul-de-sac with the repair shop and waiting for the pair to show up.

As luck would have it, a local cop showed up first. I saw him across the street coming from a coffee shop by the service road, a sweaty iced drink in his hand. His peaked hat was raised high over his pale forehead, letting it breathe in the hot spring morning. He seemed young, barely out of the academy, with steely-gray eyes and blond fuzz on his cheeks. He turned to the sidewalk first, his gaze briefly pausing on my car as he took a few steps heading north. Then he stopped and turned to take another look at me.

Well, shit.

I watched him cross the street and approach my car. He stopped about five feet from the vehicle and made a spinning gesture, pointing at my window.

"What can I do for you, officer?" I asked, rolling the window all the way down.

"You can't park here, ma'am."

"Oh, I'm sorry about that." I gave him my most charming smile. "I didn't realize that. Just waiting for somebody, that's all. I'll be moving in no time."

"You can't park here," he said again and pointed to a sign

attached to one of the support beams. He was still smiling but only with his mouth. Those steely-gray eyes took on a hard quality.

Damn rookies, I thought. *Never know when to quit.*

"Listen, Officer Simmons," I said, reading his name off a silver tag. "I'm a PI, and I'm on a case. I used to be a policewoman, just like you. A detective, as a matter of fact. Can you do me a solid and let me stay here for another ten, perhaps twenty minutes? And then I'll be out of your hair."

He leaned closer, the friendly look completely disappearing from his face. "Listen to me, *used to be a policewoman*. You can't park here. You said you are a PI. Do you have any weapons on you?"

"Not at the moment, no."

"License and registration, please."

"Are you kidding me?"

"License and registration," he repeated robotically, his eyes shooting daggers.

I took the license from my wallet and fished the registration from the mess in my glove compartment.

He studied them for a few seconds and handed them back to me. "Please move your vehicle, ma'am. I'll give you ten seconds before this becomes a bigger issue."

"Fine. I'll go." I stuck the license back in the wallet and reached over the central console toward the glove box when the registration slipped from my fingers and flew under the passenger seat. I cursed as I dug under it, but my fingers found nothing but the bumpy surface of the rubber mat. I'd have to deal with this later. I raised my chair, pressed the brake pedal, and started the engine. "Can a former detective give you a friendly piece of advice, Officer Simmons?"

"What's that? Five seconds left."

"Learn to pick your battles."

"Three, two..."

I put the car into drive and climbed off the cobblestone patch. As I did, an old working van rolled out of the cul-de-sac, blew through a stop sign, and took off heading north. I caught a glimpse of Rico behind the wheel and roared after him.

The van turned east on the next corner and then north again once it hit Fourth Avenue and picked up speed. I stayed a few cars behind, following the vehicle, and a few minutes later, it slowed down and took another right turn.

I followed, and as the van pulled into the driveway of a small two-story house with dirty beige siding between a youth center and a barber shop, I kept going. When the van was out of my direct line of sight, I pulled up next to a hydrant, got out, and headed back on foot.

By the time I got near the house, the vehicle was empty, and neither Rico nor Lopez were anywhere to be seen. The van was a beat-up Ford Econoline that used to be white at some point in its life. Most of it, including the side windows, was now covered in graffiti. I glanced around as I approached the ugly beast and then peeked into the car. The inside of the van was a mess. There were boxes with tools and rolls of copper wire, and the entire floor was littered with burger wrappers from a local fast-food joint. But what caught my attention was a small, carefully arranged pile in the corner covered by a tarp held in place by another roll of wire. By the looks of it, the items under the cover had rectangular shapes. Like boxes.

"Que pasa, chica?"

I spun around, startled by the voice. Rico was standing at the end of the driveway, watching me. He was a short, chubby man in his late twenties. He wore a pair of old dirty jeans and a simple white T-shirt. Thick, black hair was buzzed on top and shaved on the sides of his large, squarish head. Surprisingly, I saw no tattoos—at least, no visible ink. His eyes, under the bushy eyebrows, watched me closely. Rico had the bulging, beady eyes of a dead rat. I didn't like them one bit. He may have been at the bottom of a totem pole of the Diablitos gang, but this man had killed before. I had no doubt about that.

"Oh hey, you startled me." I gave him a nervous laugh that didn't require much faking. "I'm not snooping or anything, but I saw your van and was wondering if you're possibly interested in selling it. See, my cousin and I want to start a business together, but we can't afford a new vehicle, and I saw yours and thought it'd be perfect for what we need it for. We'd give you a good price."

He gave me the smallest of smiles as if to show he saw straight through my bullshit. "Not for sale, chica."

"Okay," I said, backing away from the van. "It's too bad. I guess we'll keep on looking. You have a good day."

"Don't come here anymore, chica," he said in a quiet voice, still smiling. "You're too pretty for this neighborhood. It'd be a shame if something happened to you."

I backed out onto the street, turned around, and started walking away, throwing glances over my shoulder to make sure Rico wasn't following me. As I did, another tall and gangly man came out of the house's side door and stood there next to my dear friend, Rico. Lopez was also dressed in a pair of old jeans and a simple white T-shirt. I wanted to make a snarky mental note about their uniform but failed. The boxes were in that van under the tarp, I was sure of it, and for whatever reason, they weren't even opened yet. But now I blew it. Now that Rico and Lopez knew somebody was interested in their contents, they were going to move the boxes somewhere else. After that, it might not be possible to find them. But I still had a shot. I'd just need to break into the house of a man with the eyes of a dead rat and steal the merchandise from him.

When I got back to the car, I pulled out my cell phone and dialed Morton. Before I broke into anyone's house, I needed to know what I was looking for.

FIVE

When John opened his eyes, the sun had already climbed halfway to its zenith. The bright light filtering through the peach-colored tulle swaying in front of the window filled the air with a soft, subtle glow.

He lay still for a few moments, watching the dust motes dance in the rays of light, his mind pleasantly blank, hoping he'd drift back to sleep. It seemed, however, that Morpheus had already packed up and left, and John blinked, rubbed his eyes, and stretched.

A slight headache was building in the back of his skull, but nothing a cup of coffee couldn't fix. He rolled to the side and gingerly sat up, moving the blanket away. He gazed vacantly at himself for a moment, wondering why he wasn't wearing any underwear.

Then it hit him. The image of Lilly riding him hard, her thighs squeezing his sides, her perfectly round breasts bouncing up and down with every move. Her head was thrown back, her skin slick with sweat. He shook his head and spun around, expecting to see her laughing at him, acting weird and lost, but the bed was empty.

"Hello?" he called out. "Lilly? You here?"

There was no answer, and he got up, started walking toward the bathroom, and then, suddenly ashamed of his nakedness, came back and put on a pair of boxers and a T-shirt.

The shower was empty, and so was the kitchen.

"Damn," he said out loud as he looked at the bright-orange box with bold white letters on its side in the middle of the round table. He poured a glass of water, took a small blue pill out of the container, and popped it into his mouth, wondering if Lilly had noticed the anti-depressants.

He wandered around the place, picking up the trail of his clothes that led from the front door all the way to the bedroom. There were no traces of anyone else, and if not for the scratches on his back, he might've doubted something had happened at all. He turned around a few times, making sure he didn't miss anything, and winced as a sharp pain flashed behind his eyes. He needed some caffeine.

A few minutes later, the old drip machine was spitting hot brown liquid into his cup, and John was digging into a piece of hot toast with a thin layer of butter. The headache disappeared halfway through the second cup.

He took his favorite spot on a worn-out loveseat, facing the back-yard with the magnolia tree, and opened the manuscript on his laptop. Lately, Saturdays had been his most productive days. Sunday was still ahead, the buffer between him and the madness of the new work week. The wealthy whining widows claiming the insurance of their dead husbands couldn't touch him now.

He smiled as he scrolled to the end of the file. Forty-nine pages. It still wasn't much, but it no longer felt as daunting as when he had first opened a new document, staring at the large empty space on the screen, petrified of hitting the first key.

Writing a novel wasn't much different from running a marathon. He did it once, many years ago. Despite all the training before the race, as he stood with his group watching the mighty span of the Verrazzano Bridge, clutching the competition number on the front of his shirt, the task ahead of him seemed all but impossible. Surely, no human could walk—let alone run—for over twenty-six miles. But then he took the first step and then another. Before he knew it, he was already in Brooklyn, running through familiar streets, the crowds lining up the sidewalks, cheering him on with shouts, music, and the rhythmic clanking of the iconic cowbell. Now, as he looked at the lines of text on the screen, he felt the same rush as he did during the race. It was no longer an impossible task. A fantasy conjured up in a moment of fancy, ready to shatter when it met the unforgiving reality. On the contrary, it was impossible for him not to finish it.

His fingers hovered over the keyboard for a few moments and then started their dance.

Luca opened the drawer and took out his journal. The soft leather felt good in his hands, and he spent a few moments admiring it, tracing his fingers around its edges. Even without opening it, he could see the progress he'd made. The pages he'd used to meticulously document each ritual were thicker than the rest. They were swollen with ink, their edges wavy, moving as he turned the journal around. Alive.

Luca opened the book and took out his gold-coated Montblanc. He'd used this pen for the last twenty years. It was more than a pen. It had character. It demanded precision. He knew every scratch and dent upon its surface. His thumb traced a long scrape on one side. It happened after Luca had consumed the first spirit.

John stopped typing and closed his eyes. There was an image of Lilly's face close to his. Her lips parted, eyes sparkling. He shook his head, trying to get it out of his mind, but all he could see was the dark outline of her body against the window. He opened his eyes, staring at the document for a moment, and then gave in, closing the laptop. He put it aside, got up, and looked at the garden. He was too distracted, he realized, to write today. He needed to see her again, or at least hear her voice.

John took out his phone and searched for Lilly's number that she'd given him at the bar. He hesitated for a few seconds, looking at her name, and then pressed the Dial button.

"Hello?" a woman said after the first ring. The voice was pleasant, matter-of-fact but higher pitched than he'd expected. He frowned, taking the phone away from his ear and looking at the number for confirmation.

"Hello?" the voice repeated, the last syllable going up with annoyance.

"Hey, Lilly," he said, "it's John."

"You've got the wrong number," the woman said and hung up.

He cocked his head in surprise as he stared at the phone for a few seconds more and then redialed the number.

"Who's this?" the same voice said, impatiently this time.

"Um," he mumbled, "I'm sorry, this is John Levy. Is Lilly around? She gave me this number last night."

"Moron," the voice said, and the line went dead.

John sat straight on the edge of the loveseat and then threw the phone on the table.

I'm such an idiot, he thought—*the drunk idiot who can't even write a number down.*

He tried to think back, recreate the conversations in his head, and remember the numbers, but it was all in vain. They'd had two rounds of drinks by then. All he could remember was the taste of her lips. He groaned.

He stumbled into the shower and turned the water as hot as he could handle. He needed to clear his head and get back to writing if he couldn't call Lilly. She surely would call him. After all, she had his number.

She is going to call me, right? Would she...call me? Or would she think I was satisfied with a one-night stand and move on?

John tried to push the thought away. He stuck his head under the running water and concentrated on the book again. He'd outlined most of the story by now, but he still hadn't decided on the paranormal angle. As he had told Lilly on the train, each approach had pros and cons. Leaving Luca human, a deranged man in pursuit of madness, made it more real. More believable. More gripping, perhaps. But giving him extraordinary powers made it more exciting. Pushed the story into the realm of "what if." He sighed. It was a hard choice to make. And then there was the ending. Was Luca going to get away with the murders? If he left Luca free and the book turned out to be successful, he could potentially write a sequel. Everybody says they hate sequels, yet people always flock to movie theaters and bookstores to find out what else their favorite characters were up to. If the stars aligned just right, he could turn it into a powerhouse of a franchise. He laughed out loud at the thought. It might have been his first novel, but in his mind, he was already competing with James Patterson, Dan Brown, and Thomas Harris.

He got out of the shower, put on a bathrobe, and returned to the loveseat.

Before he could settle, his phone rang, making him jump, and he scrambled to his feet, snatching the cell off the table.

"Lilly?"

"Eh, what?" a man's voice said. "John?"

"Who's that?" he asked, then looked at the phone. "Oh, hey, Phil. I thought it was somebody else."

"No kidding," the man said, chuckling. "For a second, I thought I dialed the wrong number. Who's Lilly?"

"Nobody. This woman I met yesterday on the train," John said. His cheeks grew hot. "We kind of hit it off."

"That's about time, my friend," said Phil. "Listen, I know it's short notice, but it's nice out, so we decided to throw some meat on the grill. Why don't you come over? The girls will be delighted to see you. And you can tell me all about this Lilly person."

"Sure," John said after a brief hesitation. "I was planning to write, but maybe it's not in the cards today. Not much to tell about Lilly, I'm afraid. Besides, it looks like I didn't get her number right. I called her this morning, only to have someone to tell me off."

"That's a shame. I'm sure she'll call you back. She'd be crazy not to. We'll see you soon, right?"

"Yep." He glanced at his watch. "I'll be there in an hour."

John and Phil went back a long way. They first met at a local pre-k, fierce rivals at once, competing for rides on the biggest slide and the best toys. Before long, they were inseparable. They went to the same high school and parted only for a few years when Phil went down to Washington, DC, to get his undergrad.

After graduation, Phil went to work for a white-shoe law firm, quickly rising through the ranks and becoming a partner, while John built an equally impressive career in finance. But despite crazy schedules, they stayed close. They went to each other's weddings, first John's, when he married his coworker, Grace. Then, Phil tied the knot with his high school sweetheart, Kathy. Life was good for a while, until Grace didn't make it home one night. It'd been all downhill since, and if not for the unwavering support of his friend and his family, John sometimes wondered if he'd still even be around.

A clock chimed on the wall, bringing John back to the present, and he put the phone down and started to get dressed. He could use some company.

He grabbed his sneakers, wore washed-out jeans, a black T-shirt, and a leather jacket, and headed for the door. He paused momentarily and looked back at his apartment, thinking of last night. His eye caught the bright-orange box in the middle of the kitchen table.

"Seriously!" he said out loud, going back.

John grabbed the box, opened the drawer, threw it inside, and shut it closed. He started to walk back to the door and then froze in place. His rib cage contracted, the air coming out of his mouth in quick, shallow breaths as the taste of bile coated his tongue.

He walked back to the kitchen table and slowly touched the drawer's stainless-steel handle as if a coiled viper was waiting for him inside. Then, slower still, he pulled it wide open.

The box of antidepressants was sitting on top of the mess of whisks, graters, spoons, tongs, and peelers. He took the pills out, and there, at the bottom of the drawer, nestled between a can opener and a spatula, sat a gold-coated Montblanc.

His hands shaking, John took the pen out of the drawer, holding it to the light. It wasn't a new pen. It'd been around. Its once shiny gold surface was matte and covered in scuffs. John turned it this way and that, and his limbs grew cold and rigid as he looked at a lengthy scrape next to the pocket clip.

He knew every scratch and dent upon its surface. It had character. It demanded precision.

John's thumb traced a long scratch on the side of the pen. It was deep, its edges rough and bumpy under his skin.

It happened after he'd consumed the first spirit.

"No," he finally said out loud, vigorously shaking his head. He flipped the pen back and forth, studying the marks on its surface, and finally put it in his breast pocket. "No, no, no. There must be an explanation for this."

He locked the door, walked down the two flights of stairs, and burst into the bright, sunny April day. The air was warm and smelled of blossoms and wet grass. He was sure he'd forget about the pen when he got to Phil's, and the world would be right again.

SIX

"I apologize, but Mr. Morton is out. Traveling. He should be back in two days. Would you like me to leave him a message?"

"No." My fingers drummed impatiently on the steering wheel. As much as I wanted to explain the reason for the call, I couldn't jeopardize his client's secrecy. That would only piss him off and possibly get me fired altogether. "Just tell him I called."

I hung up and stared at the house with the dirty beige siding across the street. The second floor was dark, but a bare lightbulb on the ground level was still on, its harsh, overly bright light seeping through the half-drawn blinds.

Shit. Morton couldn't have picked a worse time to be traveling. After my clumsy attempt to check out the van, the safe deposit boxes were probably already gutted, their contents moved elsewhere. I wasn't counting on finding whatever Morton's client held precious at Rico's and Lopez's abode. But I hoped there were still some clues in the house. I just wished the lawyer told me what I was looking for.

The lightbulb went off, plunging the house into darkness, and I slid down in my seat, making myself small. The front door swung open, and Rico's squat outline emerged from the doorway, followed by a tall, gangly one. Lopez. They climbed into the van, and a moment later, the ugly beast sputtered and coughed as if struggling to catch its breath. Then the engine roared, the tailpipe spewing a big black cloud, and Rico maneuvered into the street, picking up speed.

I waited a few minutes to make sure and then exited the car. It was already dark, but the streetlamps hadn't turned on yet, the houses on the block flicking their lights on one after another like decorations on a Christmas tree. I jogged across the street, keeping my head down and shoulders hunched. The screen door wasn't locked, and the main door, a solid three-quarter-inch slab covered with a thick layer of old, peeling white paint, was secured with a simple pin-and-tumbler cylinder lock. I glanced around, ensuring nobody was watching me, and kneeled in front of the door, pulling out a tension wrench and a pick. A few moments later, I heard the pins click in place. I picked up the tools, snuck inside, locked the door behind me, and turned on a flashlight.

Apart from the musty smell of an old house, the place looked spartan and surprisingly clean. A kitchen island cut the first floor in half, with the prep space by the farthest wall. There was a small dining room to my left with a cheap rectangular table and six rattan chairs. A small plain vase sat on a white doily in the center of the table. If I hadn't known any better, I would've thought the house was used as a modest Airbnb rather than a place to crash for two violent gangbangers. Not quite what I expected after seeing the insides of the working van. Were neat gangbangers better than messy ones?

I almost chuckled at my own joke when something else occurred to me. Rico and Lopez might not be as simple as their white T-shirt and dirty jeans uniforms suggested. The van wasn't just messy on the inside and dirty on the outside. It appeared precisely how you expected a vehicle of two poor men working at a car repair shop to look like. And then there was this house. There was a non-zero chance that, at least to some degree, guys like Rico and Lopez were on the radar of the local precinct. It could be because someone in the department had suspicions about their true career aspirations. Or, perhaps they were even a known entity, left alone in the hope they'd eventually lead the cops to a bigger fish. One way or the other, some overly zealous detective could pay them a visit once in a while. Just to see which way the weathervane was pointing. It was part of a standard tactic. You keep them on their toes, put some pressure on them. Sooner or later, they get paranoid and start making mistakes. Leave some merchandise in the wrong place. Talk to a person they weren't supposed to be talking to. But these two didn't seem like a pair of novices. All a visitor would see was a neat first floor. An honest man's house. Hardly a place that would justify a search without a warrant.

But the good stuff was here somewhere. I had no doubt. It just needed to be found. My money was on the basement, but I climbed the stairs to the second floor first, just in case, only to find more of the same. Two separate rooms. Two tidy beds with clean sheets. A simple wooden cross on the wall above each headboard. No personal items of any kind, except for a shared closet, mostly stuffed with white T-shirts and jeans.

I went down to the first level and went for the door to the basement, only to find it locked. It was another pin-and-tumbler, and after some jiggling, the lock clicked. I swung the door open and stared at the rough-hewn brick walls and unfinished wooden stairs leading into a cavernous dark place.

"Bingo," I murmured as I switched on the lights and looked at the neat rows of durable, industrial metal shelves stuffed with what I could only imagine were illicitly acquired goods. Boxes of electronics, smartphones, laptops, and gaming consoles. A few rows of counterfeit designer handbags and watches. A section lined with small, clear plastic bags filled with white powder. If the top part of the house was Dr. Jekyll, this was definitely Mr. Hyde. A treasure trove for any cop if they could find a compelling reason to make their way past the faux facade of clean rooms upstairs. But I couldn't worry about any of that. As I quickly scanned the shelves, I saw no traces of safe deposit boxes or anything that could have come from them.

A sturdy safe was in the corner of the room, and a small desk with a pile of papers next to it. The thick steel box with a standard combination lock surely had some interesting stories to tell, but I had neither the skills nor the tools to open it, so I concentrated on the documents. There was some kind of a ledger—a thick notebook, its pages covered in neat, cursive notes—and I quickly flipped through it, snapping pictures on my cell phone. When I was done, I spread a handful of receipts on the wooden surface, smoothing out the most crumpled ones, and took a picture of them as well. It seemed there was nothing else for me to find here. It was my cue to leave.

I turned to the stairs when I heard the front door open, followed by a man's voice saying something in Spanish. I rushed to the light switch, flipped it off, and stepped back into the darkness. The floors creaked above me, and then there was a muted rumble of the television—a weather channel by the sound of it.

I silently groaned. This was just how my luck worked. First, the van, and now this. Pete swore to me that these two clowns were at the shop six days a week, every single week. And yet here they were, seemingly settling in for the night while I was stuck in a dark basement, praying neither decided to come downstairs. As far as I could see, there were only two options. I could hide out, hoping that both of them would take off sooner or later before checking their precious stuff. Then, I would leave once the house was empty. Or, I could try to storm out of the basement, using the element of surprise to my advantage. I wasn't kidding myself. I'm a proficient fighter in multiple martial arts and no easy mark for a rando on the street. But I also weigh a hundred and ten pounds, and there was no way I could overpower two fully grown men in a prolonged fight. But if I struck fast and hard, I'd have a good chance of breaking through them.

"Puta madre!" The door to the basement swung open with a loud bang, the lights flooding the cavernous space. It seemed there was a third option, and the decision was made for me. I backed up more and went low, putting the shelves in front of me as I heard the rapid steps going down the stairs. I frantically looked around for a weapon and settled on a slim laptop.

"You!" Rico immediately spotted me behind the shelves, and I stood straight.

So much for trying to hide.

His face twisted in a scowl. "No good, chica. I told you not to come here."

"Can we talk about it?" I tried to keep my voice level. "This is just a giant misunderstanding. I don't want any trouble."

"Si, chica," Rico said as he walked toward me, planting his feet wide like a sailor just off the boat after a long stint at sea. He spread his arms open, ready to catch me. Blocking my escape route. "You can talk."

I swung the laptop, aiming at his chin. He saw it coming, angling his face away at the last moment, turning what would have been a crippling strike into a glancing blow and sending the laptop flying. Then, there was a blur of his hand, and he landed a solid slap across my face, sending me tumbling back. My vision blurred, my head ringing from the impact.

He lunged, trying to pin me to the ground, but I arched, pushing myself off the floor, and kicked him in the face as he reached for my throat. There was a sickening crunch, and Rico landed on his ass, blood gushing out of his nose. I rushed forward, grabbed a fistful of his thick hair, and drove my knee into his chin as hard as I could. His body crashed back with a thud, and I rushed toward the stairs, stepping on his torso as I went. He gasped as my foot got buried in his stomach and went quiet.

But I didn't get a chance to celebrate for long. As I arrived at the foot of the stairs, I saw Lopez. Alerted by the commotion, he was heading toward me, an ugly kitchen knife in his long hand and an even uglier look on his face. I rushed up the stairs before he could process what he saw, hoping to throw him off-balance. He paused for a moment, the blade slashing at my face, and I ducked under it, grabbed his ankles, and pulled with all my might. A flash of hot pain struck my shoulder, but Lopez went down with a bang, his head hitting the rough edge of the wooden steps, his eyes momentarily glazing over.

I pressed my advantage and pulled his body down, his head counting each step as it went until it reached the basement floor. I saw Rico stir from the corner of my eye, but the path ahead of me was open, and I flew up the stairs, taking two steps at a time. When I got to the kitchen, I dashed across the floor, heaved the dinner table up, and then crashed it down on its side, jamming the door to the basement. Then I bolted out of the house toward the car. A few seconds later, I was speeding down the street, my hands squeezing the wheel in a death grip.

I gingerly touched my face where Rico's meaty hand made contact. It was numb, and as I shifted for a moment to see myself in the rearview mirror, there were the first signs of black and blue around my left eye.

"You should see the other guy," I muttered. The week wasn't even over yet, but I'd already broken two noses and possibly cracked another skull. I giggled as reality set in, and then a burst of manic laughter rattled my entire body. If anyone saw me now, speeding down the empty street, my face swollen, my nose bleeding, cackling like a witch, I'd surely get sent to a place with nice padded walls and smiley male nurses with overly muscular arms. Well, screw them. Everybody works through shock in different ways. Some cry. Some get depressed and drink themselves into a stupor. Apparently, I howl like a lunatic after getting slapped around, stabbed, and barely making out of the cartel's safe house alive.

I stopped laughing as something warm and wet ran down my back and into my underwear. Then came the sharp pain in my shoulder. The car swerved as my vision blurred, and I gripped the steering wheel even harder, smashing my foot into the pedal. I had no idea how bad the wound in my shoulder was. I needed to get home, and fast. Bleeding out wasn't an option. I had a case to solve.

SEVEN

Levy took a cab to Sunset Park, lost in thought. As the car raced up Shore Road, he watched the boats on the Narrows and occasionally glanced at the shiny top of the Montblanc pen sticking out of his pocket as if to check it was real. It didn't disappear, its hard outline pressing firmly against his rib cage, but the hypnotic view of the bay calmed Levy down. When the taxi pulled up in front of a small townhouse with a waist-height wrought-iron gate, he pushed the thought aside.

"How are you, old man?" Phil ignored Levy's outstretched hand and pulled him into a bear hug. "Come on in. Want a cold one?"

"Sure," he said. "What you got?"

"Let's see." Phil walked through the living room, stepping over toys and into the kitchen. "I've got some Brooklyn Lager, unless you want wine. Or something stronger, perhaps?"

"Nah, beer's fine," he said, looking through the French doors. Two girls chased each other in the backyard, running around an empty inflatable pool. "They're getting big."

"Yeah." Phil handed him a sweaty bottle. "Doing their best to destroy the house while I try to keep it straight. They are winning. Resistance is futile. Cheers."

They clinked their bottles, and Levy took a sip, watching his best friend do the same.

"How are they doing?"

"Great. Emily got accepted into the gifted and talented program. Clearly, she is taking after her nerd father. And Sarah," Phil pointed with the bottle at the backyard, "I think we might have a prodigy on our hands. She's getting good with the violin. It's just incredible. I don't know where she's getting it from. Kathy is no musician, but at least she can hold a tune. I can't even properly whistle. But she's just killing it. Maybe if you're lucky, we'll be able to cajole her into playing something for Uncle John later."

"I'd love that."

Phil's house was the only place where he felt safe these days. There was no internal pressure, no mental itch that drove him crazy most of the time. It was different today, though. Last night had already thrown him off-balance. With the fountain pen burning a hole in his pocket, Levy found himself struggling to maintain control.

"John? You okay, bud?"

"Yeah." He forced a smile. "Let's go see if you ruined the meat."

They went outside, and Levy found himself under the assault of the twins demanding that *Uncle John* listen to their stories and participate in their games.

"Leave Uncle John alone," he heard Kathy's voice as she came out of the house with a plate of vegetables and dips. "Hey, handsome."

"Hey." He picked up the plate from her hands and kissed her on the cheek. "You look better every time I see you."

"You hear that, Phil? You should be taking notes."

It was a good place to be. John sat at the wooden table, soaking up the warm sun, listening to the girls, and wolfing down the best burgers on the east side of the Mississippi.

They asked him to stay for dinner when the sun started to go down, but he declined, unwilling to impose. He kissed the girls, gave Kathy a peck on the cheek, and shook hands with his friend.

"Call me if you need anything, will you?" Phil held his hand briefly, looking him in the eye.

"I will," he said, smiling. "I'm fine, though. Stop looking at me like that."

"Okay."

He closed the door and went outside. The cherry trees on both sides of the street were now in full bloom, filling the air with the flowery smell and covering sidewalks with petals.

He crossed to the sunny side of the street and started to walk to the subway stop. The train car was weekend-empty, and Levy took the opportunity to do some people-watching. Sometimes, observations like these gave him fodder for book characters: a gesture, an accent, how someone dressed or moved.

He took out a small pad and the Montblanc. It felt weird in his hands, but it was a good pen, and he decided to put it to use.

I must've bought it, John thought, looking at the scratches on its dull surface. He thought about the box of antidepressants with suspicion. *Could it be side effects?*

It was unlikely, he decided. He'd been taking them for years now and had no problems whatsoever. He took a deep breath and tapped the top of the pen with his thumb. *I just forgot about this thing, that's all.*

He went back to people-watching. There were only four passengers close enough for him to see. He started taking notes.

An Asian man. Red windbreaker, green khaki pants, thick glasses. Talks to himself.

A guy in a gray suit. He crossed the words out. Boring.

A teenage boy. Skinny jeans, a New York Yankees hat, and a dirty backpack.

A sleeping laborer. John tilted his head, looking the man up and down. This was an interesting character. *Bright-orange hoodie pulled over his head. A hard hat, paint-stained jeans, and work boots covered in dust. The sleeves rolled up, showing off powerful arms covered in exotic tattoos. A handsome face with a strong jaw.*

The train stopped, and a woman walked in. She took a seat on the long bench right next to him.

He watched her scrolling through her phone, oblivious to everyone on the train. John glanced at the screen of her phone over her shoulder as she read through what appeared to be an article about a murder in a local newspaper. The picture of a victim caught his attention.

Olive skin. Makeup is a touch too heavy. Nice long eyelashes, though. Pretty. Twenty-something. Dark, wavy hair down to her shoulders. White shirt peeking out of her coat. Green sweater. Cheap faux leather bag and a diamond stud in her nose.

John closed his pad, put his pen away, and let his mind wander. It would be difficult to find Lilly, he thought. He knew almost nothing about her. An accountant who works in a downtown office and lives in Brooklyn? Good luck with that. He could try to go to the same German bar, but he'd been there many times before and was certain he'd never seen her.

I could leave work early and wait for her on the subway platform, he thought. *But would she even want to see me if she didn't call me?*

He watched the woman with the phone get up and walk to the door. A tiny diamond shone in her ear like a raindrop in the morning sun. The woman touched it with the tip of her right index finger as if checking it was in place. Then the train stopped, and off she went, her long legs striding purposefully up the stairs and out of John's view.

He frowned, watching her go. There was something about the diamond that triggered the mental itch again. A sticky feeling hidden deep in the dark corner of his brain.

He got off at the next stop and walked back to his apartment. The sun was getting low now, and the spring warmth was quickly dissipating from the air.

His apartment was cold, as it usually happened when it was

warm enough outside for his landlord not to have an obligation to turn on the heat, but cold enough to make the building's residents wish he had. John took off his shoes, hung his jacket in the closet, then went to the kitchen and put a kettle on. *A hot cup of tea should do the trick.*

He went back to the living room and turned the laptop on. Perhaps, he thought, he could write a couple of pages before he went to bed. He scanned the last few words he'd typed.

His thumb traced a long scratch on the side of the pen. It happened after he'd consumed the first spirit.

John stared at the text for some time and opened the document with the manuscript's outline, looking for ideas and thinking of where the story was going. His left hand moved almost on its own accord, his pinky pressing Ctrl as his index finger hit the F.

Diamond stud, he typed into a search box and pressed Enter. Nothing came up, and he drew a short breath, then chuckled. He wasn't crazy after all. He hit the backspace a few times, watching the words disappear.

Diamond stu
  Diamond st
  Diamond s
  Diamond

The panel on the left of his screen blinked, highlighting the found text in bright, venomous yellow. He stared at the word *diamond* as cold drops of perspiration started to form on his forehead. The hair on the back of his neck stood up.

diamond gleaming in her nose, the only possession he allowed her to keep.

While she was unconscious, he bound her legs, threaded the rope through a small wheel contraption attached to the ceiling, and pulled her up until her hands were dangling about four feet from the floor. That's when she woke up, screaming for help and trying to scratch him as he was binding her wrists. But her gentle frame was no match for his muscular bulk.

He wasn't worried about her shouting, either. The room was soundproof, and he'd tested it himself. If he couldn't hear heavy metal blasting at full volume from a powerful stereo in the adjacent room, there was no way somebody would hear her cries.

Luca threaded the rope, binding her hands through another machine attached to the floor, and started to turn the wheel, tightening the cables.

Her body stretched like a string of a longbow, her olive skin glistening with sweat. She was having difficulty breathing, and shallow gasps for air replaced her screams.

Luca watched her struggle. He knew the demon inside her would try to tempt him. She was in her mid-twenties, her body in perfect shape. His finger traced a line from her knee down to her thigh, then over her flat stomach and around her small, firm breast, lingering for a moment when it touched her nipple.

"Why?" she managed.

He ignored her, his finger going lower, tracing her neck and then resting on her cheek as he squatted next to her. Then he stood up and stepped back, observing. Her heavy makeup ran down, leaving dark streaks on her temples and forehead. Her black, wavy hair swayed back and forth as she pulled in raspy breaths.

Luca fought the urge to touch her more and retreated farther away.

He had to stay pure. He picked up the remnants of her clothes: a white shirt, a green sweater that he'd cut off her, a bra, and a pair of plain beige panties. He packed the pieces into a garbage bag along with her cheap faux leather purse and black sneakers. He needed to burn her things before he could start the ritual.

He shuddered. He had been preparing for this for so long, and now he was about to absorb his first spirit. Soon, he'd be too powerful for anyone to stop him.

Levy slammed the laptop shut and stood up, the sound of the chair dragging across the kitchen floor reverberating through the apartment. He drew a shaky breath, trying to calm down. Then, not giving himself a moment to reconsider, he sat down again, re-opened his computer, and switched from the word processor to a browser. His fingers flew over the keyboard, typing in the few elements from the story he read over the woman's shoulder on the train. A few seconds later, he was staring at the victim's photograph. The picture was taken in Central Park. The woman was sitting on a bench, a broad smile directed at the camera. She was young, perhaps in her mid-twenties—dark, wavy hair. Levy drew in another shaky breath as his eyes went from a tiny diamond sparkling in her nose to the wrinkled collar of a white shirt sticking out of a green wool sweater.

He closed the browser and opened the document again, staring at the page. There was no rational explanation for this, yet he knew the photograph he saw online was of the woman he described in his yet-to-be-finished book. It was madness. Something no one would be able to understand, no matter how he tried to explain it. And yet, it was real.

Levy reached for his cell phone and dialed Phil's number.

"Hello?"

"I hope I'm not interrupting anything."

"No, no. Is everything okay?"

"Yeah," he lied. "I have a weird question for you, if that's okay."

"Shoot."

"Say, hypothetically," he said, "I needed a detective to find someone, but it's not something you'd go to the police with. What would I do?"

"Well," there was a soft chuckle on the other side, "hypothetically, if you can't go to the police, I'd say you need a private investigator. Is this about the woman?"

"The woman?" Levy tensed, frantically thinking of a benign explanation.

"The lady you've met. What was her name? Lillian?"

"Oh." He exhaled with relief. "No. That's not for Lilly. This is something else. Do you, by chance, know of any PIs?"

"As strange as it sounds, I do," Phil said. "Give me a few, and I'll text you their contact information. My firm used them awhile back. There was this insurance fraud case. I don't know anything about the guy, but from what I hear, he was excellent."

"Okay. Thank you."

"No problem. Are you sure you're okay?"

"Yeah," he said, adding as much cheer into his voice as he could muster. "Peachy. Good night. I'll wait for your text."

He hung up and stayed in the chair, motionless, staring into the void. The likeness of his character to the real-life victim was uncanny. But if the woman in the news was the same as in his manuscript, it was just the beginning of his troubles. She was the first of the twelve gruesome murders that he had meticulously planned in his outline. The carnage was only starting.

EIGHT

I uploaded the pictures from my phone that I took during the raid on Rico's house and was ready to close the laptop when I noticed a lonely figure 1 next to the Spam folder. There was a message with the subject line HELP. Half expecting to see an ad for penis enlargement pills, I clicked on the link.

The email was from John Levy, who wanted to discuss some confidential business. Apparently, Mr. Levy thought I was a man, as the message was addressed to *Mr. Watts*. In his defense, he wasn't the first person to make that mistake and surely won't be the last.

He didn't want to meet in my office, which was unusual, but instead proposed meeting in a Starbucks a block away. Odd, but I can do odd. What I can't do is meet people I don't know in abandoned places, no matter how compelling their story is. Learned it the hard way.

I decided to take the bait and wrote a short reply to John Levy. The ledger from Rico's house was a hard nut to crack. Nothing was written in plain English. Or Spanish, for that matter. Just numbers and codes. I needed a break after staring at it for the past few hours.

Besides, I've juggled multiple cases before, and now that the Black American Express wasn't going to make any appearances in my life any time soon, I could surely use the money.

I got to the coffee shop ten minutes early. Call me paranoid, but I like to observe a potential client before we shake hands. People behave differently when they are not aware they are being watched. You can learn more about a person in a few minutes than they'll tell you in an hour.

I bought a large cappuccino and claimed a table in a corner, watching the door.

Mr. Levy showed up two minutes before the appointment. He wore dark jeans, brown dress shoes, and a slim, salmon-colored shirt, just like he said he would. He ordered a cup of black coffee, clutched a laptop under his left arm, and sat by the window.

He looked ordinary. Average build. Average height. A pleasant but somewhat plain face with a pair of sad, green eyes. He seemed nervous, fidgeting in his chair and running his hand through his curly, salt-and-pepper hair.

A Burberry shirt and a pair of distressed jeans from Ralph Lauren said *money*. If you ask me, two kinds of people wear expensive clothes. Those who want others to know they wear expensive clothes, and those who wear them because they suit them. The first are usually broke, though it's more of a guide than a rule. Watching as Levy put his elbows on a questionably clean surface of the cafe table without as much as wiping it with a napkin, I decided he was in the latter category.

I couldn't tell what he did for a living, but I could tell he wasn't a lawyer. A pity. But you have to work with what you've got. Overall, he didn't seem threatening, and I got up and walked to his table.

"Mr. Levy?" I offered a hand. "Alex Watts."

"Hi." He stood up and took my hand into his. The handshake was warm and firm. A good start. He smiled awkwardly, his eyes, for a brief moment, studying the black-and-blue on the left side of my face. Whatever conclusions he might have made, he kept them to himself. I liked that, too. "Call me John, please. It's nice to meet you. And, please forgive me about the *Mr. Watts*. A good friend of mine recommended your agency, but I guess I should have done my own research."

"That's okay," I said, taking a seat. "Not the first time and probably not the last. My full name is Alexandra, but you can call me Alex. How can I help you?"

He squirmed in his chair as he pondered the question.

"I have a rather unusual request. I want you to track down a person for me," he finally said.

"It's not that unusual."

He fished in his pockets for a moment and then produced a small, crumpled piece of paper. "Here's the description."

"Do you know this person?"

"No." He shrugged, almost apologetically, and put the note on the table before me. "Not exactly."

I looked at the paper with a few short lines of neat cursive and frowned.

"A thirty-year-old woman named Naomi. A butterfly tattoo on her left shoulder blade. Slim build, brown eyes, dark hair. About five foot five. Southern accent." I stopped reading and looked up. "Is this a joke?"

He vigorously shook his head. "Not at all, Miss Watts, er, Alex."

"If you want me to find a thirty-year-old woman named Naomi with a butterfly tattoo in a city of eight million people, you'll have to do better than that."

"It's all I've got, I'm afraid."

"Are you related?"

"No."

"Romantically involved?"

"No."

"Worked together?"

"No."

"Have you met her?"

"I don't believe so."

"Why are you looking for her then?" I was starting to lose patience.

I've done weird cases before. Drive from this address to that and back in your black Range Rover? Okay. Make a show of taking pictures of your wife in public to ruin her affair? No problem.

You want me to go on a wild-goose chase and spend some of your money? I'll do that. But something about John Levy's inquiry was starting to feel off, and I tried to stay the hell away from cases that felt off. Also learned that the hard way.

"Why are you looking for Naomi?" I repeated.

"I can't tell you," he said. His face twisted in a mask of desperation. "And this is all I know about her. I'll pay you well. I have money."

"I'm sorry," I said and got up to leave, "but I'm afraid I can't help you. Best of luck."

"Wait."

I ignored him, left the coffee shop, and started toward my office. With some luck, the codes from Rico's ledger would reveal their true meaning to me sooner or later. I had no intention of losing Morton's bounty.

"Alex, wait."

I turned around, watching Levy running after me.

"You have to try," he said, as he caught up to me, "if—"

"Look, Mr. Levy," I said, cutting him off. "I'm sure there are many people out there who'd gladly take your money for a few weeks and tell you how hard they worked looking for her, but that's not how I do business."

"That's quite all right," he said, a painful look on his face. "We don't have weeks, anyway. I believe we only have three days. Until Friday, to be precise. Take this case just for three days. Please."

Something about how he said that, the way he looked at me with those sad, puppy eyes, made my stomach churn. I didn't like it.

"Why do we only have three days?" I finally managed.

He stood there for a moment, looking at me as if deciding what to do. Somewhere in the distance, church bells started to toll. He sighed and finally looked away.

"Why do we only have three days?"

"I don't have more information about Naomi, I'm afraid," he said, ignoring my question. "But I thought someone of your skill set could figure out how to find her."

"You haven't answered my question."

He looked down at his shoes, as if unable to meet my eyes.

"John," I said, surprising myself. "Why do you think you only have three days?"

His eyes met mine, a look on his face I couldn't quite understand. "Because in three days, Naomi will die a terrible death."

I recoiled in shock, studying his face. "How do you know that?"

"I'm sorry," he said, pressing his palms to his cheeks, his laptop precariously balancing under his arm. "I can't tell you that. You won't believe me."

"Why don't you go to the police?" I pressed him. "That doesn't sound like a job for a PI. If you know someone's life is in danger, you should go straight to the cops."

"They won't believe me either. They'll think I'm crazy."

"I'm already starting to think you might be crazy," I said, stepping closer. "Or, perhaps, you're the person who's planning to hurt Naomi. Or maybe somebody else."

It was his turn to look horrified. He took a step back and stumbled, almost losing his balance. The color drained from his face.

"I'd never." He took another step away from me. "I'm sorry. This has been a mistake. Goodbye, Miss Watts."

"John."

"I'm very sorry. I have to go." He turned and started to walk away from me, slowly first, then faster and faster, almost running, his arms comically swinging back and forth as if he wasn't sure he could walk straight. I was afraid his laptop would fly away on one of those swings.

I watched him go and then disappear around the corner as I stood there with my mouth open, debating what to do. But what could I do? Despite what I said, I didn't think he was going to kill anyone. Not really. He didn't seem the type. I know it sounds stupid when somebody says it, but I spent a few years looking at all kinds of people who end up taking another person's life. They all have something in common. I don't know what it is or how to describe it because they are so different. There are shy ones, the rejects. There are aggressors. The explosive types.

But there's an underlying tone of being a predator. Like a door left ajar in a large house that lets the cold air in. You don't know where it is. You don't even know what it looks like, but you can feel the draft making you shiver.

I imagined calling 911.

Yeah, I thought. *That would go just great. Hello? I know someone looking for a woman named Naomi, and they say she will die in three days. A horrible death, they say. How do I know that? They wouldn't tell me. Okay, sure, I'll hold. What's my name? Yes, I was a detective. Why am I no longer a detective?*

That was going straight to my former partner, and I'd rather die a horrible death in place of the magical Naomi than talk to Detective Dominic Deluca ever again.

I snapped my mouth shut and turned on my heels. If my gut told me to stay away from this case, that's precisely what I would do.

I crossed the street and walked up Third Avenue to my office. The place on the corner, with a large glass wall and a neon sign *ALEX WATTS, PI* that works most of the time, doesn't look like much, but it serves its purpose. It gives me a separate address from my home, which is important in my line of work. You piss people off enough to trash your place, you want it to be your office, not your house.

It also gives my practice a touch of professionalism and strokes my ego. I like seeing my name on the flimsy sign in bright pulsating letters, and if you think it's shallow, then sue me.

The best part of the office was how cheap I got it. The butcher, a very nice Italian guy the entire neighborhood only knew as Jim, who occupied the space before me, went out of business just as I needed a place. It's also the worst part about my office. Despite a coat of fresh paint and a dying lemon tree in the front of the window, it still hits you with the funky smell of dead meat the moment you step through the doors. It doesn't matter how many times I washed the floors with fragrant soap or how many scented candles I burned; the smell just doesn't want to go away.

My phone rang, and I cringed, looking at the name.

"Hello?"

"Hello, Alex."

"Hello, Tina." The amount of silent superiority my sister managed to stuff into a simple *Hello, Alex* was truly impressive. But I was newly single, thirteen and a half grand richer, and I wasn't going to let her ruin it. "What's up?"

"We are going to Carnegie Hall on Saturday night, and we were planning to have dinner at the Petrossian before the show," she said, "but our babysitter is down with the flu. I'd hate to ask—"

"That's no bother at all," I said before she could finish the sentence. If there was a side gig I didn't mind, it was babysitting my niece, Olivia. Maybe by the time she graduates from high school, her mother will finally convince her that Aunt Alex was an irredeemable screwup. So far, her efforts haven't been successful. The kid worshipped me. "I'll be there."

"Thank you, Alex. I'll have my driver pick you up at four."

I rolled my eyes. That's how she always talks. It's not just *we are going out*. No, it's *we are going to a show nobody else has tickets to*. It's not a *restaurant*. It's *the Petrossian*. To be fair, I don't know if she even does it on purpose. But even if it's because this is just something that feels natural to her, it doesn't make it any less irritating. "There's no need. I can take my own car. I'm perfectly capable of driving myself to your place."

"Okay, then. Please, don't be late."

"Sure thing. I'll see you Saturday." I kept my tone cheerful. It's hard to grind teeth when you're smiling.

NINE

The sky was cloudy[10] when John Levy opened his eyes. He stayed motionless for a few seconds, clinging to the scattered fragments of a vivid dream as he watched the gray outside the window. He couldn't quite remember the details, just that he was in a bright, sunny place full of flowers and exotic plants, and he was happy and safe. But as he stayed in bed, the images frayed like a spiderweb in a strong wind. Eventually, they disappeared, leaving nothing but a faint echo bouncing around the deepest corners of his mind. Close and yet out of reach.

Reluctantly, he moved the blanket aside, the cold air whisking away the last remnants of sleep, and sat up straight. After the unsuccessful meeting with the private investigator on Monday, he called in sick, took the rest of the week off, and locked himself in the apartment. He was disappointed but couldn't blame Alex for not believing him. He wouldn't have believed his story if the roles had been reversed, either. But knowing that did nothing to lift his spirits.

As he stayed in, John's mood spiraled downward with each passing day, as if being swallowed by a vast and all-consuming darkness.

On Tuesday, he spent the entire day online, combing through newspaper articles and blog posts for details about the first murder. More than anything, he wanted to find inconsistencies between the fate of the woman in a green sweater, whose picture he had first glanced on a phone of a fellow subway commuter, and the unnamed character in his story. Something that could, without a doubt, prove once and for all they were not the same person.

It turned out to be more difficult than he had envisioned. Not to say there were no discrepancies. Most news outlets listed the crime as a stabbing, if they even reported it at all. While the fictional character also died from the blade, Levy suspected that most people would have used a different word to describe her gruesome death rather than simple *stabbing*.

Levy found the lack of details about the murder frustrating. One of the fringe online blogs that followed true crime even went as far as to claim that there was a cover-up by the NYPD. The blog didn't specify what kind but strongly implied that some of the specifics of the crime were never released to the public. It could, of course, mean that there was more to that murder than simple stabbing. However, other posts on the blog were dedicated to UFOs, witches, and poltergeists, which didn't exactly inspire confidence in its source material.

By the end of the day, Levy had gathered as much information as he suspected he would ever find without direct access to the NYPD database. He learned that the woman had only recently moved from the South to New York City and worked as a waitress in a Midtown cafe. In the book, the first murder took place on Valentine's Day. That's how he calculated Naomi's upcoming demise, as the second killing was supposed to happen seven weeks later—on the first Friday of April.

When the woman in a green sweater was actually killed was unclear. Still, the same blog claimed that it took the police a long time to identify the victim because no one came forward for a while. She remained a Jane Doe for over a month until her coworker saw the photograph on the news and reached out to the police. It *could* have happened on Valentine's Day, but Levy couldn't prove it one way or the other.

As Tuesday drew to a close, he was still as far from being able to make a conclusion as he was in the morning. The lack of details about the woman in a green sweater was just a part of it. Another problem was the manuscript itself. He had written the first murder as a flashback from Luca's point of view in the scene where the killer examines the pen he used to catalog his victims. Levy had done it on purpose. Each of Luca's successive hunts and the eventual murders would be described in greater detail as the book progressed, building tension and keeping the reader on the edge of their seat.

For now, however, even if he were to accept that the real-life victims were the same as his characters, Levy didn't have much to draw from. Naomi most likely could not be found from the scant details he had shown Alex, even if she were real.

Frustrated and uncertain, Levy gave up. After all, if the private investigator, a professional who looked for things and people for a living, couldn't find Naomi, what chance did he have?

That left him with two more days to waste before the fateful Friday would arrive. Normally, he would have jumped at the opportunity to continue working on the manuscript. But now, with the possibility of the impending murder of another young woman, writing was entirely out of the question. Levy tried to keep himself busy and think about anything but the murders. After all, there was a great chance that the connection was just a figment of his imagination, and Friday would come and go just like any other day. If it did, Levy would be free again from this curse, ready to move on with his life.

The plan seemed to work for some time. He spent most of his Wednesday doing routine tasks. He cleaned the apartment, prepared meals for the entire week, and took an hour-long shower. Then, he alternated between binging TV and catching up on his reading list.

Whenever he thought about the murders, he'd poured himself a drink. By the time the sun started to set, his liquor cabinet showed signs of significant damage, and Levy was so drunk he barely had enough strength to crawl into his bed and pass out.

He had intended to spend Thursday in a similar fashion, but now, as he sat at the edge of his bed with one more day to go, he was restless again, unable to think about anything else but the woman with a butterfly tattoo on her shoulder. If she were real, somewhere in the city, a tall, muscular man was about to snatch her off the street and then, after a day of horrible torture, take her life in a room with soundproofed walls. The thought was driving him mad.

He tried to reach Alex again, but the call went straight to her voicemail, and he hung up without leaving a message.

"Wait a second," he said out loud, his body tensing. He never wrote it into the story, but now it occurred to him that he thought about the tattoo when he was imagining the scene. And in his mind's eye, it wasn't just a butterfly. It was a butterfly with a pair of dragon wings. He even recalled considering giving it some greater meaning and expanding a scene where Naomi proudly told someone about recently getting it at some fancy parlor at St. Mark's Square in the East Village.

He jumped off the bed and raced to the kitchen, only to stop mid-step as a vicious headache reminded him of the drinks the night prior.

"That was dumb," he grumbled, gingerly rubbing his temples. "Easy now."

Levy put on the coffee drip and sat down at his laptop as the machine gurgled and hissed. He opened a search engine and pulled up every tattoo artist who operated in the East Village in and around St. Mark's Square. Twelve in total. As he sipped on one cup of coffee after another for the next hour, he pored over the pictures on their websites. There were a lot of butterflies. There were a lot of dragons. There were also a lot of flowers, snakes, Chinese and Japanese characters, geometrical designs, lightning bolts, and more. What he didn't see was a butterfly with a pair of leathery wings of a dragon.

He was getting nowhere. He pulled out a notepad, wrote down each business's name, and then picked up the phone.

"Julia's Art Inc." A cheerful voice answered the call on the first ring. "This is Irene."

"Hi." He sat up straighter in his chair. "I have a strange question for you. I'm looking for someone. A woman named Naomi. She's in her late twenties or early thirties. Slim build, brown eyes, dark hair. About five foot five. She grew up in the South, so she's got a bit of an accent. I believe she recently got a tattoo on her left shoulder. A butterfly."

"We do a lot of butterflies," the woman said. "And we care for the privacy of our clients, too."

"Look," he leaned forward, squeezing the phone hard, "I believe she might be in danger. And the tattoo is fairly unique. It's not just a butterfly. It has leathery dragon wings. I must find the woman. I need to warn her."

"All right." The woman paused, as if considering what to do. "This is...weird. Let me ask Julia, but I wouldn't hold my breath if I were you."

"Okay." He sat on pins and needles for a few moments, straining to hear the sounds coming from the other side of the line. Finally, he heard the steps coming back and the rustling as the woman picked up the phone again.

"Hello?"

"I'm still here."

"Julia says she hasn't done a tattoo like that. At least not recently."

"Okay. Thanks for checking."

"What kind of trouble is she in, anyway?" the woman asked before he could end the call.

"I'm not really sure." He sighed. "A bad person is looking for her. That's all I know. I just want to warn her."

"You should go to the police then," she said. "Well, good luck. Sorry I couldn't help."

He hung up and stared at the phone for a few seconds. Then, he crossed the name off the list and dialed the next one. Considering that the woman from the first shop almost blew him off, Levy changed tactics. This time, he pretended that he was looking to get a similar tattoo and that the work someone had done on Naomi had impressed him so much only the same artist would do. It took him another thirty minutes to call every parlor. After some back-and-forth, everyone told him the same thing—nobody remembered a woman named Naomi getting a butterfly tattoo. All but one. A woman at East Side Patterns told him she thought one of the artists might have done a similar job in the last few days.

"He's not in yet," she said. "But he'll be here in about forty minutes. You can call back if you'd like."

"I'm going to be in the area," he lied. "I'll stop by. What's his name?"

"Kendrick," she said. "Or you can call him Ken. He's cool either way."

"Okay, great. I'll see you in a bit."

He changed into jeans, a black T-shirt, and a leather jacket. A few minutes later, a cab pulled up by his building, whisked him toward the bridge and continued north on the Belt Parkway. As the car sped toward the city, he watched the dark skies hanging low over the Narrows harbor. The air was warm, but there was a promise of a storm, as if the heavy clouds held their breath in anticipation.

Levy had never been inside a tattoo parlor before. His imagination had drawn a small, darkly lit office with shabby couches and cramped workstations. Instead, East Side Patterns was a bright and open space. Reprints of Basquiat and Andy Warhol soaked up natural light coming from the big, floor-to-ceiling windows. The walls, painted with a neutral color, were lined with bookshelves. Soft instrumental music flowed from speakers hidden somewhere in the industrial exposed ceiling.

"May I help you?" the woman at the counter asked. Her smile was genuine, and her posture relaxed.

"Hi. I spoke to someone about a butterfly tattoo. I think her name was Serena. I'm here to see Kendrick."

"Oh, right." Her face lit up even more. "That was me. Nice to meet you. You're in luck. He just came in. John, right?"

"Yes." He gave her a timid smile.

"He's right there." She pointed across the floor at a young man going through the drawers of a workstation.

"Thanks."

He walked across the polished floor, self-conscious, his hands damp. "Kendrick?"

"What's up, man?"

"I was told you might have done a tattoo recently for a friend of mine, Naomi." He chuckled. "As you can see, I don't have any tattoos, but hers was so beautiful, I thought maybe I could do something similar."

"That's cool." The young man smiled in response. "I get lots of first-timers. It's addictive. You get one, you'll have to have another, I promise. What kind of a tattoo did she get?"

"A butterfly," he said. "But the wings were these leathery wings of a dragon. It was very realistic."

"Hmm." The man cocked his head. "I don't recall a job like that. I did a dragon last week, but no butterflies. But I'm happy to look at a few designs with you. I'm sure we can find something you like."

"No." Levy shook his head. "It has to be the same exact tattoo."

"And she said I did it?" There was some confusion on Kendrick's face.

"No. I thought she said it was this place, but it seems I was wrong. I guess I'd have to ask her when she comes back. She's traveling, you see."

"Okay." Kendrick shrugged. "If you change your mind, I'm happy to give you some options."

Levy thanked the man, walked outside, and stood there for a few minutes, leaning against the warm bricks of the building next door. His heart, until now fluttering like a bird in a small cage, was slowing down. He took a deep breath, unclenched his fists, and headed toward the subway station. There was no woman named Naomi with a butterfly tattoo, and John Levy was planning to do some people-watching on his ride home. He had some writing to do.

TEN

By the time I got to Carroll Gardens, it started to drizzle, the wipers startling me as they scraped across the windshield. Perhaps the tall, handsome weatherman was right after all, and we would get a cold spell in the next week or two.

I turned onto Willow Court and drove around the silver stretch limo parked next to my sister's driveway. The chauffeur, a man in his late fifties dressed in an impeccable black suit, looked at me as I rolled by his window and nodded. I shook my head. It wasn't the first time I saw it, but it amused me to no end every time. I didn't know anyone else besides my sister who takes limousines anywhere other than to a wedding reception.

Before I could stop myself, I anxiously glanced at the clock. It was 4:15 p.m. I was on time and yet, strangely, felt guilty as if I was an hour late. Tina had that effect on people.

I pulled into the driveway and parked next to the red stone porch leading to a massive oak door painted in bright yellow. Tina's house, a magnificent four-story that sat on the border of Cobble Hill and Carroll Gardens, two of the most expensive neighborhoods in Brooklyn, was one of a kind. It's been featured in one of those *Architectural*

Digest journals, the glossy magazines you find in a waiting room in a dentist's office. I had no idea how much she and Chad paid for the building or the subsequent renovation. It's easy to look up, but I'm not sure my self-esteem could handle looking at that many zeroes.

"You're here," she said, opening the door while looking at her phone. It sounded more like a question than a statement. She wore a simple, long black dress, the kind that hugged your body and show-cased your best features in the most subtle ways. For a second, I wondered if it could cover my car loan if I sold it.

"Hello, Tina. You've asked me to be here before 4:30, so here I am." I patiently watched as she finished typing, the ring with a diamond the size of a basketball on her finger throwing sunbeams into my eyes.

"Right." She finally looked up from her phone, tilted her head, and made a face.

"What?"

"What's that?" she asked, vaguely pointing at me with her chin.

"Huh?" I stared at her for a moment, and then it dawned on me. "Oh, the bruise."

"Well?" She raised an eyebrow. "Oh, never mind. Olivia? Alex is here."

"Hey, Chad," I said as Tina's husband came out of the kitchen and half walked, half jogged across the family room, fixing his bow tie as he went. He mumbled something without as much as a glance in my direction and disappeared into the bathroom.

"Make sure you come back together from dinner, eh?" I said, addressing my sister.

"Of course. Why?"

"Because I don't think Chad knows who I am. He might call the cops."

"Oh, stop it, Alex. You know how he is. He's just got a lot on his plate." She turned around and yelled into the house, louder this time. "Olivia! Come on down. Alex is here."

"Coming!" A moment later, I saw the girl, her short hair wildly swinging this way and that, as she bounded down the stairs, her mouth split in a huge grin from ear to ear. "Alex!"

I threw my arms wide open, and she barreled into me like a meteor, almost knocking me off my feet and crushing my ribs in a ferocious squeeze.

"Air," I gasped, rolling my eyes as if I was about to pass out. "Air!"

She disengaged from me and tilted her head back, studying my face. "What happened to you?"

"This?" I touched the cheek. "That's nothing. You should see the other guy."

"Come." She tugged on my arm, toward the stairs. "I have to show you this new game I've been playing."

"Sure." I followed her. "Maybe we could watch a movie before dinner? My pick, this time."

"Okay. But can we have Chinese? Please?"

"No fast food. Maria will be here by six," Tina called after us. "She'll cook you a proper meal."

"Sorry," I mouthed to the girl, and she silently rolled her eyes and shook her head.

I didn't hear when Tina and Chad left. Olivia and I played a tycoon game on her tablet. After a while, we settled in to watch some television.

"*Jumanji?*" I suggested.

"I've seen it." Olivia shrugged.

"All of them?"

"I think so. Maybe we could find some documentaries?"

"How old are you again?" I gave her a look. "Sixty-one?"

She looked sideways at me and then looked away as soon as we made eye contact. "Alex?"

"Yeah?"

"Well, never mind." She fidgeted on the couch and tucked a bright-blue throw pillow under her elbow. "Let's just watch something."

I reached out and ruffled her hair. "What's on your mind, kiddo? You can tell me."

She hesitated for a few moments. "I'm being bullied in school."

I studied her face, my heart racing. "What do you mean? Who's bullying you?"

"It's these two guys. High schoolers. They've been following me around and calling me names. I usually just ignore them, but it's been getting worse. Last week, one of them shoved me in the hallway while no one was looking and took away some of my things. Nothing important, but it's just annoying."

"What the hell?" I sat up straight. "Have you told the school?"

"No. I don't have any proof, and they don't like it when you just come to them and accuse people."

"What about your parents?"

"No."

"Why not?"

"You know how my mom is." Olivia shrugged. "She'll go ballistic, and then everyone will know me as *that* girl, and I'll have to change schools. And I really like this school. All my friends are here."

"I see." She had a point. And it *was* one of the best private schools in the city. "Tell me about the kids."

"One is Ben Nowak. Everybody calls him Big Ben because he's really tall. And the other is Tommy Lombardi. He's the one who pushed me. He's the nasty one of the two. Ben is big and scary but follows Tommy around like a puppy. Tommy is the mastermind of all their shenanigans."

"Do you know who their parents are?"

"I'm not sure about Ben," she said as she watched me. "I think his dad is a dentist? I don't know. Tommy's father is Jacob Lombardi. He makes sure to tell everyone about that."

"As in *with Lombardi on the case, you're all set, no need to pace?*" I quoted one of the most annoying jingles on television. "The ambulance chasers?"

"I think so."

"Oh gosh." I cringed. "No wonder you don't want to tell your mother. She'll eat them alive. Don't worry, kid. I'll take care of it."

"You will?"

"I promise."

"But how?"

"The less you know, the better." I gave her a wink. "Plausible deniability."

"Thank you, Alex." She scooted closer and gave me a hug. "You're the best. You know, I'm not really in the mood to watch movies. Do you mind if I just flip through the channels? I like watching the news."

"Sure." I stood up, hearing the doorbell. Maria, Tina's personal chef, was here. "I'll work then, while you are browsing."

"A new case?"

"Yeah."

"Did you crack it yet?"

"No." I smiled. "But I will."

I went downstairs, letting the woman in, and went outside to grab my laptop from the car. It stopped drizzling, but it was so humid the fine mist just hung in the air, clinging to my skin. I shivered in disgust.

When I came back, we settled in the kitchen, and I tuned out the noise of the television, trying to concentrate on the receipts from Rico's house. Most were handwritten notes of various amounts, none larger than five hundred dollars. One ticket was slightly bigger than the rest, and I zoomed in, looking at the faded blue ink, as my heart raced.

It was a pawnshop ticket, written by the Bargain Bazaar, to someone named "RL" for nine hundred ninety-nine dollars. The description cryptically stated "miscellaneous valuables," and the ticket was signed by Dev Mehta, presumably the shop's owner.

I took a deep breath—this was my first solid lead. Shady pawn-shops have been essential to many criminal organizations, helping to move stolen merchandise and launder the money. The Diablitos wasn't any different. The police always tried to connect with the local pawnshop owners to ensure they alerted the authorities if someone brought them anything suspicious. And most people did. But some played for both teams. It's always the pull and the push. What's greater—the fear of getting in trouble with the police or the financial reward and the intimidation level coming from the gangs? I don't envy those who run those places, but to quote Hyman Roth from *The Godfather*, "This is the business they have chosen."

Olivia and I might have wanted Chinese for dinner, but Maria cooked us a fresh Mediterranean salad with grilled salmon, and we chatted as we wolfed down the food. I felt strangely aloof as I sat there, listening as my niece recounted her recent school trip to Vermont. I didn't belong in this house with a polished kitchen island in brilliant white and a personal chef styling a perfectly crispy fish on expensive china plates. I'm fairly sure if not for Olivia, Tina and I would have drifted apart long ago. Maybe I was the screwup my sister always considered me to be.

"You okay, Alex?" Olivia reached out and touched my arm. "You have a funny look on your face."

"Oh, yeah." I gave her a reassuring smile. "Never better."

The limo pulled up in front of the house close to midnight, the powerful beams of light sweeping the foyer and the living room. By then, Maria was long gone, having cleaned the kitchen. Olivia and I were parked in front of the TV in the family room, watching a *Jeopardy* rerun.

"How did it go?" I asked as Chad walked through the front door.

He smiled, nodded, and did his half walk half jog again, disappearing into the second-floor study.

"I guess that's my cue," I said, giving Olivia one more hug and getting up as Tina walked through the door.

"You guys had fun?" She looked tipsy, her cheeks flushed.

"Oh yeah." Olivia came to the door. "Always. Thank you, Alex. For you know...the thing."

"What thing?" Tina asked, her tone suspicious.

"Oh, that's nothing."

"It's good that you are no longer a detective," the girl said, her face serious.

"Why is that?"

"Didn't you hear?" She turned and pointed at the TV. "The story earlier? About the Valentine Killer?"

I could feel my cheeks growing hot and cast a sideway glance at my sister. I didn't hear about the Valentine Killer, but there was a significant chance someone would be murdered in this house. "No. Maybe—"

"They were talking about this murder," Olivia continued, oblivious to the growing tension around her. "There was this woman who was killed back in February on Valentine's Day, but nobody said anything about it because they thought it was just one lady. But now, they found this other woman, and they are saying it's a serial killer because they were both killed the same way. They said he cut them open and took their organs out. Really gross stuff."

"Is this your idea of appropriate entertainment for an eleven-year-old?" Tina's voice dropped an octave. "For once, Alex, can I trust you? For once?"

"I'm sorry, Mom," Olivia said, realizing her mistake. "It's not Aunt Alex's fault. She wanted to watch a movie, but I didn't feel like it. I was just flipping channels, and this was on TV. It's not a big deal, really. It's not like they were showing anything inappropriate."

"It's not your fault." Tina padded her on the head. "You're a kid. That's why we have adults. Who can supervise and make adult decisions. But apparently, Alex here isn't one of them."

"Look," I started to lose patience, "I'm sorry she heard that, but you can't keep her in a cocoon either. People talk about that stuff, too. It might be better if she hears something like this on the news, not from some high schoolers with a bunch of scary boloney attached to it. It's a rough world out there. Sooner or later, she'll learn about it."

"Well, that's my decision, isn't it?" She turned to me and pointed her perfectly manicured finger at my chest. "When you get a kid, you can make whatever decisions you want. Until then, I'll decide what is or isn't appropriate for her to see."

"I'm sorry, Mom," Olivia repeated, trying to get her out of the zone. She turned to me. "Do you think they'll catch him?"

"They will, kiddo." I leaned over and kissed her forehead. "They always do. NYPD are the best of the best. He doesn't stand a chance. Good night now, I've got to run. I'm beat."

"I hope so." She tilted her head. "It's scary, though. Poor Naomi."

A year or so ago, I read an article about what a human would feel if exposed to the vacuum of space. The sudden drop in pressure paralyzing the lungs. The struggle for the oxygen that wasn't there. I wasn't in space, but now, looking at my niece, I knew exactly how that felt. "What did you say her name was?"

"Naomi something," she mumbled, a terrified look on her face. "Why?"

"Nothing," I said, my face numb. "I'll see you later, kiddo."

Then I walked outside and stood on the porch, staring into the void.

ELEVEN

John Levy whistled as the knife scraped against the toast, the blunt, rounded blade pushing soft butter in tight semicircles until it covered the entire golden-brown surface. Satisfied, he walked to the window, a cup of coffee in one hand, toast in another, and took a big bite, savoring the crunch as he watched the magnolia tree in the yard. The sky was cloudy and gray, making the flowers' bright, luscious pink hues look pale and subdued. The courtyard, dim even on the sunniest days, today looked particularly gloomy, like the bottom of a deep well. But none of it bothered Levy at the moment. On the contrary, as he watched the melancholy scenery outside, he was at peace.

It hadn't started this way. The sense of relief he had when none of the tattoo artists in St. Mark's Square seemed to remember a woman with a peculiar butterfly tattoo was short-lived. As he sat in the corner of the subway car on the way home, watching the crowd, looking for colorful characters for the book, his mind wandered. As the train slowly rumbled from station to station, Levy grew increasingly agitated. By the time the R took him to the last stop in Bay Ridge, his anxiety was back with a vengeance.

He hardly slept that night, tossing and turning under the sweat-soaked sheets until he couldn't stay in bed a second longer. He was up by four in the morning, pacing the room back and forth between the kitchen table and the couch, obsessively watching the news. He was spiraling out of control. A few times, he opened the drawer that kept the bright-orange box with antidepressants, but then he would close it again. The mystery of the Montblanc pen still haunted him, and he thought the pills might have been to blame.

In the book, Naomi's body was found almost immediately after the murder. Luca, his confidence growing after the first successful hunt, became careless and nearly got caught as he disposed of the corpse in a public park at the crack of dawn. By late morning, every news outlet in the city was supposed to buzz with gruesome details of the murder.

But as the day progressed and Levy kept switching from one news channel to the next, there was nothing. There was plenty of crime, of course. There were murders and robberies. Rapes and domestic abuse cases. A three-alarm fire in Queens and a flooded basement in Staten Island. The city was big, and someone—some-where, somehow—was going to get hurt. But every time Levy held his breath when a crime segment came up on yet another channel, they talked about something other than a dead woman named Naomi.

By late afternoon, he was calm enough to order a pizza, and he ate it in silence as he sat at the table facing the window and occasion-ally glanced at the muted television. When night fell on the city, Levy finally turned off the screen, had a glass of wine, and went to bed. If he had dreamed of anything while he slept, he had no recol-lection of it in the morning.

There was nothing on the news, but Levy dutifully watched the morning shows while making himself a cup of coffee and toast. He turned off the television, had breakfast by the window overlooking the tree, and sat in front of a laptop. It was clear now—there was no woman named Naomi. Not one who was going to die at the hands of a crazed man convinced she was possessed by a demon, anyway.

And now that the dread of an inevitable disaster had disappeared, the writing itch was back.

He read the synopsis of the following few chapters again to refresh his memory and got to work, his fingers flying over the keyboard as the story continued. The killer was on the hunt again, stalking a new victim, a young man named Benjamin French.

John was particularly proud of this curveball. Too many serial killer novels and movies followed the predictable path where the sociopath hunted for a specific type of person. Most of them were women. Many carried a distinct trait that triggered a long-suppressed trauma of the killer. Red hair. Blue eyes. A certain age. Levy's fictional Luca had none of those needs. He believed that he collected demons no matter what shape they took. Young or old. Handsome or plain. None of it mattered. Because Luca had no type, it also made catching him much more challenging. Levy was looking forward to writing the finale, revealing a long string of subtle clues he would plant along the way that could have led the police and the private eye to the killer. At some point, he'd have to decide if Luca would get caught. Or get away with murder.

But that would come later. For now, in the book, the killer believed that Benjamin French would unlock the next demon spirit. Within days, Luca would learn Ben's habits and rituals and find the best time to strike. Then, he'd make a move, and the poor young man would find himself in the same soundproofed room as Naomi's final destination.

By late afternoon, Levy finished two long passages leading up to the kidnapping. He read them out loud, catching a typo here and there and polishing a few sentences until he was satisfied with the result. By then, the next chapter, the abduction sequence, and the murder scene, was etched into his mind, clear as day, ready to jump onto the screen. And yet, after he typed the chapter heading at the top of the page, Levy sat still, staring into the void. He started to type a few times, putting down a sentence or two, only to strike them down again the next moment.

After several unsuccessful tries, he stood up and pushed the chair away from the table. Naomi might have been only killed in his mind, but he couldn't bring himself to write another murder. At least not today.

"Perhaps a few days' break won't hurt," he said out loud.

Levy closed the laptop and placed it on his nightstand. Then he put on a windbreaker and a Yankees hat and went outside. A fine mist hung in the air, clinging to Levy's face and clothes. The sky was getting dark now, a murky shade of gray, and the clouds loomed low as if burdened by the weight of the city below. He took Third Avenue all the way to Shore Road. Then he made his way down to the promenade along the strait, leisurely strolling the path as he watched the hulking silhouette of the bridge jutting over the bay.

The boardwalk was unusually empty at this hour, and John quickened his pace as if trying to outrun the tension that had settled over him. But it was no use. For a moment, he imagined that he was the only living soul left in the entire world, unknowingly having crossed into the realm of the dead. Walking the endless path by the dark river that separated him from the living.

He stopped momentarily, trying to regain his equilibrium, and was about to turn back when he caught a glimpse of a silhouette in the distance. As he squinted through the falling darkness, he thought it was a woman. There was something familiar about her. About the elegant curve of her back as she leaned on the railing. The tilt of her head. He took a few steps toward her, unsure of himself, not wanting to startle her. But as he got closer, the figure became animated and waved at him, and suddenly Levy found it hard to breathe.

"Lilly?"

"John? I was just out for a walk, and I thought I saw you," she said, her voice carrying on the wind.

He closed the distance between them and hugged her tightly. She smelled like lilac and jasmine, just like he remembered.

"What are you doing here?" she asked, her eyes scanning his face, a half-smile playing on her lips.

"I was taking a break from my writing," he said. "Needed to clear my head. You?"

"I wanted some fresh air, only to find this apocalyptic scene." She nodded at the bridge, half-hidden by the fog. "The only thing missing is the howl of the Baskerville hound."

"Yes," he said, letting her go. "It would be fitting."

"I have to say," there was a glint in her eye, "I'm a bit surprised you've never called."

"I did. But I think I got your number wrong," he said. His cheeks were burning. He pulled out his phone and scrolled through his contact list. "Look."

She studied the screen for a moment, reached out, and tapped her manicured nail on the last number. "That should have been seven, not eight."

"Darn it. I thought you ditched me, to be honest. Gave me the wrong number on purpose. It wouldn't be the first time. I'm sorry." He took a step closer, hesitant, waiting for her to stop him. To pull away. She didn't, and he leaned into her, his mouth finding her lips. She tasted like strawberries.

"You want to get out of here?" she asked when he finally came up for air. "I'm getting cold."

"Sure." He turned around, and she linked her arm through his as they walked, their steps perfectly in sync. "We could hit that German bar, but I'm sure we can find something closer? There are plenty of good places on Third Ave. A couple of drinks will warm you right up."

"We could." She gave his arm a soft squeeze. "Or we could see what we can find at your place? Surely you have something?"

He took her back to his building, her hand in his, his mind racing. They walked up the stairs, and Levy fumbled with his keys in the hallway. Then, finally, the lock clicked, and they stepped into a dark foyer. The savory, tangy smell of the pizza he had the night before still hung in the air. Levy reached for the light switch, but Lilly pushed him up against the wall, her hands searching his body. Hungry. Demanding.

They stumbled through the place and made their way to the bedroom. The blue lights from the window danced on her naked skin, and Levy's world spun out of control as he let himself go. Tumbling headlong into the unknown.

"Are you going to disappear in the morning like you did last time?" he asked as they lay later in bed side by side, his skin electric where it touched hers.

"I'm not sure." She chuckled. "I haven't decided yet."

"Funny. Do you want that drink now? I have some wine, or perhaps I can fix something stronger?"

"No." She propped herself on her elbow. "But I'm hungry. That pizza smell is driving me crazy. It is pizza, right? Do you have anything? Don't answer. Just stay here. I'll look myself."

She got up and walked to the kitchen before he could say anything, not making any attempts to cover herself. She plucked an apple from a vase on the table and turned back, taking a big bite.

"Wow," was all he could manage.

"What have you been up to?"

"Work. Mostly." He couldn't take his eyes off her, standing so freely in the middle of his apartment, the blue light accentuating her curves.

"Ugh. Sour." She put the apple back on the table and walked toward him in slow, deliberate steps. "How's your novel going?"

"In stops and starts." He glanced at the laptop on the nightstand. "Mostly in stops."

"How so?" She climbed on the bed and straddled him, guiding him in. "I thought it was going to be a masterpiece?"

"I don't know. I'm having doubts," he said. His thoughts were scattered, his mind dizzy.

She rode him. Slowly at first, then faster and faster. He grabbed her sides as she leaned close to him, her face right next to his.

"You shouldn't be afraid," she whispered, her breath hot on his skin as she drove her nails into his chest. "Conquer your fears, and greatness will follow."

TWELVE

When Morton called, I was pulling up into a tight parking spot next to the Bargain Bazaar in the shadow of the overhead highway. I let the phone ring while I squeezed between a beat-up Dodge Caravan and a Jeep that was brand new during the Reagan administration, put the car in park, and only then hit the Talk button on the steering wheel.

"Mr. Morton. It's kind of you to return my call."

"Not at all." He didn't take the bait. I could almost see a condescending smirk on his plump lips. "What can I do for you? Any updates?"

"Some." I stayed quiet, letting him stew, as I watched the pawn-shop. It was nestled between two dilapidated buildings, its faded sign barely visible from the street. The grimy windows—two dark gaping holes in a graffiti-covered wall—were secured behind thick metal grates. "I have a solid lead."

"Good."

I silently cursed. A real talker, this one. "You said you'd tell me what it was if I had something concrete."

"Do you have something concrete?"

"Two low-level Diablitos had the items. I suspect they were the ones who lifted them from the bank in the first place. I saw the boxes intact but couldn't retrieve them in time. But whatever was inside is now in the wild, getting laundered."

"I see."

"I got lucky," I said. A big statement, considering my adventures at Rico's house and the sorry state of my face. "I found a pawnshop where I think they left the merchandise. I'm about to go in. It would be hugely helpful if I knew what I was looking for."

He stayed quiet for a while. There was a wet sound on the line, as if he sucked on his lip.

I waited. One of the tricks you learn as a cop is the power of silence. People aren't comfortable with the quiet. They want to fill it. If you just keep pushing, even the biggest cowards tend to push back sooner or later. But most of them will spill when you give the person enough information and then have the patience to shut up just long enough. So, I sat in the car, listening to Morton suck on his lip and contemplate.

"Look," he finally said. "I appreciate where you're coming from. But I don't think my client would be comfortable sharing this information at this point."

So much for the pregnant pause. "Okay. But you gotta give me something."

"However, I can tell you what it isn't. It's not documents. Give me a call when you have more, will you?"

He hung up before I could answer. I wanted to do some lip chewing of my own now. The secrecy around the object was starting to get old. But this was something, at least. It sounded like Morton's client was after an object. Considering the dimensions of the safe deposit boxes, it couldn't be anything large, either. Jewelry perhaps? Or a weapon? It would get dicey if it was a weapon. But I'd have to cross that bridge when I got there. For now, I had a pawnshop broker to talk to.

I pushed the door open, and a small bell chimed above me,

signaling my arrival. The shop was long and narrow, the air thick with the smell of mildew and stale cigarette smoke. On the right was a counter made of stained, worn-out wood, behind which sat a man in his mid-fifties with greasy hair and a thick mustache. His dark, almost black eyes met mine, and he gave me a silent nod of acknowledgment. To my left, there were shelves with merchandise. The thick protective glass was covered in grime and filth, a window into a world of sordid deals and desperation.

"Hello?" The man's voice was high-pitched and raspy. A life-long smoker's voice. "Looking for anything in particular?"

"Perhaps." I took a slow walk along the showcase.

He stood up, the chair making a scraping sound as he did, and walked around the counter until he stood in front of me, his nicotine-stained fingers leaning on the smudge-covered glass. "Want to see something up close?"

"Sure. I'd like to look at what you paid a thousand dollars to Rico and Lopez for."

He remained still, but I could see the flicker of recognition in his eyes. "I've no idea what you're talking about."

"Come on, Dev. I'm not going to rat you out to the cops. This is just business. Don't you need to sell it, anyway? I'll buy it from you. Kill two birds with one stone."

"You're out of your mind, lady. I have nothing to tell you, and unless you have something to buy or pawn, I'd suggest you get going."

"I have a receipt. For nine hundred and ninety-nine dollars, to be exact. Signed by someone named Dev Mehta of Bargain Bazaar. Isn't that you?"

"Get the fuck out of my store before—"

"Before, what? You call the cops? I'd love to see that."

He said nothing and skulked behind the counter, only to emerge from there with a baseball bat.

"You don't want to do that." I placed my hand on the small of my back, my fingers touching the rough surface of the pistol grip. Since my adventure in Rico's basement, I was taking my P30SK everywhere I went. Call me paranoid, but I'd rather have an unpleasant conversation with a cop if they happened to see me carrying than find out the local cartel guys were just as bad as their cousins across the border.

"Get out. Now." He stopped a few steps away from me, visibly conflicted. He didn't seem to believe I had a gun but wasn't trying to find out for sure, either.

"Look, Dev. It doesn't have to be this way. But I really need what Rico and Lopez brought here. You can either sell it to me and make money, or I'll go around town telling everyone I meet how much you hate those two nice gentlemen and can't wait to give them up to the local precinct."

"What?" He waved his hand in exasperation and then angrily stabbed the bat toward my face. "You have no idea what you're getting yourself into. No idea."

I shrugged and waited. Pregnant pauses and all that.

"You're going to get me killed." He put the bat down, looking deflated.

I said nothing.

"How do you know Rico?"

"It doesn't matter. They took something that didn't belong to them. Now you have it, and I want it back. It doesn't have to be complicated. Let me buy it, and you'll never see me again. Everybody wins."

"It's not that simple." He walked back, threw the bat under the counter, and sat in his chair. "I know what you think of me. But I'm an honest man, just trying to survive."

"Sure."

"Oh, you think you have me all figured out," he bristled. "I didn't choose to do this. It's not like that show on TV where people bring cool random shit to the pawnshop, and everybody walks away with a decent deal. I saved a little cash and borrowed more from my cousin to open this place. All I wanted was a chance. Isn't it what they say? This is America. If you work hard, you can build your dream here."

I said nothing.

"One day, these two clowns showed up and asked me to work for them. Said they'd pay me well. All I needed to do was to buy stuff from them. Cheap. Said I'd make a good profit." He sighed and lowered his head. "I chased them off with this very bat."

I watched him sitting on his chair, his mustache somberly pointing down. "What happened?"

"Nothing for a while. A few weeks went by, and I forgot about them. It's a lot of work to run this shop. At least it used to be. Then one day, they showed up, and this white man was with them. He was small and skinny, yet I was shitting my pants the moment he walked in."

The way he said it sent cold shivers down my spine. "What did he do?"

"They didn't touch me," he said. "Just told me to sit down, and Franky, that man's name it was, showed me a video."

The hairs on the back of my neck stood up. "What video?"

"There was this man," Mehta said, his voice breaking. "He was on the ground. A steel collar around his neck. Two men held his legs, and another stepped on his face to keep him from moving. And there was this Franky guy with a knife... At least he said it was him. All I could see was his hands and the blade. I can't... The poor son of a bitch was still alive as this man...this man..."

He broke down, crying as I stood there. "I'm sorry."

"Look." He wiped his face with the back of his hand and stared back at me. His eyes were hard now, determined. "I don't have what you're looking for. Franky took all of it. He didn't even pay me this time, so I'm out a thousand bucks. I have a family; I can't risk this. I'm begging you, don't talk about them to other people."

"What was in those safe deposit boxes? Can you tell me that, at least?" I walked over to the counter and stood in front of him. "Tell me that, and I swear I'll walk away from here. You'll never see me again."

"It wasn't much," he said. "Some passports, real estate papers, a living will. Some jewelry, a few gold coins. Nothing worth risking your life over."

"Were there any weapons?"

"Weapons? Like guns?" He shook his head. "No. No weapons. It was all cheap stuff, really. There was this necklace that I thought might be worth something. The stone was rather unusual. But I had my precious stone guy look at it, and he said it was a couple of hundred bucks at most."

I thought about it. Could those coins be rare and worth much more than the pawnshop broker suspected? Or was it the necklace with a strange stone? *It wasn't the papers*, Morton said. That didn't leave a whole lot of choices. "And Franky took all of it?"

"Yes."

"How do I find him?"

He looked at me as if I were a dim-witted child and then spoke slowly and deliberately. "The only people who know how to find Franky are Rico and Lopez. I don't know where Franky is. I don't *want* to know where Franky is. And *you* don't want to know where Franky is."

I sighed. "But I do. Somebody's paying me good money to find what was in those boxes."

"I don't know how much they are paying you." Mehta rose to his feet, signaling that the meeting was over. "But I can assure you—they are not paying you nearly enough."

"Fine." I turned on my heels and headed for the door. "As promised, I won't bother you again."

He said nothing as I pulled on the handle.

"Actually..." I paused as the doorbell chimed, this time announcing my departure. "One more thing. What was the name of that unusual stone in the necklace?"

"I don't remember." He stroked his mustache with a yellowed finger. "It was a weird name. Sounded like a *parasite*."

"Did you say a parasite?"

"Yeah. I know it sounds strange, but that's what he said. But it was worthless. The necklace itself was made of stainless steel. It was finished to look like white gold, but it wasn't fooling anyone. And the stone looked pretty, but I already told you; my guy said it wouldn't fetch much. Whoever stored it in that safe deposit box probably had other reasons to keep it. Sentimental value, perhaps. People get attached to the strangest things. I see it all the time. They bring their trinkets to the shop thinking they'd get something for them and then get all pissy because nobody cares they got them from their grandpa."

"And the coins? You're sure they weren't rare?"

"I'm sure. Just your run-of-the-mill gold coins."

"Thanks."

I stepped outside and closed the door behind me. Despite my bravado, Dev Mehta was right about one thing—I didn't want to know where Franky was. Whatever they had shown to the pawnshop broker must have been horrific. But I took Morton's money. This was the business *I had chosen*. I had to see it through.

I looked up and down the street, making sure no one was watching me, got into the car, and started the engine. While I couldn't ask Rico for Franky's whereabouts for obvious reasons, it didn't mean I was out of leads. I still had one. My informant, Pete. He wasn't going to like it, and I suspected even if I managed to squeeze the information out of him, I wouldn't get away with a few crispy banknotes as payment. This was too big. If Pete knew what was best for him, he'd use it to finally get off my hook.

I sighed. This job sure looked like it was going to burn some bridges. I pulled out of the parking spot, maneuvered the car around the Caravan, and headed for the highway. A few heavy raindrops hit the windshield, and the wipers moved, smearing the dust across my view. As I sped down the highway, heading back to my house, I couldn't help but wonder—what was so special about whatever Morton's client was looking for? I was missing something, and it troubled me. Whatever it was, the promised bonus money no longer seemed generous.

THIRTEEN

The light tap-tapping of the rain against the windowpanes roused John Levy from sleep. He blinked and squinted at the gray outline, his eyes tracing the raindrops as they raced down the foggy surface. He propped himself on his elbows and looked around the empty room. The sheets on the other side of the bed were crumpled, but the woman was gone; the only evidence of her ever being there was a lingering scent of jasmine.

John swung his legs off the bed and sat up straight, listening. The city was never a quiet place. The soothing pattering of the rain outside was interrupted by the rumbling cars in the distance, occasionally punctuated by an angry horn. There was a gentle humming of the refrigerator coming from the kitchen and the muted sounds of conversations drifting through the pipes and the walls from other units in the building. But there was no sound he wanted to hear the most—the sound of another person walking around his living quarters.

"Lilly?" he called out into the apartment, just to be sure, but no answer came. He stood up and walked through the place, checking the shower and the kitchen. Nobody was there, and he shook his head and smiled as he stood in the middle of the room.

He had hoped he would find her still next to him in the morning. Now that she wasn't there, he should have been disappointed, but somehow, he was not. It felt different. He didn't mind being patient. Lilly was wild and independent, strong-willed, and...he drew a short breath...wonderful. It may have started as a spontaneous fling, a one-night stand. But something was happening between them. He was sure of it now. Something was happening *to him.*

He didn't know what it was, but there was a softness in the world around him for the first time since he had received that dreadful phone call about Grace. It was as if the room had been dark for the longest time, and then somebody finally lifted a heavy curtain, letting the morning sun in.

He rubbed his face with both hands, erasing the silly ear-to-ear smile, but it returned a moment later, and he let it stay.

He took a quick shower and drank strong coffee, whistling as he went. The fridge was empty, the lonely piece of a two-day-old pizza staring at him from the top shelf, and Levy decided to take a short walk to the farmers' market and pick up a few things for lunch.

He wore a light jacket, pulled up the hood, and went down to Third Avenue. The rain fell in a light drizzle, the pitter-patter of drops echoing in his ears and splashing his face as he wove through the crowded stalls. The vibrant colors and pungent smells of the market assaulted his senses. John stopped there for a moment, taking it in, watching the crowd move, hands reaching out and touching and probing the fruits and the vegetables. Listening to the vendors calling out and touting their fares.

He bought a head of lettuce, a box of cherry tomatoes, some cucumbers, and a ripe avocado. Then, giving in to temptation, picked up a pair of flaky croissants and a jar of dark local honey.

As he made his way back to the apartment, the rain picked up, and John jogged up the road, clutching the paper bag to his chest, the raindrops beating against his face like thousands of tiny fists.

He was soaked to the bone and shivering by the time he stepped through the door, but to his delight, the croissants were still warm, the buttery scent wafting through the air as he opened the bag. John put a kettle on and slathered the pastry with honey, his mouth salivating in anticipation.

A minute later, the kettle was whistling. John carefully put the saucer with the croissant on the kitchen table and turned toward the counter to make a cup of tea. His eyes flicked back to the table as his fingers reached for his favorite mug. His laptop sat between a saucer and the vase that still had the apple with Lilly's bite in it.

He frowned, his heart skipping a beat. He had been certain that he had left the laptop on the nightstand in his bedroom. He tried to retrace his steps. Had he moved it in the morning without realizing it? Or had Lilly brought it to the kitchen table before she left?

He hesitated before reaching out and flipping open the lid. John felt a cold knot form in his stomach as the screen flickered to life. The manuscript was open, and he saw that more text had been added to the novel.

He sat down in front of the computer, mechanically scrolling through the document. There were multiple pages of new text starting right where he left off.

Luca heaved the massive door open and looked at the bound figure on the floor of the soundproofed room. The young man was still uncon-scious, but his cheeks were no longer pale, taking on a healthy pink glow. The man would wake up soon, and Luca wasn't ready.

He went back to his study and put a mask on. Then he pulled a small bottle without a label and a square rag from the top drawer of his desk and walked back to his captive. He kneeled next to him, squirted some liquid into the rag, and pressed it into the man's face, counting out loud, the sounds muffled by his mask. He let go when he reached twenty. That was going to keep Benjamin French asleep for at least another hour.

Content, Luca left the room, pushed the heavy door back in place until it locked with a satisfying click, took off the mask, and returned to his office.

There was a leather-bound journal on his desk, and Luca picked it up, pulled on a bookmark ribbon, and opened it, looking at his notes. There was the description of the ritual he performed on the late Naomi Williams, and he re-read it, making sure he hadn't missed anything. When he was done, he flipped the journal to another page, his massive index finger tracing three names written in a neat cursive at the top. Two women. One man. Three vessels waiting for him to find them.

- Isaac Greenberg

- Emily Rivera

- Ruby Wong

Below the names was a wall of text detailing everything he knew by now about Ruby Wong. He had no information on the other two. Not yet. But it would come in time. The hunt for these three was going to be his most dangerous. Unlike the demons he had already captured, these were of a higher rank. Stronger. Faster. Smarter. The ritual could kill him if something went wrong.

But there was a weak link. He didn't know how, but the book said these demons were connected. If he performed the ritual on all of them at once, they'd stand no chance against him.

Luca closed the journal and reached for the phone, a gray rectangular office model with a bulky wireless receiver. He dialed the number and waited.

"Hello?" The woman's voice was cheerful and honest. She seemed confused about an unknown number's call, yet she sounded polite, almost to a fault. Telemarketers must have loved Ruby Wong.

Luca smiled broadly before answering. He'd read somewhere that a smile came across in phone conversations, and he smiled when he talked to people over the phone ever since. He made his voice sound deep and reassuring. "Ruby Wong? My name is Hank, and my wife saw your ad in the online marketplace for the cookies you're selling. We are having some friends over, and she thought it would be a nice *touch to have artisanal cookies for dessert. Not a huge party by any means. Just four people. I personally don't know much about cookies, but she was really gushing over your product, so here I am."*

Ruby Wong gave a polite laugh and switched into selling mode as she ran down the list of reasons Luca's imaginary wife was making the right choice.

He made his smile even wider when she stopped talking. "Well, it's settled then. Would you be able to get them done by tomorrow? I can meet you somewhere in the city that is convenient for you, but it would have to be after eight in the evening, if that's okay. I work pretty late."

"Of course." She sounded enthusiastic.

"It's a deal, then," he said after negotiating the price. "I'll call you tomorrow afternoon to confirm the pickup time and the place."

John Levy stopped reading and carefully lowered the lid of the laptop. He sat there for a few moments, perfectly still, the air growing thick around him. For some reason, he thought about the honey he had bought, wondering what it would feel like to be a fly stuck on its syrupy, viscous surface. Struggling as his legs sunk deeper and deeper until the liquid came up to his face, covering his mouth and nose, choking him in its nauseating sweetness.

A painful pang hit him in the stomach with the force of a sledge-hammer. Levy doubled over; his body contorted with spasms as he vomited with the force of a pressure hose. The acrid smell filled the air, making him even more queasy. He fell to his knees, panting and gasping for air, and retched again, heaving as his now-empty stomach cramped, trying to expel liquid that was no longer there. He trembled as he tried to regain his balance, his face twisted with pain. Sweat rolled down his temples, and he steadied himself with a hand on the ground, taking deep breaths to calm his churning stomach.

Gradually, the nausea subsided, and he shakily forced himself to his feet, wiping his mouth with the back of a hand.

He walked to the bathroom and splashed some cold water on his face. It helped, and Levy filled a bucket with soapy water, picked up a mop, and got to work. He scrubbed the floor until the mess was gone, trying to find comfort in the monotony of physical effort.

When finished, he put the mop in the corner, threw the croissant into a garbage bin, and washed his face.

Calmer now, he took his cell phone and dialed Lilly's number.

"That didn't take you long," she said, picking up after the first ring, startling him.

Now that she was on the line, he realized he didn't expect her to answer. He wasn't ready for how she sounded, either. The words teased, but her tone was light and playful.

"I wondered if you would last twenty-four hours, but now we know the answer."

"I hoped I'd find you next to me in the morning."

"I don't recall making promises."

"True."

"Did you have something important to ask or did you just want to chat? I need to get some things done. I can call you later, and we can talk."

"Oh, nothing important." He squirmed, not knowing how to ask about the laptop without accusing her.

"Okay."

"Wait. It might sound like a weird question—do you recall seeing my laptop yesterday?"

"Why? Is it missing?"

"Oh no, not at all," he said quickly. "It's here. But I could have sworn I had left it in the bedroom, and this morning, I found it on the table in the kitchen."

There was a pause on the other end of the line, and John held his breath.

"I didn't pay attention," she said. "I don't recall seeing it at all. Wait, did you think I moved it there?"

"No," he said. "Trying to get my bearings. It was probably one of those sleepwalking things."

"I promise you; I didn't touch your laptop. I would never do something like that without your permission."

John closed his eyes and rapped his knuckles on his forehead in frustration. "Of course. Never mind, forget I asked. I'm like that in the morning sometimes."

"Okay. I've got to run. Call me later then." She hung up before he could say anything else.

He stuffed the phone in the back of his jeans and groaned. *Somebody* wrote those pages on his laptop last night. There could have been a few explanations of how that happened, and John didn't care for any of them. For starters, his laptop was password-protected. For Lilly or anyone other than John, accessing his novel would require hacking his computer first. And if he wrote those pages himself... He didn't even want to go down that path. First, there was the mysterious pen. Now this.

He shook his head. Perhaps he was overreacting. The deadline was behind him. Naomi couldn't be dead; he was sure of it now. Whatever happened on the pages of his manuscript wouldn't hurt anyone, regardless of who typed the words.

He crossed the kitchen, opened the drawer with antidepressants, and took a pill out of the bottle. He stared at it for a moment, contemplating, and then poured a cup of cold water and washed the bright-blue capsule down with it.

Then he went to the living room, sat in front of the TV, and flipped it on. The voice of a female reporter cut the silence in the apartment like a razor slicing through flesh.

Who made the gruesome discovery. Naomi Williams was only thirty years old and had just moved to New York City last summer. Her friends described her as an eternal optimist and a caring soul, always ready to help those in need.

. . .

John Levy clicked the television off and closed his eyes. But even then, the world around him spun on.

FOURTEEN

I didn't like the way my house smelled. It wasn't a sweet odor of something rotten, a violent and offensive scent that would assault your senses if you got close enough to the source of it. It was more like a pungent whiff of ozone or a burning wire. It was subtle, and I wouldn't have noticed it if I had marched through the door as intended. But the key refused to come out of the keyhole, yanking my arm back as I tried to clear the threshold and, for a moment, I was stuck in the middle of the doorway, my feet inside of the house, and the rest of me leaning out at an awkward angle.

That's where it hit me. I stood there for a moment, sniffing the air like a hunting dog on a trail, fully aware of how I must have looked to any passersby, but there was something peculiar about that smell that sent shivers running down my spine.

I freed the key from the lock and pocketed it, stepping inside the house and closing the door behind me. Then, I unholstered my pistol and crept through the hallway, straining to hear any sounds of an intruder. There were none, and as I made my way through the house, checking one room after another, my heartbeat slowed, the rush of excitement gone.

After inspecting the second floor, I returned downstairs, holstered my weapon, and went to the bathroom to splash some cold water on my face. When I turned to grab the towel from the hook next to the small mirror, a hairbrush caught my attention. It was a cheap, medium-sized oval brush with a long, ribbed handle colored to resemble polished wood. I had used it in the morning before I left the house, and it was just where I had left it, on the right side of the sink. But the more I looked at it, the more I didn't love the angle of the handle pointing directly at me as if it were an accusatory finger.

I squatted next to the vanity and inspected the brush closely. It looked ordinary, a few strands of my hair sticking out between the rows of steel bristles. I reached out and touched the very tip of the handle with my wet index finger, and the brush spun a few degrees counterclockwise as it rested on its slightly curved back. That's what it must have been. It turned after I had laid it on the counter.

I pushed the images of Rico and Lopez breaking into my house while I was at the pawnshop out of my head. Cartel guys were anything but subtle. They'd probably torch my house if they knew who I was and wanted to leave a message. Sneaking in and moving a hair brush an eighth of an inch to screw with my head wasn't exactly their MO.

I dried myself and sat in my favorite chair, firing up my laptop. Pete, my go-to snitch, wouldn't be roaming the streets for a couple more hours, which meant I had some time to kill.

For now, I could concentrate on what was really baking my noodle—how on earth did John Levy know about the death of Naomi. The initial shock after hearing her name from my niece's lips had waned, and while it might come across as cynical, it wasn't exactly my problem. I didn't believe Levy was the killer; the woman was already dead, and nobody paid me for my troubles. Finding Naomi's murderer, whether he was a serial killer or not, was best left to the talented people at the NYPD.

Most importantly, I had bills to pay and a paying client to take care of. Ezekiel Morton didn't exactly strike me as someone who would take kindly to wasting his time and money.

But the mystery gnawed at me. And now that I had a couple of hours of free time with no leads for Morton's case, my mind kept going to the poor woman. Perhaps, before I attempted to answer how Levy knew about Naomi's impending death, I needed to learn more about the man himself. Something I probably should have done in the beginning.

I started with the usual—a general Google search to get to the low-hanging fruit first. I typed *John Levy* into the box, and when I hit Enter, the search engine spat out over a hundred thousand hits, with the top one being some jazz cat who'd been dead for years. I ignored the links and went straight to the images. I scanned a few rows, and there it was, at the very bottom of the first page—an old photograph that was undoubtedly a younger version of the John Levy I had met. He was dressed to kill, on a stage somewhere, smiling like he owned the world. His face was rounder then and more relaxed, but it was definitely him.

I clicked on the link to an article in the news section of a wealth management company—LMR Partners. The event, ambitiously titled "The Future of Wealth Management," was headlined by one of the managing directors, John E. Levy.

I exited the article and went to the About Us section of the website to look at the big cheese. There were three, two women and a man named Theodore Karalis, but no John Levy. Confused, I went back to the original picture and took another look at it. It was him, no doubt. I swapped the page again, returned to the management section, and inspected the bios of the two women. Jennifer McCarthy and Kathy Reed. Levy, McCarthy, and Reed. LMR. It fit, but it seemed that Levy was no longer employed by the company that still bore his name.

I opened a new tab, pulled up LinkedIn, and ran another search. Levy's profile was at the very top of the results page—almost a carbon copy of the Google result. It listed him as the managing partner for

LMR up until five years ago. There had been no job listed since. It seemed like a dead end, as were his social media profiles, as Levy didn't maintain any.

I sat motionless for a few moments as I considered my options. I could run a standard background check but was reluctant to go that route. At the first meeting, he gave me an impression of a wealthy man, and his position at LMR, even though it was no longer current, only solidified that opinion. Running background checks on wealthy people is tricky. You never know what trip wires they might have set in place that would let them know someone was snooping around their lives. I didn't want Levy to know I was curious. Not yet.

For now, I decided to run a newspaper archive search that turned up precisely two articles. One was about Levy's nomination for the 40 *under* 40 list. Another was an obituary for Grace Isabelle Levy, who was survived by her husband, John Levy, and her younger brother, Sam Becker. I checked the date—it was five years ago and two months before John Levy's employment ended.

I was starting to get somewhere. Although the obituary didn't state Grace's cause of death, the wording made me think it wasn't a prolonged battle with a deadly disease. At this point, my imagination was running wild, conjuring up the images of a robbery gone wrong or a home invasion, but another newspaper search turned up a short paragraph in the online edition of *The New York Globe* that put an end to that theory:

In a tragic accident that occurred today in the city, a scaffolding erected around the Gotham Heights Tower on Madison Avenue collapsed and buried three people underneath. Two of the victims are expected to survive the incident, but unfortunately, Grace Levy, the wife of well-known financier John Levy, succumbed to her injuries. Mister Levy was in Zurich, Switzerland, at the time of this writing and unavailable for comment. The incident has left the city in shock, and authorities are investigating the cause of the collapse. Our hearts go out to the family and loved ones of the deceased during this difficult time.

I slammed my laptop shut and gnawed on a ragged nail, lost in thought. Losing a wife was a life-changing event for John Levy. That much was obvious. By all accounts, he seemed to be in the driver's seat of his life right up to that point. A great school and an incredibly successful career. Philanthropic endeavors. And then, a freak accident kills his wife, and his life derails. The man practically dropped off the map. Was it connected to the murders somehow? And more importantly, was I wrong about him not being the killer?

I dug deeper, poring over every detail, following every lead. There was no apparent link between the incident five years ago and two murdered young women. Atlas General Contractors, the company doing construction in the Gotham Heights Tower, had no ties to LMR. Atlas was later sued by the city and lost, ultimately forcing it into bankruptcy, and I couldn't find Levy's connection to the lawsuit either.

But perhaps there was something more? What if the women were related to those responsible for the scaffolding collapse, and Levy killed them to get back at those who robbed him of his loved one? Trying to make them suffer the same way he had suffered? I was grasping at straws and knew it.

I sighed, put the laptop away, and glanced at my watch—it was time for me to make another trip to Sunset Park. I put on a jacket—it stopped raining, but there was a noticeable chill in the air—and got in a car, hoping it wouldn't take too long to find Pete. He didn't have a permanent spot in the neighborhood, but the cartel's business was like any other business. Each sales rep had his own territory, and I knew where Pete's territory lay.

Fifteen minutes later, I found my informant leaning on the wall by the bodega. The cracked and crumbling sidewalk in front of him was littered with garbage, the air thick with the stench of decay. The storefronts that lined the street were all closed and boarded up, save for the bodega, a check-cashing place two doors down, and a sex shop right next to it. It was still early, but soon, the street would be lined with working girls, their haggard faces hidden behind a thick layer of makeup, their eyes hollow and empty. It was Pete's world, and his skinny silhouette glued to the wall looked like it was just where it was supposed to be, waiting for his clientele to show. Ready to provide a short-lived bliss packed into a pill in exchange for a few dollar bills. Small or large, crisp or tattered, he'd take them all.

I could see him stiffen as he recognized my car. His eyes darted up and down the street as if he considered bolting, but then logic prevailed, and he stayed, his posture relaxing. He hated our meetings, but causing a scene would be detrimental to Pete's reputation and his standing with Diablitos. Pete's fear of the cartel was much greater than his dislike of me.

I leaned out of the window and waved him over. "Get in."

"Meeting so often is not good for my health," he said as he climbed into the passenger seat and shut the door behind him. "And yours."

"Something came up." I put the car into drive and pulled into the street traffic. "We'll just circle around a few blocks, and I'll leave you right where I found you."

He threw me one of his sullen glances but said nothing.

"I need information," I started.

"You always need information."

"And you always need money."

"What do you want?"

"I'm looking for someone." I took a pause and said the name as nonchalantly as I could. "Franky."

"I don't know a Franky."

I glanced at Pete, but he was looking dead ahead, his jaw set. "Yes, you do. He's an enforcer for Diablitos. I'll pay you well for this information."

"Pull over," he said, finally turning to me, his eyes burning with so much hatred it made me recoil. "Let me the fuck out."

"Pete. I need to find Franky."

"No, you don't. You don't find people like Franky. They find you, and then you wish he didn't."

"I'm on the job."

"You're always on the job. I don't care. Let me out."

"No." It was my turn to push back. "Listen to me. You'll tell me how to find Franky, and that's that."

"Or what?"

I stayed silent, letting him stew on it. Whatever punishment he was going to imagine in his head was undoubtedly worse than whatever I could come up with on my own.

"Fine."

I waited.

"Under one condition." He leaned toward me and spoke with a ferocity I had never seen from him. "I never see you again. No favors. No spying shit. No information on no one. Nothing. Zilch. Nada."

"How much?"

"Zero." He shook his head. "Some things are just not worth it."

"Deal."

He hesitated briefly and then told me the address and the time. "Now let me out."

I pulled over. It wasn't exactly the same place I had picked him up from, but it would have to do. "Thanks, Pete."

"For your own sake," he said, glancing over his shoulder as he exited the car, "don't look for him. He'll kill you. Or worse."

"Or worse?" I asked, but Pete was already gone, his skinny legs carrying him away from me at a pace that could almost qualify as running.

My phone rang before I could contemplate what might be worse than getting killed, and I pressed the Talk button on the wheel without looking at the number.

"Alex? This is John Levy. We need to meet as soon as possible."

"Why?" He sounded frantic, and I didn't like it for one second.

"There are going to be more murders," he said. "At least four more."

FIFTEEN

I saw John Levy through the window as he jogged across the street, clutching a laptop in his hands. He wore washed-out jeans and a simple black T-shirt under a leather jacket. His eyes were squinted against the wind, and his curly, salt-and-pepper hair, neat and proper last time I saw him, now flew wildly in the wind.

Levy paused in front of the office, glanced at the neon sign above it, and then pushed the door wide open, letting a gust of cold air in.

"Lock it and pull down the blinds," I said instead of a greeting. He gave me a curt nod and did as instructed. I could see him wrinkle his nose, no doubt catching a whiff of the ghost of a butcher shop smell, but if he had something to say, he kept it to himself. "Now sit down."

"I'm sorry about this," he said, sitting in an armchair before my desk. The chair, a monstrosity of soft black leather with a high back-rest and plush, rounded arms, was my pride and joy. It was by far the most expensive item in the entire office. I read somewhere that clients were more likely to part with their money when they were warm and comfortable. I still didn't' know if that was true, but it seemed like a logical enough argument to justify the splurge at the time. If only I could herd more people into the soft jaws of the leather monster, perhaps I could come up with meaningful statistics about the return on my investment.

"You said you knew about more murders."

"Yes." He tapped his fingernail on the laptop he kept pressing to his chest. His long fingers were soft, with carefully manicured nails. Not perfect enough to have been done at a nail salon, but I saw no evidence of a jagged line left after a cheap nail clipper either. His face was smoothly shaved, and I could smell the light touch of a high-end cologne every time he moved. Under different circumstances, I'd call him *dapper*, but only if I liked him. And I hadn't decided if I liked John Levy just yet.

"Go on."

"I wish you'd listened to me when I told you about Naomi, but I understand how it must have sounded. Frankly, I wasn't entirely convinced myself. It won't be easy to believe this even now, but I can show you some proof."

"Good," I said, revealing my pistol and lowering it on the table between us. "But it better be convincing."

"That...won't be necessary." Apart from some color draining from his face, he showed no fear. "I have one of those. *Had*, rather. There was a time I seriously considered using one on myself."

"When Grace died?"

He stiffened, but only for a moment. "You've done your homework."

"I'm a PI, John."

"Of course." Slowly, as if not to spook me, Levy extended his arm and placed the laptop on the table's edge.

"Is it why you killed Naomi? And planning to kill more? Because those people are connected to Atlas?"

"Atlas?" He tilted his head in confusion, but then there was a spark of recognition in his eyes. "The scaffolding company? What do they have to do with it?"

I stayed quiet.

"Oh." He raised his face skyward. "I'm an idiot. Do you think I killed them because they are related to the company? A vendetta of sorts?"

"Did you?"

"No." He looked at me as if I were a child. "I wrote a book."

It was my turn to look confused. "You wrote a book?"

"*Writing* is a more appropriate verb, as it isn't finished. You see, I was in a dark place the first three years after Grace's death. She was…" He paused, looking for words. "It doesn't matter. It was easier right after she died because there were so many things to take care of. The funeral, the arrangements. People have no idea how much work goes into a funeral. You have to organize the wake, take care of insurance, and call friends, relatives, banks, and credit card companies. Order a catering service. It's almost like arranging a wedding, just the circumstances are shitty. But then, after everything was finished, I found myself in a giant empty place, all by myself. Going insane."

I said nothing.

"I thought of checking out," he continued with a vacant look. "Almost did. But in the end, I convinced myself it wasn't something Grace would have approved of. Instead, I sold my apartment in the city, moved to Brooklyn, and tried to live a simple life. But even here, I was tempted. Two things saved me. One was my childhood friend, who bullied me into taking up therapy. I hated it in the beginning. Spent the first three months sitting on the couch without saying a word only because I made a promise to go there. But over time, I started to see the point."

"And another?"

"The book." He nodded toward the laptop. "My psychologist made a suggestion. I had never had any interest in writing fiction before. But then, one day, I came home from therapy and got this mental itch. Before I knew it, I was writing an outline for *Madness*."

"Madness?"

"That's the working title."

I glanced at his laptop. I'd heard some outlandish stories before, both as a cop and as a PI. Wherever he was going with this was going to top them, I had no doubt. "All right, I'll bite. What's this book about? And what does it have to do with Naomi?"

"Everything." He leaned toward me, a feverish look on his face. "I thought it was a clever plot. A serial killer who believes that he is collecting demons to become Lucifer himself. But I fear it is much more."

I listened, reluctantly at first, as Levy told me his story. He sensed my disbelief, too. I could tell. But he continued to weave his tale, recounting his reaction when he first read about a woman's murder who bore an uncanny resemblance to one of his characters. As the story progressed, he grew more animated. By the time he got to Naomi and his frantic hunt for a tattoo artist, I couldn't help but feel his passion. When he was finished, he leaned back in his chair, his face covered with a sheen of sweat and his breath ragged, as if he ran a mile or two. I still didn't know if what he told me was true. But unless I'd lost my touch, the man sitting across the table from me believed it was.

"You think Luca is real?"

"I don't know if his real name is Luca, but yes." He shivered. "Even after I found the similarities between the woman in the manuscript and the dead woman I saw on the news, I didn't want to believe it. It could've been just a coincidence. Millions of women would vaguely fit the description. The diamond in her nose and the clothes she wore were generic enough. Perhaps I read something in the news, forgot about it, and then subconsciously used it in the book. I checked the dates—that part was written after the woman's disappearance, so it was entirely possible. Hell, I even convinced myself that Naomi didn't exist until I saw the news about her murder plastered all over the TV channels."

"And you believe he's going to kill more women?"

"Not necessarily women. May I?" He pointed at the laptop, and I nodded. He opened it, scrolled through a document a few times, and then turned it to me so I could see the screen. "His next victim is a young man, Benjamin French."

"He kills men, too? That's rather unusual for serials. They all have a type."

"I don't think gender matters to him. A demon can possess whatever body is convenient at the moment. They can jump from one person to another, too. This means Luca needs to be very specific about the timing of his killings. Or else he risks killing a person without the benefit of freeing the demon. As crazy as it may sound, he doesn't want to kill the wrong person."

"I don't even know how to ask this, but is it something that has an origin story? Like in the Bible? Or is it just your invention?"

"No origin story." He tapped his temple with his index finger. "All my ideas, I'm afraid. I've never been religious in any shape or form."

"Let's say I believe you. And I'm not talking about the demons part. Say you do, somehow, have a connection to Luca. Last time we met, you gave me so little to work with, I couldn't find Naomi even if I tried. Why is this time going to be any different?"

"There's some good news." He fidgeted in his chair. "The way I had planned the book was to give more details to the reader as the story progressed. The first murder isn't even described. It's only mentioned in passing, as Luca leafs through his journal. With each subsequent murder, I had planned to give the reader more, eventually describing Luca's hunt for the last victim in real-time. There's also something else. I told you about Naomi's tattoo. What I hadn't mentioned was that it was unique. In the manuscript, it's described as a butterfly. But then I recalled when I imagined the scene, it was a butterfly with dragon wings. There was no information like that on the news, but if that part matches, we'll know my head might hold more clues independent of the novel. For example, I think French will be found in a dumpster under a graffiti drawing of a goat."

"And the bad news?"

"The bad news is that details about his next victim are still sparse, and if we don't stop the killing of Benjamin French, next time, Luca will kill three people at once."

I stared at him for some time as he squirmed in the chair under my gaze. There were so many things wrong with this conversation I didn't know where to begin. And John Levy was the key to it all. How could an Ivy League grad, who once had a successful career in a highly pragmatic field, even entertain the possibility of what he just told me? A psychic connection to a serial killer who believed in Lucifer and gutted his victims? John Levy was damaged goods, that much was obvious, but he wasn't a kook. And I still didn't think he was capable of murder, or else he wouldn't be here with his laptop and his crazy story. The gun between us was more to put him on edge than for my protection. It was easier to read people when they are nervous.

I didn't believe in demons or psychics. Or Lucifer, for that matter. Somewhere there must be a logical explanation for all of this. I just needed to find it. I would play along until I had something concrete to grab onto. For now.

And there was something else that was nagging me. John Levy wasn't telling me the whole story. Perhaps he didn't want me to know it. Or maybe he hadn't arrived at the point where he understood it himself. One way or another, a piece of the puzzle was missing.

"Why don't you change it?" I finally said, breaking the awkward silence.

"Change what, exactly?"

"The book. It isn't finished, you say. Why don't you write a chapter where the serial killer does something foolish while trying to catch this Benjamin French guy? That way, instead of killing the man, he gets caught himself and goes to jail for the rest of his life? Maybe even write *The End* after that chapter for good measure."

"I don't think it would work."

There it was—the unspoken. "Why not?"

"It's hard to explain."

I said nothing.

"You know that feeling when you go to someone's house for a party? You ring the bell, waiting for somebody to open the door, and you hear the steps coming from the other side. In your mind, there's probably an image of someone opening the door and inviting you in. It's most likely the host or someone else from that household. There's a certain quality to that expectation. To that image in your head. It's lifelike. It's real."

I nodded my head but said nothing. I had no idea where he was going with this, but I let him continue.

"Now picture yourself at the same door," he said. "And right before it opens, I tell you to imagine that a white elephant wearing a tuxedo will greet you. You can imagine it because that's how imagination works. You can think up pretty much anything if you try hard enough. But it wouldn't feel real. It would have a cartoonish quality to it no matter how hard you try."

"You're saying it won't come true unless you mean it?" I spread my arms wide, which, considering the loaded gun between us, wasn't the wisest of moves. "Then mean it when you write it."

"I've tried, but I don't think I can," he said. "I also don't remember writing the past few chapters about Benjamin French. I didn't want to write them. Even when I wasn't sure about my connection to Naomi, I had trouble writing another murder. It didn't seem right. But then, one day, I went to sleep, and when I got up the next morning, it was on my laptop. French was already caught, and Luca was calling up the next victim on his list."

And there it was again. He wasn't telling me the whole story. I let it go and made a decision. "Fine. Something compels you to write the manuscript. We will deal with this later. Tell me what you know about the murder of Benjamin French."

SIXTEEN

I closed the car door and turned on the engine. Then I cranked the heater on full blast and placed my hands above the vents. At the pace the temps had been dropping in the past few days, we'd be ice skating by June.

When my fingers started bending again, I dialed Morton's number. To my surprise, he answered the call himself after the first ring.

"Is it a necklace?" I asked, skipping pleasantries.

"What necklace, Alex?"

"Don't beat around the bush," I said, "because I'm starting to rethink our entire arrangement."

"Why is that?"

I chewed on my lip before I answered. Telling the client how dangerous the mission was isn't as straightforward as it sounds. Some won't believe you, thinking you're fishing for more money, and cut you loose. Others will believe you but get spooked and cut you loose. Either way, it's a bad outcome as long as you want to continue paying your bills. "I'm about to meet a cartel enforcer. I think he has the contents of the safe deposit box. Or at least knows where they are."

"It doesn't mean—"

"A grown man cried, telling me about meeting this fellow. And my loyal informant of many years quit, didn't take the money I offered, and said he'd never work with me again after telling me how to find the guy."

There was silence on the other side of the phone. My imagination obligingly drew a picture of Morton in his giant tufted brown leather chair, his sausage-like fingers pinching the fat under his chin as he deliberated. "Fine."

"Fine, what? Was it a necklace?"

"Yes. Stainless steel with a pendant made of olivine pallasite."

Pallasite. Not *parasite*. I'd never heard this word before. No wonder Mehta was confused.

"Expensive?"

"Not in a traditional sense, no."

"Morton," I said, my patience wearing thin. "I spent the last half hour freezing my ass off and learning escape routes should I need to bolt from a man capable of extreme violence. I'm not in the mood. I need details, not coded messages."

"You could buy it for less than a thousand dollars if it were in a store. But it's important to its owner, that's all. I can't tell you too many details because I don't know them myself. All I know is that it has something to do with the Holocaust. It was lost but then miraculously found, and since then, it passed through the family."

I chewed on my lip again. From Nazis to the cartels. Fate can be a cruel bitch, sometimes. "How badly do they want it back?"

"Badly enough."

"Will they pay for it? I doubt the guy will hand it over to me out of the goodness of his heart."

"My client is willing to pay. Fifty thousand for the return of the necklace. Cash. No questions asked."

"Okay. I'll let you know how it goes."

"Alex," he said before I could end the call.

"Yeah?"

"Take care of yourself."

"Careful there, Ezekiel Morton. God forbid I start thinking lawyers have souls."

"That'd be a tragedy," he said and hung up.

I looked through the window at the bar across the street, psyching myself up. It was a shoddy place built into the basement of a two-story brownstone. A flight of rough-hewn steps led to a thick wooden door with a bright neon sign. *The Purple Lounge.* A few other, smaller signs shone through the dirty narrow window, informing any potential patrons that the place had a backyard patio, served some local brews, and had a live band. I doubted anyone was camping out on the deck, given the weather. Or that the place had ever seen a live band.

I took a few deep breaths and came out of the car, steeling myself against the cold and hoping my face didn't reflect the summersaults my stomach was doing inside my rib cage.

The pungent odor of stale beer hit me in the face as I entered a long and narrow, dimly lit room. There was a bar on the left side with a heavyset man watching a game and a row of small booths by the right wall. Their red plush seats would look more at home in a Midwestern diner than in a Brooklyn bar. The place was almost empty at this hour. I scanned the faces of the few patrons until I saw a short, slim man matching my informant's description. Franky sat at the table all the way by the farthest wall near the exit to the patio. At the moment, he was working on a plate of a burger and French fries in front of him. Two large, burly men occupied a booth next to him. Apart from two glasses of iced water, their table was empty. I averted my eyes before they made eye contact and headed straight for the bar.

A bartender, a short, bearded fellow with a puffy face and the eyes of a rat behind round glasses, watched me warily as I made my way to the counter.

"A pint of lager, please," I said, taking a seat and slapping a twenty on the sticky wooden surface. "Keep the change."

He nodded and poured me a glass, the twenty disappearing in his meaty hand.

"Some weather," he said as he set the drink on the coaster with the bar's logo in front of me. I made a noncommittal grunting noise, hoping he'd get the message. He did not. "Never seen you here before. Just moved?"

"No." I took a sip of the beer. It was surprisingly good. "Just looking for someone."

"Is it me you're looking for, honey?" the heavyset man said, half turning to face me. His eyes went up and down the length of my body, lingering on my chest. He raised the glass in a mock salute. "Happy to buy you a drink."

"I don't think so." I fixed him with a stare until he turned away, mumbling something under his breath.

"Don't mind him," the bartender said. "Mike's harmless. Just lonely. Is your friend going to join you here later? I can get you settled in one of the booths if you'd like."

"I think my friend is already here." I stood up and headed toward the end of the bar, not giving the bartender a chance to answer. I needed it to be over before I completely lost my nerve.

As I got within a few feet of the slim man, two of his burly pals stood up in unison, like a pair of puppets jerked to life by a puppeteer, blocking my way.

"The bathroom is that way," the man closest to me said, pointing in the direction I had come from. An intricate tattoo covered his entire neck, crawling all the way up to his mouth. It moved and stretched as Tats spoke, as if it were alive. "It's on the right side of the bar."

"I'm not lost," I said, pointing at the slim man at the table with my chin. "I'm here to talk to him."

"I don't think so," Tats said, stepping toward me.

I stayed put, defying every instinct in my body urging me to turn around and run.

"It's okay, Tony." Franky pushed away his plate with the half-eaten burger and was also staring at me. He wore a biker's leather jacket and dark jeans that half covered sturdy black working boots. His pale, almost ghostly face was skinny, just like he was. It was unnaturally sharp, as if somebody took an axe to a clay model of his head and shaved off just a tad too much from his ears to his nose. But his most striking feature was his eyes. They were large, which made them look even more prominent on his thin face, their color such a light shade of gray they could have been made of ice. The eyes are the window to the soul, they say. Franky's eyes were a window all right, but I would want to pluck my own eyes out before I peered through.

Franky was a short man. He didn't get up, but I was sure that the top of his head would barely reach my eye level if he did. But as I stood there, transfixed by the hypnotic stare of his haunting eyes like a rabbit frozen in front of a python, all I wanted to do was curl into a ball and cry.

"Sit." He waved at the chair on the other side of the table from him. "You hungry?"

"Not really." I sat down, pulled a French fry from the plate before me, and took a bite without tasting it. As long as I kept my hands moving, I could keep them from shaking. "Thanks for allowing me to talk to you."

"I'm not opposed to talking to anybody."

Hearing Franky talk was a jarring experience. His voice was a pleasant baritone devoid of the sharp corners of a Brooklyn accent. It was young, smooth, and sophisticated and couldn't be further from the rough image I saw across the table. Suppose I had heard him on the phone. In that case, I'd imagine a mid-level manager in a financial firm or an ambitious lawyer. A young kid from a good school, making his way to the top.

"What can I do for you, Miss..."

"Alex Watts," I said, suppressing the shudder, as if I was relinquishing a small part of my soul to this monster by giving him my real name.

"What can I do for you, Miss Watts?"

"A local bank in Bay Ridge lost power not long ago. It looks like when it was restored, a few objects from safe deposit boxes went missing. I've been hired by someone to locate one of the items. It has no real-world value, but it is important to the owner. I thought you might be able to help me retrieve it."

"I've read about the robbery in the paper." Franky tilted his head in a sharp, bird-like movement. "Sounds like a miserable affair. I might be wrong, but as far as I know, things with no significant value aren't usually kept in safe deposit boxes."

"Very true. But this one might be an exception."

"I wish I could help." His smile was almost genuine. "But I wouldn't even know where to begin. If the owner had hired you, I'd wager you have the skills to find it."

"Look." I leaned closer. "I don't know or care what other items there are. I just need one. It's a necklace. Polished steel with a cheap stone. A few hundred bucks at most. But it's important. The owner's family lost it during the Holocaust but found it again after the war. They are prepared to pay for it. Twenty-five thousand."

"A necklace, you say. From the Holocaust?"

"Yes."

"That's some tough luck," he said and pulled his plate closer, signaling that the interview was coming to its close. "Like I said. I wish I could help."

"Fifty thousand. Cash. That's as high as I can go."

Franky studied my face for a few seconds and then glanced at Tats, giving him a nod. The bodyguard moved closer, making me freeze in terror. But instead of grabbing me, the man pulled a small electronic device from his pocket. He waved it around my head a few times first. Then he moved it up and down my body, staring at a small screen. "She's clean."

"Good." Franky did his bird move again. "Just a precaution. I'm sure you understand."

I nodded, not trusting my mouth to say anything.

"I like you, Miss Watts. It is so refreshing to see bold people. It almost never happens. I miss it sometimes."

"Will you help me, then?"

"I can't." He shrugged, almost apologetically. "For two reasons. One, I have a reputation to uphold. I might lose some influence if I start giving people what they ask for. In my line of work, that would be unfortunate. Perhaps, in your case, I could make an exception. A good cause and all. But, alas, there's another reason."

"Which is?"

"The necklace has already found a new owner, I'm afraid. Someone I greatly respect took a liking to it and gave it to his wife." Franky picked up the burger and bit into it. He took his time chewing and then licked his fingers. "Forget it. That's the only advice I can give you."

"Thank you for your time," I said and stood up. I panicked for a moment as Tats stayed immobile, but Franky gave him another short nod, and the bodyguard took a step back, clearing my path.

In a daze, I walked back through the bar and into the freezing rain outside. The cold snapped me back to reality, and I ran across the street, taking shelter inside my car. A few moments later, I was driving up a ramp and getting on the Belt Parkway, heading home. There was a decision I had to make. There had been tough assignments before in my relatively short career as a PI. Some were worse than others. I've completed them all anyway. But then again, I never needed to retrieve an item from the head of a cartel. El Jefe himself. This could be the first case I was going to fail.

SEVENTEEN

Ben Nowak, aka Big Ben, was a rare case when a nickname was right on the money. He slouched as he walked, the way some large people do to minimize their height, and yet his red, spiky hair floated at least a foot above the crowd. Standing next to him was a pudgy, pimple-faced kid with slicked-back hair that belonged on a used car salesman. Tommy Lombardi, I presumed. He was short, which made Nowak look even bigger and gave the pair an almost comical quality.

Two groups from Harrington Academy were scheduled to visit the science museum that day. My niece's classmates had the luxury of wandering the halls and enjoying the exhibits while the high schoolers worked as their chaperones. At least most of them did. I watched Ben and Tommy fall behind the main group and peel away, heading toward the gift shop. They lingered there for a while before shoplifting some trinkets and then making their way to the planetarium. They didn't strike me as kids fascinated with astronomy. Most likely, they were planning on getting higher than the stars that would soon be projected on the curved dome of the theater.

Little did they know, I had other plans for their immediate future.

It is astonishing how easy it is to break into a maintenance closet at a science museum. I arrived at the museum an hour before the school bus did. After familiarizing myself with the layout of the building, I stuck around the solar system exhibit and watched the door with an Authorized Personnel Only sign for a few minutes. No card reader was next to it, and I suspected it opened with a regular key.

To my amazement, after a short wait, a middle-aged woman wearing a uniform walked up the stairs from the lower level, went into the closet without as much as pausing in front of it, and left a few moments later with a bottle of cleaner in her hands.

"No key," I whispered. "Things can go right for a change."

I glanced around, walked businesslike toward the closet, and pulled on the door, still half expecting it to be locked. It wasn't, and I ducked inside the small room. It was narrow and cramped, with shelves overflowing with janitorial equipment lining the walls. A large, heavy-looking folding ladder leaned against one of the shelves in the back. I ignored the supplies and made a beeline for a neat pile of freshly laundered uniforms.

A few moments later, I emerged from the closet and vanished into the crowd, wandering through the exhibits and waiting for the school bus to arrive. When it finally did, I had no trouble spotting my targets, the two bullies who had tormented my niece.

I intercepted Ben and Tommy before they got near the line into the planetarium. I cut in front of them, blocking their way, and put a broad smile on my face. "You boys look like someone I could use. Could you help me get a ladder from the utility closet? It's too heavy for me."

"Um, sorry," Tommy said, trying to sidestep around me. "We are watching some kids. Gotta get back to them."

"Right." Ben nodded in agreement.

I mirrored Tommy's move, blocking his path again. "You kids are from Harrington Academy, aren't you? Dr. Charlotte Pembroke is a good friend. I'll make sure she knows you volunteered to help. Will only take a moment."

I saw them exchange glances at the mention of their school principal, and then Tommy gave me a fake smile. "Sure thing. No big deal."

"Thank you, boys," I gushed and led them away from the line toward the utility closet.

"Where is it?" Ben asked.

"Right there," I said, swinging the door open and pointing at the tall ladder. After they entered the room, I shut the door behind me and stood in front of it.

"What are you doing?" Tommy said. He was instantly suspicious, his eyes darting between me and the exit, but there was still some hesitation on his plump, acne-covered face.

"You shut it, *troll_lover69*," I said, using his handle from a popular porn site. I could see the bewilderment on Ben's face as he mouthed the username, repeating it after me.

"What are you talking about?" Tommy tried to play dumb, which would have worked if not for the brightest shade of red that spilled across his neck and face, highlighting his zits.

"Look, I don't judge. Want to watch some troll-on-troll action? Be my guest, although I have to say two hours a day does seem excessive. But hey, it's a very confusing time to be a teenager."

"Do you know who my dad is?"

"Oh, I do, and I'm sure he'd love to know that *NFC* on the statement for the credit card he lets you use is not for the science club and stands for *NaughtyFlix dot com*. And his friends would also enjoy that information. Not to mention Dr. Pembroke. Now let's talk about you, my friend," I said, turning toward Ben. He backed into the wall, clearly wishing he could disappear into thin air. "Opening crypto accounts under your mother's name? Do you realize she works for a financial firm and needs to report all her assets and everything she trades? You could cost her her job."

"What do you want?" Tommy said.

"You stop with the bullying. Leave Olivia Spencer alone. I will not ask twice."

"Spencer? Fine." He made a move toward the door, but I blocked his path.

"And," I said, pointing a finger at his chest. "You'll make sure nobody else bullies her either. Is that clear?"

Tommy nodded, but I wouldn't let him off so easily. "Is that clear?"

"Yes, ma'am," he finally said, and I stepped away from the door. "We'll look after her."

"Bruh. For real? Trolls, man?" I heard Ben whisper as they walked away.

"Shut up."

I smiled, took off the uniform, and folded it neatly on the shelf. My work here was done.

When I stepped out of the museum, a blast of icy wind hit me square in the face, stealing my breath. I yanked my collar as high as I could and jogged toward my car, eager to escape the biting cold.

Just as I was about to slide into the driver's seat, a faint sound reached my ears. It was pitiful and small, like the cry of a lost soul. I waited and stepped out of the car when it didn't repeat. There it was again, insistent and needy. I looked around, but there was no sign of any other living thing in the desolate parking lot. Just me and the wind. But then, as I glanced down, I saw it. A tiny kitten, gray with black spots, cowering behind my front tire.

"What the hell am I supposed to do with you?"

The kitten didn't respond, just blinking at me with wide, green eyes. I glanced around, but there were no signs of other cats or any indication of where the little one might have come from.

"Oh boy." I sighed and carried it back to the car, settling it onto the passenger seat. It meowed softly, curled into a ball, and didn't move a muscle as I drove back to my office.

When we returned, I set her on the floor and went to the little refrigerator behind my desk.

"You're lucky I'm not one of those people who take their coffee black," I said as I poured milk into a saucer. The cat rushed to it, burying its face in the white liquid.

I returned to my desk just in time to see John Levy coming down the street and knocking on my door.

"Don't you live south from here?" I said. Call me paranoid, but when I see people I don't entirely trust come from a different direction than I expect them to, I want to know why.

He gave me a puzzled look and pointed at the cat. "I'm not coming from home. Just got back from the city. You got a cat?"

"She was sitting behind the front tire of my car. Long story."

"She?" He bent over, gripped the skin at the back of the cat's neck between its shoulder blades, and picked it up. "That's most definitely not a she. That's a boy."

"Oh."

"He got a name yet?"

"No." I looked at the cat in Levy's hands. *He* seemed perfectly content for the moment.

"All right." Levy brought the cat close to his face. "In that case, you shall be known as Spots."

"I don't like that name," I said. "And I probably shouldn't keep it."

Levy shrugged and returned the kitten to his meal, but Spots seemed to have had enough milk and went behind my chair to investigate. "You wanted to talk about Luca."

"Right." I mentally shifted gears. "We need a profile. I've read your manuscript, but you said sometimes you have more information in your head."

"I do." Levy took a seat in the leather chair and crossed his legs. "I went to a bookshop in the city. Secret Scrolls. They sell rare books, first editions, that kind of stuff. Wanted to see if they have something that matched a description of the book Luca was using, which is also not in the novel."

"Any luck?"

"Apart from making the clerk uncomfortable when I tried to describe a demonic book with a horned angel on the cover and grooves in bonded leather for sacrificial blood? I'm afraid not."

"I see."

"Let's talk about the profile." He steepled his fingers and looked up as if trying to remember. "He's tall and powerful. Blond hair. Extremely intelligent."

"Psychopaths usually are. They are also charming as hell. Manipulative."

"Right."

"He must be wealthy. Or powerful. Perhaps both."

"What makes you say that?"

"Just think about it. A soundproofed room. A Montblanc pen."

"I guess." Levy fidgeted in his chair and gave me a weird look.

"But the strongest clue is how he handles the victims when he brings them in. And when he takes out the bodies. He dumped both of the women in the city. Unless we get some new information, I think it's safe to assume he lives in one of the boroughs. But he must have a pretty nice house."

"How do we know that?"

"Access to and from whatever place he's using as his killing ground. Imagine if I were the killer and wanted to bring a dead body into my office. Hauling a large human-shaped bag while double-parked on a busy street isn't exactly the stealthiest thing to do."

"Or," Levy said, "he has a service entrance somewhere. A warehouse or a loading dock."

"It's possible. But my gut tells me he's wealthy. Not necessarily a billionaire, but very well-off. Makes me think..." My phone pinged, and I paused, looking at a small block of text.

"What?" Levy said.

"Nothing. I get alerts when the NYPD has a press conference." I scrolled through the article, ready to put the phone away, and then stopped, my eyes catching a familiar name. A frown settled on my lips.

"What is it?"

"That's DD," I said. "Dom Deluca. My former partner. He's rarely in front of the cameras unless there's something important."

John gave me a look but didn't say anything. He didn't have to.

I fished for a remote, clicked the TV on, and switched to a local channel just in time to see a young reporter step in front of the camera.

That the NYPD has called for an urgent press conference. According to the preliminary information we have received, the police have discovered a young man's body whose injuries are consistent with the two female victims found in the past few weeks and were thought to be the work of the so-called Valentine Killer.

At this time, the identity of the victim is unknown. The NYPD has assigned a veteran detective, Sean Gallagher, to lead this investigation along with his partner, Detective Dominic Deluca. These two experienced detectives have been working around the clock to gather evidence and track down the perpetrator responsible for these heinous crimes.

Before we proceed, I must warn you that the details we are about to share may be disturbing to some viewers. The police are still in the process of piecing together the facts, but we know that the killer is still at large and should be considered armed and extremely dangerous.

The camera panned to the podium, showing the grumpy face of my old partner, unseasonably dressed in a suit and tie, standing next to a tall, muscular man with a slicked-back undercut of straw-blond hair. I heard a weird noise and glanced at John to make sure he was watching. His mouth was wide open, his face as pale as if he was struck by lightning.

"Now what?" I asked, not sure if I wanted to know the answer.

He pointed at the screen with a trembling finger. "This tall man looks *exactly* how I imagined Luca would look like."

I turned to the screen, studying the man beside my old partner. As if sensing our turmoil, Spots made a pitiful meowing sound somewhere behind me. I reached back without looking to touch him. The kitten was shaking. And so was I.

EIGHTEEN

I didn't sleep well. One part of the problem was Spots, who refused to stay on a soft old towel I set up for him in the corner of the bedroom. Every time I left him there, he'd stay there just long enough for me to return to bed and get comfortable. After that, he'd climb onto the mattress, clawing at my linen and purring like a diesel engine in subzero temperatures. Then he'd try to snuggle next to my neck, poking me with his cool, wet nose.

When he did it for the third time, I gave up and offered him a compromise by moving his towel onto the bed next to my feet. It worked, but by then, I was wide awake. I lay there for a while, staring at the ceiling in the dark, listening to the sounds of the city outside, and thinking about Benjamin French.

When the realm of Morpheus finally took me in, the nightmares came. I couldn't remember what I saw every time I woke up, shivering and drenched in cold sweat. Just the cold, sticky feeling of terror that seemed to be bleeding me dry. When morning came, filtering gray, cold light through the bedroom's blinds, I was more exhausted than before I went to bed.

I wanted to stay in, watch something mindless on TV, and mope for a while, but who was I kidding? Although in Levy's book, the murders of the next three people took place almost a month later, I had no idea if that would be true in reality. Benjamin was supposed to have a few more days, too, but now he was dead, and I felt personally responsible. We needed to find Luca. Which meant I had to make not one but two very unpleasant phone calls.

First, I needed to drop Morton's case. The lawyer wasn't going to be happy. My bank account was going to be upset, too. But Levy seemed willing to pay for my services, which would cushion at least some of the blow. That also meant I'd need to do something I had been avoiding like the plague for the past few years—talk to my former partner, Dominic Deluca.

"What do you think, Spots? Should I call Morton first?" I scratched the cat behind the ears. He purred and stuck his head out, offering me his neck. Then, as if after careful consideration, he fell on his side, scooted closer, and gave me his belly. "Yeah. I guess Morton it is."

I dressed and headed to my office, stopping for coffee and a bagel. The storm seemed to have abated since last night, but the crisp chill was still in the air, more appropriate for late February than early May. Fat, heavy clouds hung low in the murky sky above like shadows of prehistoric beasts, long dead but still haunting the living. I stuffed the paper bag with the bagel under my arm and held the hot cup with both hands as I hurried down the street.

"Good news, I hope?" Morton asked as soon as the line connected.

"If by good news you mean that I'm still alive after talking to one of the scariest people I've ever met, then yes. Other than that, not so much."

"He doesn't know where it is?"

"Oh, he does." I took a sip of the coffee, burning my lips. "And this is where I tell you I must pay you back the retainer."

"I don't think I understand."

"The boss has it," I said. "His wife, to be exact. I'm not sure why Franky, the guy I saw, even brought it to El Jefe, considering the necklace is practically worthless. But he did. The boss liked it, and then his wife liked it. She's got it now. You see my dilemma?"

"I do."

"Just tell me how much I owe you, and I'll send you a check."

"Don't do that just yet," Morton said, his voice as cheery as always. "I didn't know how exactly your meeting would play out, but I had a conversation with my client, trying to figure out some contingencies. Just in case."

I said nothing.

"My client understands the stakes are significantly higher now. Your payment would be higher, too."

"I don't think—"

"You will get a fifty-thousand-dollar bonus if you deliver the necklace."

"I thought the fifty was for the purchase."

"No." He chuckled. I had a vision of the Cheshire Cat's smile plastered on his thick lips and the waves the chuckle created on his vast belly. "This is in addition to. And the pot stays the same. You can keep the entire hundred if you get the necklace without spending the money."

I bit into my lip. One hundred grand was going to solve a lot of my problems and give me a buffer should my arrangement with John Levy prove to be short-lived.

"Can I think about it?"

"Of course."

"You understand that even if I decide to give it a shot, the chances of me getting it back are pretty slim at this point, right?"

"Alex," Morton said, his voice turning serious for once. "I can't make that decision for you. But don't feel pressured. My job here is to provide options. You are to choose what option suits you. Whatever you decide, you don't have to repay me. I'd rather my client didn't get the necklace than you got hurt."

He disconnected before I could answer. I sat silently for a few minutes, my foot tapping a nervous rhythm under the table. I supposed I could play coy with Morton, but I wasn't going to lie to myself—I couldn't pass on this opportunity. And it wasn't just about the money. The story of the necklace gnawed on me. There was a reason it survived the Holocaust and found its way to the person it belonged to. Scum like El Jefe shouldn't be able to lay claim to what the Nazis couldn't. Perhaps when I called Morton, I didn't really want to tell him I was quitting but was looking for a reason not to. *Maybe*, a lone, dark voice in my head added, *it* was *about the money, and I just wanted to feel good earning it.*

There would be time later, when no serial killers were roaming the streets of New York, to philosophize what reason drove me to continue with the case. For now, however, I had another call to make.

I scrolled through my contacts until I found one titled DD. On the off chance he would pick up the phone, I'd better remember not to call him that. *DD* was reserved for close friends and family. The inner circle. It'd been a long time since we stopped calling each other that. Worse yet, it'd been a long time since we called each other at all. I sighed, put the phone on speaker, and hit his number.

It rang for so long that I thought his voicemail had kicked in when he finally answered, his rough, scratchy voice cutting the air like a blade. "Deluca."

"Dominic?"

"Yes. Who is this?"

I didn't know what hurt more: the fact that he didn't recognize my voice or that he no longer had my phone number in his contacts. "This is Alex Watts."

There was a sound on the line as if he opened his mouth to say something but cut himself short. I waited a few seconds, ready for him to hang up, but he didn't. "Can we talk?"

"You dialed my number. I answered. I'm pretty sure this is how those things work. Talk."

He wasn't going to make it easy. But if this was his way of discouraging our conversation, Dom should have known better. I was a big girl. And old partners giving me the cold shoulder were the least of my problems. "I saw you on TV. New partner?"

"Did you call me to ask if I have a new partner, Alex?"

"No." I felt anger rising in my chest. "But he's part of the reason that I called. I saw the press conference about the Valentine Killer case. I'm working on something potentially connected to it and was hoping you could share some details with me. For old times' sake."

"You're still a PI, I see? Running around like a chicken without a head? At least you stuck with something."

"If you didn't sell me out," I yelled, standing up and banging my fist on the table, "I'd still be at the NYPD."

He said nothing for a while, letting me stew long enough to calm down and regret what I had said. Finally, he cleared his throat. "Is that how you remember it? Me? Selling you out? Because my recollection is hazy, but I don't think that's what happened."

"You owe me," I said quietly. I didn't want to say it, knowing it'd bring pain, but he left me no other choice.

"I do," he conceded. "That's the only reason I'm still talking to you."

"Can we start over? Please? We don't need to be friends. But this is important."

"It's always important with you, Alex. Until it isn't. Talk."

"How long have you known Gallagher?"

"About three months. Give or take."

"Do you know where he came from?"

"He's been on the force for a long time, just not in the same precinct. Military before that. MP. Why?"

"Have you noticed anything off about him?" I had to tread carefully here. If I still didn't believe John Levy, DD would surely dismiss the idea of a connection between a manuscript and the murders outright. "Taking time off in odd hours? Unplanned trips?"

"Not that I recall." Dom paused for a few seconds, as if trying to remember. "Although, maybe once or twice? His mother is sick. Alzheimer's. He occasionally visits her at the nursing home. Are you going to tell me what this is about or not?"

"Look. I don't have anything concrete, but there's a chance he might be connected to the murders."

"Connected? How?"

"I'm not sure yet, and hopefully, there's nothing there, but I wanted to warn you. Keep an eye on him."

"Are you saying he might have something to do with it? Because I'm about to hang up."

"I don't know, DD."

"Don't you DD me," he said. His tone was quiet, but I could hear the fury. "If you called to accuse my partner when we are in the middle—"

"Naomi Williams had a tattoo," I said. "A butterfly. Did it have dragon wings?"

He stopped talking, his heavy breathing thundering into the phone.

"Dom?"

"How did you know that?"

It was my time to get my breathing under control. There was a crushing weight on my chest, and as much as I struggled to lift it, it just sat there, pressing me down.

"Alex? What have you gotten yourself into?"

"Just be careful, Dom," I finally managed.

"Fine."

"I have another question, though." I knew I was pushing my luck, but this wasn't the time to be picky. "Do you know who is in charge of the Diablitos cartel?"

"You think they had something to do with the murders?"

"No. This is a separate case."

"Like I said. A chicken without a head. Figuratively so far, but on this trajectory..." He trailed off.

"Please, Dom. I'm tracking a stolen piece of jewelry. Sounds like it survived the Holocaust only to be picked up by the cartel. Shitty luck all around. From what I've learned, El Jefe has it. His wife, to be exact."

"Mateo Alvarez is the guy you're looking for," Dom said. "He has a legitimate front—a large shipping company that delivers goods from South America. He's been on our radar for the past few years, but he's really careful. Everything is aboveboard. Pays more taxes than he's supposed to. Somehow, he's using his company to smuggle drugs, but apart from low-level testimonials, we've got nothing. Everything is highly compartmentalized. Nobody knows anyone beyond their immediate contacts, and when someone talks, repercussions are swift."

"Sounds like a charmer."

"He is. Whatever your client is paying you is not enough."

"Figures. And his wife?"

"Olga Ryghenko."

"Is she in on the business, too?"

"I don't know," Dom said and cleared his throat again. "But I don't think so. She's a socialite and flies all over the place. I'd be surprised if she were involved. My guess is she doesn't know what he does for a living or, more realistically, does but chooses to ignore it. Either way, I'd be cautious approaching her. They seem pretty close. Mateo is whoring around sometimes, especially when he travels, but she knows about it and doesn't seem to mind."

"Does she?"

"What? Sleep around? I don't think so, which is probably a wise choice, considering the fate of some people who have tried to cross him."

"Thank you," I said. All things considered, I got more than I had hoped for. "Please be careful with Gallagher."

"I will," he said and paused, as if weighing what he was about to tell me. "You be careful too. Alex?"

"Yes?"

"This makes us even, you hear me? No more 'you owe me, Dom' bullshit. I did, and now I've repaid my debt. Do you understand?"

"Yes, sir." My eyes stung, but I held my tongue. "You take care of yourself, Dom."

He hung up, and I sat there for a while. Staring at my phone. Determined not to shed a single tear. I succeeded. Mostly.

NINETEEN

John Levy grabbed the bright-orange box from the kitchen drawer and marched to the bathroom. He swung the door open and paused in front of the toilet just long enough to open the lid. Then, he pulled the bottle from the box, unscrewed the cap, and tipped it over into the white bowl. The little blue capsules bobbed up and down in the clear water like miniature submarines caught in a storm. Not giving himself enough time to hesitate, Levy pressed the button and watched as the man-made whirlpool took his month-long supply of medication away.

"It's fine," he whispered, staring at the water circling down the drain. "This is for the best."

As the water stopped spinning, however, doubts returned. He had been wondering if the medication made him more susceptible to whatever connection there was between his writing and the real-life serial killer. He hadn't found the answer. But something must have been responsible for the utter madness that had consumed his life in the past few weeks. There must have been a trigger. A reason. A cause. A logical explanation of some kind.

But what if he had been wrong to toss them? What if the meds made the connection weaker, not stronger? Or worse yet, what if it didn't matter what he did or didn't do, and nothing could sever the link between him and the maniac he had christened Luca in his unfinished novel? What if he was doomed to follow this cursed path wherever it led? He rubbed his face with both hands and stared at the water's surface as if waiting for answers. None came.

His phone vibrated in his back pocket, plucking him out of a trance, and he answered it without looking at the caller ID. "Who is this?"

"Did you exchange your cell for a rotary phone?" a familiar voice said. "You ask this question a lot lately."

He glanced at the screen and grimaced in frustration. Phil. He *really* didn't want to talk to his best friend in this state. Paranoid. Scared. It was as if all the years of therapy and hard work had been undone over the course of a few short days. He forced himself to smile before he answered. "Hey, Phil. Sorry, I was in the middle of something when you called. Everything all right?"

"With me?" There was a silence on the other side long enough to grow uncomfortable. "I'm fine. But you didn't return any of my calls over the past few days, which got me worried."

"You don't have to be worried."

"Okay."

"I'm serious."

There was another long pause, and Levy stifled a sigh. In their circle of friends, they often joked that Phil had a superpower—reading people. And he was never shy to call out Levy's bullshit before. The last time Levy had avoided Phil the same way was right after Grace's funeral. The story he told Alex was only half true. Grace would have wanted him to go on and enjoy the rest of his life. But had Phil not visited Levy's place one evening when John got busy cleaning the M1911 pistol, he didn't know if he'd still be around to try.

"What's going on with you, pal? You don't sound the same."

"Just busy," he lied. "Work has been hectic, and I'm on a roll with the book, that's all. I saw your calls, but it was too late by the time I got around to calling you back."

"Okay. You know, I've been thinking about your job. Have you considered that it might be time—"

"I'm sorry, Phil. You caught me right at the door. Don't want to be late for a date." He forced a chuckle. "Another reason I might not be getting back to people. I'll call you tomorrow, okay?"

"All right. A date sounds nice. Same girl?"

"Yes."

"Have fun, then."

The line went dead, and Levy stared at the phone for a few seconds. He didn't have a date to go to. If anything, as much as he would love to spend another night with Lilly, he didn't want her to see him in this state. He felt fragile. Like a vase that had been broken and glued together and now was back in its owner's favorite place on top of the mantel. Seemingly in one piece, as long as you didn't look close enough. He also wondered if his questions about the mystery of the laptop migrating to the kitchen table had ticked her off.

But he could use some fresh air. And perhaps a stiff drink or two if he found the right place.

He wore old jeans and a leather jacket over a black hoodie and went outside. It was early, and the sun was still high, but the air was cold enough to make his breath come out in white, delicate puffs.

Levy stuck his hands deep into his pockets, pulled the hoodie over his head, and headed north on Third Avenue. He didn't have a direction in mind, just the need to keep moving. Soon, he found a rhythm, his legs carrying him forward like pistons of a combustion engine. Somebody said that walking was just falling and catching yourself over and over. But then, wasn't life? Falling and catching yourself?

He hadn't intended to go to the German bar where he had his first date with Lilly, but before long, he stood before its dark oak doors with handles shaped like a beer stein. He hesitated, watching the blinking lights on the garlands hanging off the shallow awning.

Still, he was tired and cold, and the smell of grilled sausage emanating from the inside sealed the deal.

John sat at the end of a long and narrow bar and ordered a smoked bratwurst with sauerkraut and mashed potatoes. He sipped on a tall glass of amber ale while waiting for his food to arrive and scanning the place. It was too early for the regulars, and apart from a couple in their forties in the front of the dining room and an old man with a walker in the corner, the bar was empty. That suited Levy just fine.

"Waiting for someone?" the bartender said, placing a plate in front of him and laying utensils on a paper napkin.

"Nope. Just gawking." He shook his head and finished off the beer. "I'll take a martini now. Bombay Sapphire. Extra olives."

The bartender gave him a nod, and a few moments later, John's fingers were wrapped around the long stem of the martini glass. The pungent scent of gin filled his nostrils as he swirled the liquid, and he downed the cocktail in one gulp. A burst of saltiness filled his mouth, and as the drink settled, a wave of warmth radiated from his stomach outward. It was numbing and relaxing, and Levy plucked the olives off the miniature skewer and popped them into his mouth. Then he moved the empty glass back toward the bartender. "Another, please."

"You're not playing around tonight," the man said.

"No. Keep them coming." He dug into the food, briefly wondering if the remark was an admonishment, a compliment, or both. But then another martini arrived, and it didn't matter. He took his time with the second drink, taking small sips between the bites, savoring the smoky flavor of the sausage and the fluffy, piping-hot mashed potatoes. It was comfort food at its finest—heavy, flavorful, homey—and Levy's shoulders relaxed as he cleared the plate.

As the night wore on, the bar started to fill up. It was the front dining area first, mostly couples. But as the hands on the clock above the bar kept moving, the demographics shifted to a younger, more boisterous crowd. Somebody fired up a jukebox, and the funky rhythm of the Red Hot Chili Peppers flooded the place. He couldn't make out the words, just that it was about "the other side."

John lifted a finger, signaling to the bartender to pour him another martini. It was number six, and the overhead lights swam as he turned on the chair, slapping a few dollar bills next to the empty glass.

"You sure?" The bartender threw him an appraising look.

"Yes, please. I'm fine. Just need to use a bathroom." He stuck to short sentences to avoid slurring words and almost giggled at the cleverness of it. The bartender shrugged, the bills disappearing in the front pocket of his black apron, and poured one more drink.

"That will do it," Levy said, more to himself than to the man. He ate the olives first, the skewer falling out of his fingers. He watched as it landed next to the leg of his stool, rolling toward the bar. Levy put one leg down, his instinct to go after it. But the room swayed, and he thought better of it, returning his attention to the glass. The drink's surface glistened under the bar's low-hanging lights like a giant gemstone. A swirling thin layer of oil was on its surface from the brine. Its movement was hypnotic, like a psychedelic video, the olive green blending seamlessly into the clear liquid below.

Levy shook his head, breaking the spell, picked up the glass and downed it in one go. He looked around, the buzz in his ears muffling the crowd's noise and the music, planted his feet on the ground and slid off the stool. The world shifted around him as if in slow motion, and he stood there for a moment, unsteady, like a sailor in a storm. A woman passed by him, her eyes briefly meeting his and giving him a smile. He smiled back, but she was already gone, and he stared after her for a moment.

"You need a ride home?" he heard the bartender's voice, and he shook his head and headed away from the bar, across the dining room, and toward the bathroom door in the back.

He swung the heavy door open, almost losing balance, and clung to it for a moment, his vision blurred, trying to right himself. The bathroom was empty and brightly lit, and Levy squinted as he walked past the row of sinks and toward the urinals. He almost made it as his shoulder bumped into the wall, sending him sideways. Then his left foot stepped into something wet, the rubber sole of his shoe instantly losing its grip. Levy flailed his hands, trying to regain balance, but it only made it worse, and he careened backward, picking up speed, his legs not quite able to catch up with the rest of his body. Then he was airborne, and his body slammed on the hard surface of the tile floor, his head catching the worst of it.

He cursed, the lights blinking out for a few long moments and then coming back, along with droplets of water stinging his face like cold, angry bees.

He blinked, briefly wondering if he had broken some pipe as he fell, and wiped his face with the back of his hand only to realize the water was hitting his entire body.

"Watch it, you asshole," a raspy voice shouted. "If ya lay a hand on my house, Imma mess ya up."

Levy tried to sit up, squinting against the droplets hitting his face, when something crashed into his ribs, sending him tumbling again. He bit his tongue, stifling a scream as the metallic taste of blood brought the world back to focus.

He was sitting on a sidewalk in the dim light of the back alley behind some kind of a store. The rain was coming down in sheets, cold and heavy, pummeling the pavement with unrelenting force. A makeshift shelter cobbled together from cardboard and tattered rags was in front of him, leaning next to a hulking dark-green dumpster, its walls slick with rainwater. A large man, his face etched with lines of hardship, towered over him as his mad eyes flicked about.

"Where am I?"

"Didn't ya hear me?" the man bellowed, taking a step closer, the whites of his eyes shining brightly in the dark of the night. "Get out of my house. Shoo."

The man tried to kick him in the face but missed, and Levy scrambled back wildly, the rough surface of the pavement scraping his palms. The wind whipped at his face, the cold rain making him shiver. "I don't mean you any harm. I'm going to go. I don't know how I got here."

"Get outta here, I said."

Levy's back hit the wall, and he pushed himself up, raising his hands in a defensive gesture. "I'm going, man. Take it easy."

He stepped sideways and, when he was clear of the wall, moved backward until he got to the road. The rain was pouring even harder now, long sheets of icy-cold water coming down in short intervals, as if someone was swinging a giant showerhead the size of a building above the city.

"Get goin'," the man shouted at him.

"Wait." Levy kept his distance but didn't move. "Can you please tell me how I got here? The last thing I remember is that I was in Brooklyn."

"Crazy rat," the homeless man mumbled, seemingly losing interest as Levy was now outside some arbitrary zone around his cardboard home.

Convinced he was out of danger, Levy let his hands fall and started to walk away as he caught something out of the corner of his eye. He spun around in a tight circle and stared at the wall above the dumpster, a small whimper escaping his lips. Intricate graffiti of a black goat was painted above the container, the sparkling droplets of water running over it, giving it a three-dimensional quality.

Levy lowered his gaze. The heavy lid, rainwater cascading off its dirty-green surface, was askew, creating a gap. Levy walked toward it in a trance as if pulled by some invisible force, ignoring the renewed shouting of the homeless man.

"What are you looking at?" the man yelled, but Levy took the last few steps to the dumpster, the dim light from the streetlamp illuminating a pale object stuffed between the swollen trash bags.

A foot. A *human* foot. The sole was arched, and the toes were curled at odd angles as if frozen in a moment of ecstasy or extreme pain.

"Oh, shit."

He turned around, the world spinning, and ran as hard as he could. There was no direction or purpose to his mad dash. Just a wild staccato of his feet on the wet sidewalk as he pressed on. Putting as much distance between himself and the pale five toes pointing in agony at the gray, rainy skies.

"It wasn't me," he heard the homeless man shout after him. "I swear to the Lord Almighty, it wasn't me."

TWENTY

I don't know what I was expecting when I left my car in the underground parking lot and emerged at the street level at the corner of Fifty-Seventh Street and Seventh Avenue. There was a serial killer on the loose, and perhaps subconsciously, I thought there would be a dark shadow looming over the city. An invisible presence that would haunt the passersby, making them hunch just so. A slithering fear reflected in the eyes of strangers I'd pass as I walked down the street, making them avert their eyes the moment they met mine.

To my surprise, there was nothing of the sort. I don't know if the unseasonably harsh weather was the reason, but there were no signs that New Yorkers were on edge. The crowds moved with the same matter-of-fact cadence, like a great river, splashing at the concrete banks of the high-rise buildings and only occasionally creating whirlpools around the islands of gawking tourists. But when that happened, the combination of unfriendly stares and inpatient phrases like *I'm sorry*, which didn't sound sorry at all, would dissolve the congestion, and the great human river would continue its course.

Despite my best intentions to mull over the Valentine Killer case while spying on the cartel boss's wife, I found it hard to focus. I had been following Olga Ryghenko since six in the morning, and by four o'clock in the afternoon, I was so cold and tired, I was ready to murder someone myself.

If I had to compile a list of things I enjoyed about being a PI, tailing people would be firmly at the very last spot. Occasionally I'd forget that, especially during long and tedious stakeouts with dubious options for bathroom breaks. But sure enough, sooner or later, there would come a day when I needed to follow someone without being made to remind me how nice and peaceful stakeouts actually were.

The reason for that was simple—I'm a lone operator. Tracking a person with multiple teams operating different vehicles, all coordinated by a central command post that was fed a live data stream of the mark was one thing. Running alone around Manhattan on a cold-ass day while trying to follow a person with a wide-open schedule and not a care in the world? That's something entirely different.

For starters, Olga had a chauffeur. A sharply dressed Asian man in his early sixties dropped her off at different locations and picked her up at a moment's notice in an undoubtedly toasty Mercedes SUV. Two lanky lads in loose-fitting clothes, whom I immediately named Donner and Blitzen, would pop out of the car every time it made a stop to open the door and walk Olga to her destination, only to disappear a moment later in the belly of the vehicle. I was on foot, freezing my behind and relying on luck, yellow cabs, and, in one instance, my legs as I sprinted after her car for two blocks.

It wasn't much of a problem early in the morning when I first saw Olga. According to my research, she just turned forty-six last month, but the tall woman with a short, boyish haircut of blonde hair looked half her age. She reminded me of Demi Moore circa the filming of *Ghost*. Beautiful, confident, and full of purpose.

I watched her slim, fit figure clad in a pair of Lululemon leggings and a simple white T-shirt, with a fur bomber jacket thrown around her shoulders as she checked into a private Pilates class. While she worked out, I sipped a hot cup of coffee and ate a toasted bagel in a small cafe across the street from the studio. From the comfort of a warm dining room, I mused about the choices that brought the woman to a place where she married the head of a cartel. Was it a slippery slope of small, seemingly innocuous decisions she made that eventually became irreversible? Or perhaps she was the victim? Fooled by the man's legitimate facade until it was too late?

Apart from idle curiosity, the answer didn't matter to me. Olga had an item my client wanted, and I needed to find a way to get it back. If I could, an injustice a few decades in the making would be undone, and I'd be handsomely paid. Everything else was just noise.

When the Pilates class was over, I had to leave the temporary refuge of the bagel shop. From there, things got progressively less comfortable.

After the class, Olga went back to her apartment for a while. I had no way to tell whether she would call it a day and stay in. I set a timer on my phone for three hours and spent the next two sitting on a bench in a small park nearby, my teeth rattling, wishing I was one of those flask-carrying types.

But my patience paid off, and eventually, two fancy-looking ladies pulled up in an SUV with tinted windows and went into Olga's building, only to emerge a few minutes later with my target in tow. This time, the leggings gave way to an Armani pantsuit over a pair of loud Miu Miu shoes, a stylish Moose Knuckles coat, and a Birkin bag. From there, it was a whirlwind of shopping, cocktails, meals, more shopping, and more cocktails.

I'm sure some people would find this kind of lifestyle appealing. As I tracked the three women from one superficial event to another, I couldn't help but think I'd be bored out of my mind in their shoes. But then again, I was frozen to the bone and never had their kind of shoes, even when I had access to a Black American Express card. It just never felt right. Perhaps, considering the discovery of a crotchless pair of panties in my own bedroom, my modesty when it came to shoe shopping might have been a mistake.

None of it mattered. What was important was that the trajectory of my target was predictable. After a few days of suffering, I could confidently build her calendar. Better yet, she was a regular in most of the stores she went to. Personal shoppers in at least two high-end boutiques unceremoniously dropped the person they had been talking to when Olga entered and rushed to her aid. The brunch place with a view of Central Park had a table reserved in her name, which remained empty even after Olga and her entourage had left. I didn't quite know what to do with this information yet, but I was sure it would come to me in time.

At four o'clock, Olga finally returned to her apartment after giving her friends a very European two-kisses goodbye. I decided to call it a day. Perhaps she was going out again later, but by then, her husband might be back, and I had no desire to deal with extra security. I had learned enough for one day.

My car was cold, and I shivered in the front seat, keeping my hands over the air vents for a few minutes. I ignored the looks of the parking lot attendant, who clearly wanted me to move as life slowly returned to my extremities. Tough luck, young man. If a lady had to stay, then the lady had to stay.

When my fingers were flexible enough to move without the risk of breaking into pieces like a shard of ice, I put the car into gear and followed the spiral path out of the garage.

The sun was still high; it was May after all. But had I been awakened from a long coma and asked what season it was, I would say it was winter without a shadow of a doubt. The sky was gray and low, the shapeless clouds urgently rushing from west to east as if eager to escape the clutches of the land and disappear over the Atlantic.

And then there was the wind buffeting my car's sides as I navigated down Eleventh Avenue. It wasn't a gentle breeze of spring that brought the scent of blossoming trees and the promise of the hot days ahead. The wet, ruthlessly cold gale took your breath away and made your eyes water when it hit you in the face.

When I got to the West Side Highway, traffic started to build up, clogging up the flow until it came to a complete stop. After a while, we began to move again—a giant steel millipede, stretching and contracting, and stretching again.

Soon, I fell into a mindless rhythm—stop and go, stop and go. I turned the radio on, tuned to a classic rock station, and let my mind wander as Robert Plant sang of traveling time and space over Jimmy Page's hypnotic riffs.

A shiver ran down my spine as I recalled the graphic descriptions from Levy's novel. The unnamed woman. Naomi. Benjamin French. Those poor bastards. No one should die the way those people did. I tried to push the thought away, but it kept coming back like an angry hornet, buzzing in my ear, its stinger ready. A wave of panic rose in my chest, constricting my ribs and making my breath shallow.

I cranked the radio all the way up until my ears hurt, drowning out every noise, every thought, every emotion. My hands squeezed the steering wheel in a death grip. We stopped again, the red light breaking up the already lethargic flow. I looked around wildly, locking my eyes with a woman in a silver SUV sitting in the lane beside mine. She averted her eyes. Hastily, like you would when a crazy homeless man meets your gaze on the subway.

"Easy there, Alex," I said out loud. "Easy. Let's not scare fellow travelers."

Embarrassment snapped me back to normal. I turned the radio down and switched it to a news channel, the friendly banter of the host and a meteorologist calming me even more. The crazy cold spell would get even crazier with a large storm front moving in from the north. I glanced at the reading of the outside thermometer and sneered—as it was, we were a hair away from seeing the snowflakes.

My cell phone vibrated in the back pocket of my jeans, and, keeping one hand on the wheel, I fished it out. The two letters on the screen made me sit up straight. *DD.* I cursed under my breath. This couldn't possibly be good. DD made it abundantly clear the last time we spoke that he wanted nothing to do with me. And yet, here he was, calling my cell. I stared at the screen briefly and then threw the phone on the dash. DD was going to have to leave me a voice message. Whatever it was, it could wait until I returned home to Brooklyn.

And now, the radio host said, abruptly cutting off the weatherman, *we are interrupting our regular broadcast for an emergency announcement.*

I didn't know what the host with a silky baritone and a touch of a Boston accent was going to say. And yet, not a single word that came through my radio next was a surprise.

Three more victims of what seems to be the work of the elusive Valentine Killer who has been terrorizing the city for the past few weeks. A patrolman found their bodies in a dumpster area behind a rare bookshop...

"Shit!" I cried out, my knuckles white from the force I applied to the steering wheel. "You slimy son of a bitch."

We will continue to provide you with updates as they become available. Remember, your safety and well-being are our top priority. Please stay vigilant...

My palm slammed into the dashboard, almost breaking the knob off the panel, and the radio went silent, cutting the baritone mid-sentence. *A rare bookshop,* I fumed. What are the odds? The skin on my face felt so hot it could have been burning.

The phone started vibrating again, the tremors making it slide closer and closer to the edge of the dash. I caught it before it fell off and switched it to silent mode without looking at the caller ID. I knew who it was. This was going to be fun.

TWENTY-ONE

"I'm going to lock you up, Alex. You know I will." My former partner sounded furious. "If you have something that can help the investigation, I need you to spill it. Now."

I thought giving DD some time to cool off before calling him back was a good idea, but it seemed to have had the opposite effect. The intensity in his voice was so high I thought he would reach through the phone and shake me like a rag doll.

I ignored three (or was it four?) calls from him as I fought the traffic on the way back to Brooklyn. As luck would have it, there was a parking spot right next to my house, for which I was grateful. The chill of the day spent tracking El Jefe's wife got deep into my bones, and no amount of car heat could vanquish it. Once back in the house, I fed Spots, made hot tea, spiked it with a generous amount of brandy, and settled on a couch under a heavy blanket.

Only when I was halfway done with the drink did the stiff numbness finally release my body from its deathly grip. The phone vibrated again, and when I glanced at the screen, there was a text from my former partner that read *CALL ME RIGHT THIS SECOND* in all capital letters. I've known DD for years, and I don't recall a single time he texted anyone, let alone in all capital letters. He was one of those old-school guys. He'd read your messages, but instead of texting you back, he'd dial your number if he considered it worth his time. Otherwise, you'd simply never hear from him. Even his superiors, to much of their chagrin, weren't spared the *no-text* treatment.

"Dom, stop it," I said before he had a chance to elaborate on his plans to put me away. "Can we talk like two normal people? I know it's been awhile, but you don't have to resort to threats."

"This is not a threat. This is a reality. Six people, Alex," Dom said. His voice dropped low, to almost a whisper, but anyone who knew DD as I did would rather be yelled at than be at the end of this quiet, deliberate tone of his. "Six people strung up and gutted while they were still alive. Do you understand this? The city hasn't had a bona fide serial killer since the late fifties. And we've *never* had anything like this psycho. Reporters are camping around my and Sean's houses. My captain is ripping people new ones. I have feds inbound. I am not in the mood for games."

"Feds? Why are the feds coming? I thought all the victims were found in Manhattan. Did anything cross state lines?"

"Oh, please," he scoffed, "what do you think this is? An episode of *Law and Order*? You should know better. You know they'd find an excuse on a high-profile case like this. Every paper in the country will run this story on their front pages tomorrow. The mayor's having a press conference in two hours. You can bet your ass the feds will be coming."

"Right."

"My point is," Dom raised his voice again, "you need to tell me everything you know about this. It's too big now, and I won't be able to keep your name out of it, even if I want to. It won't even be me who will put you away. You know that saying about victory having a thousand fathers?"

"Sure. And defeat is an orphan."

"Not this time," he said. "If shit goes any more sideways, I'm going to be the proud papa."

I mulled it over. Dom was the most pragmatic person I had ever met. Police work is a dangerous field, and you see plenty of people with superstitions. When I was a rookie, my TO would double-tap his badge every time he stepped out of his car. Some guys would have a lucky charm. Something from the family, like a photo of their kids, or something they'd pick on the job. Silly stuff. Not because they genuinely believed in it. It was more like a "it won't hurt if I do" kind of thing. It's contagious, too. For a while, I got in the habit of adjusting the rearview mirror every time I got out of the shop. Dom had never cared for any of it. He caught me messing with it a second time and made a face but didn't say anything out loud. It irked me enough to ask him instead if he had any rituals.

Have you ever heard of bushido? He replied to my question with a question. *Those who practice it embrace death as the inevitable outcome of life. Something you can't escape from, so even trying is futile.*

Sounds morbid, I said. *All that hara-kiri stuff never made any sense to me. To most, even a shitty existence is better than death.*

That has nothing to do with hara-kiri. Bushido is a code. It literally means "the way of the warrior." Recognizing that, at some point, we will all die is not morbid. That's what people get wrong about bushido, he said. *By accepting death, you can focus on the living. Because every moment of your life could be your last. It allows you to build your legacy while you still can. Not leaving it to some hypothetical future that may never come.*

I wasn't sure I fully understood, but since then, I have seen Dominic Deluca in a different light.

Suppose I told Dom now about the manuscript. In that case, he'd certainly think I was hiding something and, instead of sharing the info with my former partner, was making fun of him. He'd lock me up for sure. I had to give him enough to get him off my back, but not too much.

Besides, what did I really have to give? While I was playing the *Can this be real?* game with John Levy, a serial killer took six lives in the most brutal way possible. Besides the fact that Dom's new partner supposedly looked like Luca from Levy's novel, I had nothing to go on. And I couldn't even explain it without going into the supernatural realm. As for what lay ahead... For all I knew, John hadn't even written any more chapters since I saw him.

"How's Sean?" I probed. "Any more unexplained trips?"

"He's fine, and no. We've been sleeping at the precinct since I spoke to you last. I don't know what your problem with Gallagher is, but you can save your accusations for someone else. He's as solid as they come. If you ask me, this looks like it could be one of the cartel guys going nuts."

"The cartel?" That was a surprising twist.

"The Diablitos. Weren't you looking into El Jefe? Why do you think I'm calling you?"

"I was, but I told you that was an unrelated case. Different client and—"

"Have you seen the *fish-out-of-water* video?"

"The what?"

"Fish out of water," he repeated, enunciating every syllable. "This is something the Diablitos use to intimidate. A couple of years back, they caught one of their own stealing from the cartel. He was a delivery guy, smuggling some of the stuff for them from the southern ports. Just a pawn. But he did well for a while. El Jefe seemed to like him enough to become a godfather to the guy's daughter. But the man got greedy. What's worse is that he struck a side deal with the Colombians. Doesn't get any worse than that. Skimming *and* sleeping with the enemy."

"I take it he got caught."

"Yes. El Jefe invited him to see a new warehouse. The guy probably thought he was getting a promotion. Found a few very unhappy fellows there instead. They chained him, put a steel collar on his neck, and pinned him to the ground. Then, one of the enforcers cut him open while he was still alive and pulled out his lungs. You could see them inflate and deflate as the poor bastard drew his last breaths like a fish out of water. It went on for a while. Unfortunately, you don't see the perp. You only see the victim and the hand with a knife carving the guy up."

"Good lord." I swallowed hard, fighting the taste of bile. That's what Dev Mehta must've seen. It made a grown man cry. "I've heard of this video. Never seen it. A pawnshop broker told me when the cartel first approached him and offered him a job, he chased them away."

"Then they showed him the flick, and he reconsidered?"

"Right."

"Don't you see the possible connection? Perhaps the victims aren't as random as they seem. We just need to dig deeper. If the Valentine Killer and the guy from the *fish-out-of-water* video are the same..."

"I know who the guy with the knife in the video is," I said. "His name is Franky, and he's the enforcer for El Jefe."

"How do you know that?"

"The same pawnshop broker. He told me Franky was pretty explicit about it."

"Does he have any proof?"

"I doubt it." I shook my head. It was a futile gesture, considering Dom couldn't see me. "I met him in person. A very charming fellow. Just a pair of the scariest eyes you'd ever see. But there are no visible marks that would make him easily recognizable. No tattoos or crazy scars. If you can round him up, by all means, do it. A guy like this shouldn't be walking the streets. But I don't think it's him."

"Why not? It makes perfect sense. I don't know anyone else capable of this violence on the East Coast. It must be him. You know what doesn't make sense?"

I knew it was a rhetorical question, but I took the bait anyway. "What?"

"The serial killer theory."

"Why not?"

"Because he doesn't have a type. They *all* have a type. Sometimes, you'd get a random murder in the mix, but that's usually a crime of opportunity. Someone got too close to the killer or something like that. Here, there's no type. Think about it. He kills both men and women. This is unheard of."

"Maybe the way he kills them is his type," I said. "Maybe it's not who he kills, but how. What if there's a religious angle?"

"Like what? A ritual of sorts?"

"Who knows," I said. "He's clearly crazy. We need to understand how he rationalizes his murders. Think from his perspective. You taught me that."

"I don't buy it," Dom said. "I don't buy it at all. We are missing something, and I strongly feel you know what it is."

I said nothing.

"Why do you keep on bringing up Gallagher?"

I bit my lip. Hard. I wanted to explain. But what was I going to tell him? That the guy fits the killer's description? And how do I have the killer's description?

"Alex?"

"I don't know." I stifled a sigh. "Call it a hunch. But I swear to you I know nothing else. Go after Franky if you can."

"Tell me about your case."

"I don't know if I can. There's—"

"You're not a lawyer," he cut me off. "There's no privilege. And I'm an actual cop. Investigating actual murders."

"All right," I said, giving up. Perhaps that would get him to back off. "Remember that robbery in Brooklyn? A new bank. Practically empty."

"When they lost power, and the alarm didn't go off?"

"Yep. That one."

"That was the cartel?"

"Yes," I said. "The lower ranks. A crime of opportunity."

"What does it have to do with you?"

"There was an artifact in one of those safe deposit boxes. It belongs to the Holocaust survivor, as far as I know. I was hired to get it back."

"Ouch. From Nazis to these assholes."

"That's exactly what I said."

"All right." Maybe it was my wishful thinking, but Dom's gravelly voice softened a notch. "Have you met the client?"

"Not directly, no. They hired an attorney, who hired me."

"And what kind of artifact?"

"Jewelry," I said vaguely. "Not even valuable in hard dollars. Just important to the client."

There was silence on the other side of the line, and I held my breath, hoping it was enough.

"Okay," he finally said. "I'll take this for now."

"Can I ask you a favor?" I knew I was pushing it, but an idea just occurred to me, and he was the only person who could find what I needed. "Can you get me a copy of this fish-out-of-water video?"

"What for?"

"Not for morbid curiosity, that's for sure. I could potentially use it to flip someone in El Jefe's circle. It would help me with the case. And it also could potentially create an inside man for you down the road. It's worth a shot."

"Do I know who that is?"

"No, and it's better if you don't. No offense. If you know, you have to put it in your reports. And if you put it in your reports, other people will read it. I'm not worried about you, but someone could talk."

He thought about it for a few moments. "Fine. But I want you to stay put."

"What's that supposed to mean?" My cheeks immediately grew hot, my pulse rising.

"You know exactly what that means." His tone was flat, matter-of-fact. "You are a person of interest in this case, Alex. Don't leave town. The last thing you want me to do is to start sending out warrants to track your phone and access your messages."

He hung up before I could say anything else, and for a moment, I sat there, angrily squeezing my phone as if I could force the connection back. *A person of interest.* What the hell was he smoking?

I had no intention of leaving town, but it didn't matter. The fact that DD was considering getting warrants on my private information spooked me. I've heard people say all the time that they didn't care if someone else read their emails or eavesdropped on their conversation. Those people are fools. There's a saying that if a cop follows you long enough, they'll find a reason to pull you over.

I knew that firsthand. You don't have to be a full-on criminal to get in trouble if somebody went through your private life with a fine-toothed comb. Jokes could be misinterpreted. Minor infractions could be turned into big issues. You paid your plumber in cash? You didn't declare a sale of an old piece of furniture? Forgot to report a few hundred bucks you earned babysitting your nephew?

One thing leads to another, and before you know it, you're out a few hundred thousand dollars in legal fees, you're fired from your job, your friends shun you, and your life is ruined. In the end, unless you actually broke the law, you'll probably clear your name. And it's not a guarantee. As someone said to me once, *there's plenty of slip between the cup and the lip.*

TWENTY-TWO

John Levy stumbled through the door into his apartment. He swung the door, catching it right before it slammed into the frame, and then leaned back, his body shaking.

He closed his eyes, and there it was again—the dimly lit alley where shadows danced their macabre waltz under the torrents of icy rain. John groaned as he saw the graffiti that adorned the weathered brick wall above the dumpster.

New York was full of rebellious art, but he could not remember seeing anything of such incredible skill. Each stroke seemed to writhe and coil, the drops of water on the rough surface of the wall making the sinuous form of the goat seem almost alive.

And then there was the paint. He'd never seen such color. He'd recalled reading somewhere that black wasn't a color at all. It was the absence of it. Something that absorbed every photon of light and returned none of it back. In real life, that wasn't the case. The black color was everywhere. But it was never perfect. Cars glistened with a metallic sheen. Briefcases of lush leather were dotted with tiny dimples. Black spots on a painting canvas were ribbed with traces of dried brushstrokes.

This was different. The blackness of the goat's paint was absolute. It was as if the cosmic void had seeped through the brick wall. Somehow, John was sure that if anyone dared to touch it, the blackness would swallow the offender and then transport them to a place from where no one could return.

John's mental image shifted from the goat to the dumpster, and he hurriedly snapped his eyes wide, terrified to see what lay beneath its worn-out lid again. The shapeless gray of swollen garbage bags inside. And between them, the pale human foot arched in indescribable agony, its curled toes pointing at the dreary skies above.

"I won't be a part of this," he whispered. His mind raced. If he couldn't write the story that had the ending he wanted, he wasn't going to write the story at all. He'd toss the laptop and force himself to forget anything remotely related to the novel: the murders, the victims, and the Valentine Killer. There was something else he needed to get rid of, he realized with a start. Levy pushed himself off the wall and raced toward the kitchen. "The Montblanc pen."

With a swift, powerful yank, he wrenched open the kitchen drawer. The sheer force of the motion sent the utensils flying. Forks, spoons, knives, peelers, and tongs briefly hung in the air as if defying gravity itself, only to clatter to the floor the next moment.

Levy glanced at the pieces scattered on the linoleum like fallen soldiers on the battlefield and dug into the drawer, pushing whatever remained aside. There was no pen.

"What the hell?" he growled.

He grabbed the drawer with both hands and ripped it out of the cabinet, the slide rails screeching in protest. He flipped the drawer over, spilling the remaining contents onto the floor.

He fell to his knees, fingers scrounging the wreckage with frenzied urgency. There was a sharp pain in his left hand, and John cried out, pulling his arm to his chest. There was a small knife on the floor, its blade gleaming, a trace of bloody drops leading from its handle to John's knee and snaking up his arm.

"Oh man," he whispered as he turned his hand over and

inspected a long, deep cut at the edge of his palm. He climbed to his feet, the rage blinding him, grabbed the drawer, and hurled it through the air. The wooden box flew across the room, crashed into the wall above the kitchen faucet, and then fell into the sink, breaking a few dishes at the bottom of the steel basin.

There was a muted shouting from the apartment next door, and someone knocked on the wall as if complaining of the noise.

"Go fuck yourself," Levy yelled in frustration. He walked over to the table, grabbed the laptop with both hands, and raised it above his head, ready to slam it. A thin stream of blood ran down his forearm and into the sleeve of his T-shirt, tickling his skin.

The doorbell rang before he could bring the laptop down, and he froze in mid-motion. His neck craned as he listened to the melodic sound. Then it rang again.

"Go away!" he shouted toward the hallway. "I never complain about your damn game shows you watch on full blast. Get lost."

He raised the laptop again, ready to bring it down with force, but an urgent knock on the door and a muffled voice stopped him in his tracks. He put the computer on the table, turned off the lights, and tiptoed to the hallway, doing his best not to make a sound.

"John?"

There was no mistake this time. It was a voice he could recognize even if a million others were shouting in his ear at the same time. It was the woman whose magnetic presence tethered him to something he couldn't quite put into words.

He stood in the middle of the dark apartment, desperate to be quiet and equally desperate to be heard. He longed to open the door. To see her. Perhaps it was no accident she came here now, at this hour. He needed someone to save him. Maybe she was the *only one* who could still save him. Pull him away from the sticky web of madness and murder.

"John?" the voice said again, and he tensed, forgetting the throbbing pain in his palm for a moment. "I can hear you. What's going on in there? Please open up."

It was as if the air went out of him, and Levy walked to the door and placed his good hand against the cold frame. "Lilly? I'm sorry, but you should go home. I'm not feeling too well."

"Come on, John." There was concern in her voice. But also, something else. Something that plucked at the innermost strings of his soul. "I know something isn't right. I can tell. Let me in. Please."

He sighed, giving up, walked to the door without hiding, and turned the lock.

Lilly rushed in, bringing the smell of the storm, the pungent mix of ozone and humidity, into the stale air of the apartment.

"Are you okay?" Her cold hands traced the outline of his face.

"I'm fine," he managed. "You're soaked. You must be freezing. Let me take your jacket."

She let him, and he took it off her shoulders, grimacing at the pain in his left hand.

"What's this?"

"Nothing." He covered the wound with another hand. "An accident."

"Come on." She grabbed him by his good hand and pulled him toward the kitchen. "You don't want this to get infected. Where's your rubbing alcohol?"

Levy tried to protest, but she was relentless, and he gave in. He let her sit him on the kitchen chair and watched her as she pushed the mess on the floor aside without giving it much thought, washed her hands, and then got to tending to his wound.

"That's much better," she said after she wrapped a tight bandage around his wrist and tied the knot. "Now, at least you won't die of infection."

He smiled weakly, watching her close. Her hair was a mess, and her wet blouse clung to her skin in a way that made his pulse jump. She smiled back at him as she caught his gaze. "I guess not wearing a bra on a day like this wasn't the smartest idea."

"I like it." He shrugged.

"What happened here?" She waved her hand at the remains of the drawer and the mess scattered on the floor of the kitchen.

"An accident," he lied.

"Oh yeah?" She glanced at the gaping hole in the cabinet row, the ripped-out slide rail hanging at its edge like a blown-up bridge. "Did you turn into the Hulk and couldn't measure your strength when operating household items?"

He said nothing and just sat there, unsure of what to do.

"Here," she said, taking a step closer, taking his good hand into hers and bringing it to her chest. "Since you've been staring. Maybe that can jog your memory."

Levy shivered. The blouse was wet and cold, but he could feel the blistering heat of the firm breast underneath. He tried to pull away, but Lilly kept his hand and then slowly moved it down, his fingers gliding over the bump of her nipple.

"I don't think it's a good idea," he said, shivering, his voice taking on an unexpected timbre, a low and husky resonance.

"To the contrary." She turned away from him, a mischievous look on her face, and unbuttoned her pants and pulled them down. The bra wasn't the only piece of underwear she had been missing.

Levy stayed frozen as Lilly slipped out of her clothes and straddled him, leaning back against his chest and resting her head on Levy's shoulder. He moaned and closed his eyes as she brought both of his hands to cup her full breasts. "I think it's a great idea."

"We shouldn't," he said as her hand traveled down his stomach. But he didn't resist as she found his flesh and guided him in, her hips grinding his thighs. He opened his eyes and watched her toned back as she rode him. Slowly at first and then faster. Hungrier.

He climaxed without warning. A powerful, blinding ecstasy that disconnected him from reality. He writhed under her hot body, blissfully unaware of the outside world. The murders and the unfinished book, the pale foot sticking out of the jaws of a hungry dumpster. They all disappeared, if only for a moment.

"See," she whispered when they finally stopped. "Things can be better."

"You have a big scar here," Levy said as his vision finally returned to him. He traced a faint outline along the spine from the cervical vertebrae almost to her waist. It was smooth to the touch and straight, as if a surgeon had laid a ruler on her back and cut the line in one long, confident move. "It must have been a doozy."

"An old accident," she said and turned to face him. She leaned closer, the smell of lilac tickling his nose, and planted a kiss at the corner of his mouth. Then another. And another, this time firmly on his lips. He tried to say something, but she covered his mouth with her hand. "Stop talking. Just take me."

When it was over, she slipped from his embrace and, not bothering with clothes, went through his liquor cabinet.

He watched, spellbound, as she moved with the deftness of an experienced bartender, the lights from the street playing on her naked body. A minute later, she gave him a glass of swirling translucent liquid and took a chair on the other side of the table.

"What is this thing?" Levy asked suspiciously as he sniffed the tumbler. It smelled of freshly cut grass, sun-kissed oranges, and early summer rain.

"A family secret." She gave him a wink and sipped her drink. "If you behave, perhaps I'll show you how to make it one day. Or not. I haven't decided yet."

He took a sip. As the liquid went down, the subtle tang of citrus teased his nostrils. He was instantly buzzed. It was potent yet smooth and colorful, if colors could be tasted. It was like drinking a rainbow made of fire.

"Wow," was all he managed.

"Now that you're better," she said, the whites of her eyes shining in the dark of the room, "you want to tell me what happened here before I came in?"

"Not particularly. If I do, you'll think I'm crazy."

She smiled and tilted her head.

"I'm serious."

"Try me."

He studied her across the room. She was leaning on the back of the chair, legs crossed, her supple breasts rising and falling with her breath. The way she sat there, utterly unfazed by her nakedness, she could have been a model in a famous artist's studio, posing for a painting destined to be hung in the world's most prestigious galleries. Or perhaps sold to a possessive billionaire, hidden from public view, so he alone could savor the perfection of her curves.

"Well?" she probed.

"The book," he said and nodded toward the laptop on the table. "I don't know how, but there's a connection between the story and what's been happening in the city for the past few weeks."

She said nothing.

"I think, somehow," he continued, encouraged by her silence, "I'm writing about the murders perpetrated by the Valentine Killer. For some time, I thought I was predicting them as they occurred exactly on the same timeline as in the book. But now I'm not so sure. Some of them were off. I thought we had more time before he caught the next victim, but I was wrong."

"Wrong, how?"

"It's happening faster than in the book. Maybe I'm writing them down in real-time."

"Have you told anyone else about this?"

"No," he said. "No one else."

"Good." She leaned forward, the drink in her hand sparkling. "You still haven't answered my question about what you were doing right before I came in."

"I did."

"No." She made a circle gesture, the liquid in the glass precariously sloshing back and forth. "You told me about a connection you may have to a serial killer. You said nothing about the destruction of your kitchen."

He stayed silent for some time, refusing to meet her eyes.

"John?"

"I wanted to destroy the laptop and the book," he said. "I tried to change the story. But I can't. And if I can't write it where the killer gets caught, I don't want to write it at all. I want to burn it to ashes."

"Oh, but that would be wrong," she said, standing up. She took a few steps until she stood right before him. "It doesn't matter if the connection is real or just in your head. It doesn't even matter if I believe you. But I can see that it will drive you mad if you don't finish the story."

"You think so?"

"I do. Besides," she downed the rest of the drink, put it on the table, and straddled him again, "I think your literary horizons are lacking. You should read more classics. Because if you had, you would know—manuscripts do not burn."

TWENTY-THREE

If the only fitting rooms you've ever been to are the ones in department stores and shopping malls, you're missing out. Don't get me wrong—until now, I'd never seen anything fancy either. I'm used to cramped, lonely spaces with bare walls and a thin, warped mirror, where a very unreliable curtain was the only thing separating your half-dressed body from the sweaty line of impatient people outside. But things changed after my handy parabolic microphone picked up a conversation between Olga and the staff at one of the boutique stores. El Jefe's wife was coming back the next day to try a custom order.

That presented me with an opportunity I couldn't pass on, and I snuck into the store right before it closed for the night, hiding in a closet of a fitting room.

Don't feel bad for me. Most hotels I had stayed in before couldn't hold a candle to this place. The room at Le Grand Couturier was spacious and well-lit. There was an oversized leather chaise with silky cushions that I slept on. It was situated next to an elegant mahogany table with a tray for refreshments and a champagne bucket. A small intercom was placed next to the bucket and could be used to request items from the ever-helpful staff. A rack on wheels stood in the middle of the room with a large assortment of clothes, presumably for Olga's choosing.

The shelves on the wall behind the chair were filled with a curated assortment of accessories. Jewelry, handbags, and shoes stood in neat rows like soldiers before the parade, waiting for their turn to be tried.

In the corner, another door led to a private bathroom with a generous selection of makeup and more custom jewelry.

But the room's best feature was that it was completely sound-proof to maintain the highest levels of privacy for the client. This meant that in the morning, when Olga Ryghenko gasped out loud when an unfamiliar woman stepped out of the bathroom and blocked her way to the door, nobody could hear her from the outside.

"Who the hell are you?" she demanded. There was the slightest touch of an Eastern European accent when she spoke. Perhaps, when she was calm, Olga could pass for a person born on this side of the Atlantic. But in a moment of danger, the primal brain took over, and her r's became too strong and her w's not round enough.

Now that I could see the woman up close, some of the magic was missing, too. She still didn't quite look her age, but standing two feet away from her face, I wouldn't confuse her with a twenty-something, either. She was still polished and refined, but even in the soft, flat-tering light of the fitting room, I could see the traces of time etched on her face. Well-hidden but not entirely invisible.

"I'm not here to harm you. But I need your help."

"That's an interesting way to ask. I don't think you know who you're dealing with." She tried to move around me. "My guards—"

I mirrored her move, blocking her way again. "Donner and Blitzen are outside in the car. They won't hear you here. All I ask is that you give me ten minutes of your time."

Despite the tension, a hint of a smile touched the corner of her mouth. "I call them Tom and Jerry."

"See, we'll get along swimmingly." I pointed at the chair. "Take a seat. I slept on this while waiting for you, so I can tell you it's quite comfortable."

Olga watched me for a few seconds as if trying to gauge where this was going and then took a seat, crossing her legs. She still looked tense, but I could tell she wasn't scared.

"You said I don't know who I'm dealing with," I began. "But I wonder if *you* know who you're married to."

"Half of Manhattan knows who I'm married to," she quipped. "At least the half that matters."

"They only know his facade." She stiffened when I reached into my jacket pocket and relaxed again once she saw a small tablet in my hands. I put it on the table in front of her. "Your husband is a criminal, Mrs. Ryghenko. And not a petty thief at that. In some circles, he is known as El Jefe, the godfather of an organized crime syndicate known as the Diablitos."

"That's a lie. I understand now why you're here. What's that?" She scowled and pointed at the tablet with her chin. "You caught Mateo with some whores and now think I'm going to gasp in horror? Let me tell you something, sugar. On our honeymoon, Mateo brought two escorts into our suite and made me watch as he fucked them. Do you know why?"

"Because he's a pervert?"

"No." Her scowl deepened. "When he was done, he told me that a man in his position has to maintain an image. And that image comes from doing certain things whether you like them or not. And that one day, someone will come and show me a tape and ask for money or favors. And then, instead of being scared or intimidated by people like you, I would laugh in your face and give you nothing. I suggest you get going."

I slowly clapped my hands. "Wow. I've heard a lot of things in my life, but *Honey, I'm fucking whores for your protection* is sure to take the cake."

"You can believe whatever you want to believe."

"You see, I've watched you for the last couple of days. And as I did, I wondered. Did she know when she married him? Or did she find out later? Or, perhaps she was the willing participant and maybe even a partner? Did she know about the bad stuff? Not the smuggling and the thievery, but about truly evil things? The killings, the torture?"

She frowned, her lips disappearing into a thin line, but said nothing.

"Somehow," I tapped the tablet with my index finger, "I think you didn't know. And when you did, it was too late to do anything about that."

"You don't know anything about me."

"No," I said. "But I want to know if you are aware of the depth of the hellish chasm your husband has crawled out of. Have you ever heard of the fish-out-of-water video?"

"The what?"

"That's funny. I said exactly the same thing. You see, your husband had an employee. A not very loyal employee. And once Mateo Alvarez realized that the man was cheating him out of money, he punished him."

She shrugged. "Don't bite the hand that feeds you. It sounds like he deserved to be punished."

"Indeed. Say you were in your husband's shoes. What would you have done should you catch someone red-handed?"

"I don't know. Fire him, obviously. I'm guessing that he was roughed up, and somehow, you got it on tape. Well, I guess that's progress. You're not here about the whores, but you are still trying to blackmail me."

"No," I said. "And no. You need to be paying attention. I told you why I was here the moment you came in. I need your help."

"What help?"

I didn't answer and pressed the Play button on the video, stepping back from the table. I'd seen the video already and had no interest in seeing it again. Just Olga's reaction.

The woman scoffed as the video started. I heard the steps and some banter in Spanish as the unsuspecting man was led into the middle of the floor of a large warehouse. Somebody said something, and there was laughter. Then, there was a sound of a scuffle, and Olga bit her lip, her eyes widening in shock. I heard the clanging noise and grimaced. The images of the hammer arcing through the air, its iron head gleaming as it struck the collar on the poor bastard's neck, flashed in my head.

"You want me to stop it before it's too late?" I asked. "It gets grisly real fast."

Olga shook her head, and I stepped away even more to ensure I didn't accidentally see the screen. Seeing this footage once was one time too many.

She gasped and covered her mouth when screaming started, her face turning so white I thought she would pass out. I couldn't blame her. It took me four tries to watch the tape from the beginning to the end, and it was only seven minutes long. But Olga seemed to have found her resolve and watched it all in one go.

"Where did you get this?" Her eyes were red, but she kept her tears at bay. If anything, there was more anger in her voice than shock.

"Did you know the guy?"

"Yes. No. I—" Her voice broke. She cleared her throat and straightened. "I didn't know him well, but I've seen him a few times at the docks. Alejandro, I think. I don't remember his last name. Mateo seemed to like him. I remember he even went to an event for him. A wedding or a christening. It's been awhile since I saw him; frankly, I didn't think twice about it. Mateo employs thousands of people. Some stay, some go. It's a large business."

"You didn't go to the christening?"

She shook her head. "I told you; Mateo doesn't bring me everywhere he goes. Not even to all of his social events. He prefers to be alone sometimes. He is the king. He needs to act like one."

I said nothing as I watched the woman.

"Can I get you anything? Champaign or snacks?" The intercom on the table quacked, startling both of us, but Olga recovered first.

She leaned forward and pressed the Talk button. "No. I'm trying a few things on. I'll call you back."

"Of course," the cheerful voice continued. "Have you tried—"

"I'll call you back," she repeated and hung up the call, then turned to me. "You didn't answer my question—where did you get this?"

"It doesn't matter."

"I won't pay for this."

"Oh," I smiled, "I'm not here for the money. When I said I needed your help, I actually meant it. I'm looking for something. A piece of jewelry that ended up in your husband's possession. Something that doesn't belong to Mateo Alvarez."

She listened without making a sound as I told her about the bank run and the subsequent hunt for the necklace.

"He really liked it," she said when I finished. "I don't even understand why. It's a pretty thing, sure, but nothing special. And it's not like I need more jewelry. I have enough pieces to last a lifetime. But he kept going on and on about how cool it was that it was made from something that didn't come from Earth."

"Didn't come from Earth? How do you mean?"

"The stone," she said. "It comes from a meteorite. I hear there are not so many of them out there in the world. A few dozen. Perhaps even less."

"So, it is expensive then?"

"You would think it would be, but no." She shrugged. "Not particularly. Our jeweler pegged it at around fourteen hundred dollars."

"It doesn't matter," I said. "I need to return it to its rightful owner. I'm prepared to pay for it."

"I can't just sell it to you. He'll know something is up, especially since you spoke to Franky about it. That rat would immediately smell a problem. He always creeped me out."

"He should be more than creeping you out. He's the guy on the video. That's Franky's hand with the knife that you see."

She recoiled back; her beautiful face contorted in shock as if I hit her. "Are you sure?"

"I can't prove it to you, but yes."

"He," she shuddered, "was watching over me on one occasion when Tom and Jerry were doing something else. There was some trouble with a rival organization, and Mateo was paranoid for a while. Thought someone was going to try to kill him. Oh my God. I spent the entire week with that monster in my house. I have to throw out the couch he slept on."

"I don't care what you do with your couch," I said. "I need the necklace."

She gave me a long, hard look. "You must have some opinion about me."

A snappy reply almost flew out of my mouth. But then my mind went back to the pair of dirty panties behind my bed, and I bit my tongue. My ex was probably not murdering people, but there was more than one parallel between my life and Olga's than I was willing to admit. I knew, *oh, I knew* who he was for the longest time. The secret phone calls, the "late nights at the office." The last-minute business trips none of his work friends were aware of. The truth was until I was presented with irrefutable evidence I couldn't explain away, no matter how hard I tried, I was content to stay where I was. To accept the convenience of his Black American Express. To sleep with him even.

"No," I said. "At least not yet. But ask me in a few weeks."

She looked down at her well-manicured nails. "It might take more than a few weeks to untangle myself from this. I don't want to end up as Alejandro."

"That's fair."

"However," she looked up at me, and for the first time, a genuine smile spread across her lips, "I know how to give you the necklace without raising suspicion. Give me your number, and I'll call you in a couple of days to set it up."

I left Olga at the fitting room and stepped out into the store, startling a young woman standing by the door like a lost puppy.

"How did—"

"Shh," I said, putting my finger to her lips. "You know how important this client is, right?"

The woman nodded, her big brown eyes wide with fear and confusion.

"Keep this a secret, will you?" In a moment of inspiration, I looked around the store and then returned my gaze to the employee, simultaneously putting a huge frown on my face. "It's a nice store you have here. It'd be a shame if something happened to it."

TWENTY-FOUR

"Oh, crap. Why would you do that?" I whispered as the door clicked open, yielding to my tools. The disappointment in my voice might have sounded strange, considering I was actively trying to pick the lock. But I really hoped the door was going to resist my assault. No such luck.

I got off my knees and looked around, but apart from the usual hushed murmur of an occupied building, the landing in front of John Levy's apartment was quiet.

I turned the handle, pushed the door open, and stepped in. It was dark, except for the muted blue glow from the bedroom window on the other side. The air was stale and strange. There was a strong scent of cleaning chemicals and a sharp note of household bleach. But right underneath it, I could smell the lingering aroma of baked bread and subtle traces of jasmine. An odd combination.

"John?" I called out into the dark after I shut the door behind me. "This is Alex. Are you home?"

There was no answer, and I ran my hand along the wall, looking for a light switch. My fingers found it, and I threw it on, squinting in anticipation, but nothing happened, and the apartment remained dark.

"John?" I said again, touching the holster sitting in the small of my back, feeling for the cold handle of the pistol with my fingertips. An army of goose bumps marched up and down my arms.

I stayed in the hallway for a few more moments, my eyes getting used to the darkness, and then I went into the bedroom. It was a place of a reclusive single man. That much was perfectly clear. There was no artwork of any kind or framed pictures. There were no flowers or splashes of color to break up the narrow spectrum of utilitarian grays. Light-gray walls. Dark-gray linens. Charcoal-gray furniture.

The room was smallish, with a queen-sized bed in the middle, a nightstand next to it, and a dresser on the opposite wall underneath a large rectangular mirror. The bed was made, and the room itself, bathed in a bluish glow from the outside, was neat. When I went to investigate the light source, it turned out to be a set of four blue spotlights showcasing a large magnolia in the middle of the courtyard. Heavy rain pounded the leaves of the tree and flickered as it passed the cones of blue light, giving it the feel of a Monet painting. I imagined it would have looked magnificent on a clear, starry sky night. Now, in the pouring rain, it was like a backdrop of a horror movie.

I went to the dresser and opened the drawers, one by one. They were just as dull as the room itself and just as well organized. Underwear and T-shirts. Pajama sets. His socks were color-coded and laid out in straight, perfect rows—long dress socks in the front and short, no-show pairs in the back. I lifted a few piles, but there was nothing underneath. No secret plans, no torture tools, no diaries. No other indication that my growing suspicion of John Levy's hidden persona was correct.

Next was the kitchen, and that's where I found some surprises. If Levy's bedroom was spartan and pristine, his kitchen was trashed. One of the drawers had been yanked out of its place and thrown to the side, leaving a gaping hole in the cabinet wall. A cabinet door next to the sink was broken and hung limply on one hinge. The floor was littered with utensils and small trash, and one of the chairs next to a small round table was broken, its legs askew.

"What the hell happened here?" I walked over to the table and froze, seeing a trail of dried blood leading to the broken chair. I pulled out my phone, snapped a few pictures, and then turned on a flashlight, trying to make sense of the chaos before me.

There wasn't enough blood for a serious wound. Whatever the injury, it resulted in nothing more than a trickle. That and the first-aid kit on the table told me it was an accident. Nobody died in this kitchen. At least not by a blade.

There was something else that caught my attention. A laptop. I went around the table, trying not to step on anything sharp, and flipped the computer lid.

After a moment, it turned on, throwing a soft glow on my gloved hands. There was no password, and it was opened in the middle of a document. On the top of the screen, I read the title: *Madness*.

"Oh boy." I pulled out a chair, sat in front of the laptop, and then scrolled up the text. From the looks of it, Levy had added a few chapters since I saw the manuscript. I stifled a sigh and started reading.

Levy was a great writer. I was cold, jumpy, and sitting in the trashed kitchen of a man I suspected could be gutting his victims alive. And yet, after a few sentences, I was transported into the world meticulously crafted by his hand. I've never read anything like that. His prose had an eerie magnetism. It wasn't flowery or overly descriptive. In some ways, it was almost crude. And yet it was precise. He wasn't a painter with his words. He wielded them like a surgeon's scalpel, parting flesh and bone and, in a few measured, practiced strokes, exposing the beating heart underneath.

I read about the three victims found behind the rare bookshop in the city. As far as I knew, the police hadn't released any details about them, and yet, as I stared at the page, I had no doubt their names would match those in Levy's novel.

- Isaac Greenberg

- Emily Rivera

- Ruby Wong

But there was more. Luca was on the prowl again, this time after a young socialite, Victoria Winslow. I'd heard the name. She was of social media fame. An influencer, whatever the hell that meant. One of those rich young people filming themselves doing glamorous things and feeding off the poor crowd who couldn't afford to follow suit but lied to themselves that one day they would.

I finished reading and flipped the lid closed. I had a decision to make. It gnawed at me. My instincts screamed that I was wrong, that Levy couldn't possibly be the killer. Yet I could find no other logical explanation. He *knew* the victims before anyone else. Their names, the places where their bodies would be found. The most intricate details that wouldn't be available even to the press, like Naomi's butterfly tattoo with dragon wings.

My intuition could scream all it wanted, but I had to make a call. I had to place my trust in the institutions I once served. If I was wrong and Levy was innocent, there would be a way for him to prove it. He was wealthy and well-connected. He could afford the best attorneys in the country. If I were wrong, he'd walk. If I were right, I'd be ridding the city I loved from a terrible monster.

I drew a long breath, pulled out my phone, and dialed DD's number.

"Let's not make it into a habit," he said instead of a salutation.

"What exactly?"

"This," he grumbled. "You calling me. Because I get ulcers every time my phone rings and I see your number come up. You keep it up, I'll have to take a medical leave."

"I have some information you want to hear. It's about the Valentine Killer case."

He was silent for a while, only a rumbling sound of his breathing in my ear. I didn't know what to expect. He told me I was a person of interest in the case, and I had vehemently denied knowing anything even remotely related to the Valentine Killer. And now I was telling him that not only had I lied, but that I actually had a suspect. There were many things DD could tell me now, and none of them would be pleasant. I could almost smell the rancid odor of a holding cell.

"How?" His tone was flat, matter-of-fact.

I grimaced. No scolding was even worse. I had been on DD's shit list for years, but this might have bumped me all the way to the top. Or pushed me all the way to the bottom. I don't know what part of the shit list was worse. "He came to me some time ago and said he wanted to prevent the murder of a woman."

"How much time ago?"

Oh, that was a loaded question indeed, and I couldn't answer it without making DD's blood boil. "He came to me claiming he needed to find someone before they got hurt. Said he didn't know many details about the person, only that it would happen."

"That's bullshit."

"That was my initial reaction as well. He's writing a book. And he says that somehow there's a connection between the manuscript and the Valentine Killer. It's like he's writing what's about to happen. He didn't put it together at first until he realized that one of the victims matched the exact description of one of the characters in his book."

"What, he says he's a psychic?"

"No." I drew a short breath. "He's actually a very down-to-earth guy. Former financial exec. The last person you'd find near any paranormal nonsense."

"What makes you think he's connected to the case?"

"I didn't say I thought he was connected. He's probably the Valentine Killer himself. A few years back, he had a personal loss. His wife. It sounds like his entire life got derailed. He left his company and almost took his life. Now works a menial job. And then, out of the blue—he starts writing this book, a thriller. And his life starts to magically get better."

"And you think—"

"I'm no psychologist, but maybe he has a split personality?"

"A Jekyll and Hyde situation?"

"Right. He's killing them in one persona and trying to save them in another."

There was more heavy breathing on the line. "Okay. Do you have anything besides a gut feeling?"

I looked around the kitchen and braced myself. "His kitchen is trashed. Broken drawers, stuff all over the floor. Traces of blood, although not enough to make me think someone was killed here. One thing is certain—he is unstable."

"For fuck's sake, Alex."

I pulled the phone away from my ear to get DD's volume down.

"You broke into his goddamned house, didn't you?"

"Technically, it's an apartment, but yes."

"Fuck." DD was never inventive in his cursing. A four-letter word was as far as it usually went. "Give me his name and address. And don't touch anything."

"Should I stay here?"

"Yes," he barked. "You should stay there, Alex. I mean, not *there* there. Get out of the apartment and wait for me on the street."

"It's raining, DD. And it's cold."

"I don't give a shit. Get an umbrella." DD got quiet for a moment. "Are you sure it's him?"

"I'm not sure of anything, DD," I said. "But I think there's a high chance John Levy is the Valentine Killer."

"Fuckity fuck," he said. "Get out of the apartment and stay put. I'm on my way."

Fuckity fuck. That was a new one. I put the phone in the back pocket of my pants and turned around just in time to see John Levy entering the kitchen.

I backpedaled, almost tripping over the chair, and pulled the gun, pointing it at the man. "Stay right there."

Levy didn't answer, just froze in the middle of the kitchen. He was wearing a leather jacket over a T-shirt and jeans. His face was pale, wet from the rain, his eyes wide and wild-looking.

"Stay there," I repeated.

"Why?" he finally said.

I could see his entire body tremble.

"Why would you say such a terrible thing? I came to you. I trusted you. It was the police, wasn't it? On the phone? You told them I'm the killer. My God. Why? Why?!"

"Because it doesn't make any fucking sense," I shouted. "A book that predicts the future? A guy who wants to become Lucifer? Can you even hear yourself, John? What do you think this is—a Stephen King novel come true?"

"I never—"

"You have their names," I said, stepping around the table. "You have their goddamn names. Nobody mentioned them on the news. Even the NYPD might not have them yet. How else could you possibly know their names if you weren't the one who killed them?"

"No, no, no, no." He stretched his hands toward me, his fingers visibly shaking. "I wanted to stop him. Why would I come to you if I was Luca?"

"Because you don't know that you're him." I took another step, getting closer. "Something happened to you, John, when your wife died. Somewhere deep inside, I think you know that. That something's wrong with you. I think you flip from John Levy to a monster and then back again. You might not remember you did those things, but when you return, there are still traces of the killer in you, like shadows. That's why you know what happens. Because you were the one who did it."

"No." He shook his head. It might have been the dark that masked the shift in his body, but I missed it. He ducked, grabbed the broken chair, and hurled it in my face, grunting.

I saw it early enough to move but not early enough to dodge it. It hit my shoulder, making me spin and fall, my back hitting something hard as I landed. I scrambled to my feet, madly swinging the pistol before me, but Levy was already gone. So was his laptop.

"Shit." I looked through the window. The rain was still pelting the backyard with large, heavy drops, the wind howling like a pack of wild dogs. I pulled out a chair and took a seat. DD was going to bite my head off once he was here anyway. There was no reason to be wet and miserable while waiting for it.

TWENTY-FIVE

John Levy pulled a cheap burner phone out of a plastic bag and gingerly sat on the corner of the motel bed. The springs creaked—a lonely, miserable sound that bounced off the room's bare walls, crawled into a corner and died there like a rat, its belly full of poison.

He powered up the device, punched in the number, and, after a moment's hesitation, hit the Talk button.

It rang a few times, and then there was Phil's voice. "Who is this?" It sounded distracted, with a hint of annoyance at an unknown caller who was surely about to try to sell him something.

"Hey, Phil," he said. "It's me."

"Wait. John?"

"Yes."

"Hang on." There was a pause, followed by the quick staccato of footsteps and the sound of a closing door. "What the hell is going on? Your face is all over the news. Are you in trouble?"

"No. Well, yes. Just not in the way they say."

"Pal, I don't think you realize the gravity of the situation. Where are you? And why are you calling me from this number?"

"I can't tell you." Levy sighed. "And it's a burner phone."

"Are you out of your mind? A burner phone? Are you in hiding?"

"Yes, but it's not important. What's important is that I didn't do it. You've got to believe me. I didn't kill those people."

"Why are you running then?" There was a touch of desperation in his friend's voice. "You realize how this makes you look, right? Turn yourself in, John. We'll sort this out, I promise you. We'll get you the best attorney in the city. Money's not an issue."

Levy's shoulders slumped. His fingers idly traced the frayed edges of the bed's cover, its coarse fabric chafing against his skin. "I appreciate you trying, but it's not that simple."

"How is it not simple? You turn yourself in, we get a defense team, prove you had nothing to do with the Valentine Killer—"

"That is exactly the problem," Levy said. "I have everything to do with the Valentine Killer."

There was a stunned silence on the other end of the line, and when Phil started speaking again, his tone was low, subdued. "I don't understand."

"It's the book, Phil. It's the goddamn book. *Madness*. I couldn't have picked a better title even if I tried."

"John..." Phil paused. "I can't believe I need to ask you this. Did you or did you not kill those people?"

"Of course I didn't." Levy struck the side of the bed with his fist. "You aren't listening. Do you remember the night you showed up at my place unannounced?"

"Yes."

"After you left... After I made you a promise and you left, I had this...revelation. If I could somehow channel my grief and sorrow into something, I could find peace. It sounds weird, but I had this image of a shapeless burden I carried after Grace died. It wasn't something you could just get rid of. It was like a giant ephemeral and impossible-to-kill leech. The only way to make it stop sucking you dry was to attach it to something else."

Phil said nothing, the silence on the line almost unbearable.

"It didn't happen immediately, and if not for the therapist, it might not have happened at all. But when I started writing, it was exactly how it felt. It was like thousands of little hooks were leaving my flesh. It hurt, and the wounds bled, but it also brought relief. I was so happy. Well, maybe not happy. Content.

"But then I found this pen. A gold-plated Montblanc that magically appeared in my kitchen's drawer, and everything was upside down again."

"Wait," Phil said. "You're rambling. What does a pen have to do with this? And what do you mean magically appeared?"

"Just that. A character in my novel had a pen. And not just any character—the serial killer himself. And not just a regular pen. A gold-plated Montblanc. I described it in great detail, and one day, right before I went to your place for the BBQ, I opened a drawer, and there it was. Exactly the same as in the book." He paused and then said it slowly, enunciating every word: "A real-life object that belonged to a fictional character I created, Phil. Do you understand how crazy this is?"

"Listen. There could be a million explanations for this. Who cares about the stupid pen. I think you need help. Please, let me help you. Tell me where you are, and I'll come to you."

"You can't." Levy put the phone on speaker, laid down, and stared at the ceiling. It was a pitiful view. Its once-white surface had faded to a sickly pallor. Cracks like varicose veins ran across its expanse, pulsating under the flickering fluorescent lights seeping from outside. He wondered how many men and women stayed here and stared at it from the same vantage point. Trying to figure out where exactly their life took a wrong turn. And where it passed the point of no return. There was little doubt in his mind that he had passed his. He was shocked by Alex's betrayal, but now, as he talked to his best friend, he understood. No one was going to believe his story. If Phil couldn't, no one else would even try. As much as he wanted to, he couldn't blame them either. The police were hunting for him, and the entire city thought he was the Valentine Killer. Most of the things were out of his hands now. But not all of them. At least not yet.

"John?"

"Yes."

"What happened after you found that pen?"

"I realized I was writing more than a fictional story. I started researching it and soon found newspaper articles about real-life murders that matched what I described in the book. And not just matched. I was writing the future, Phil. Channeling it. Down to the most intricate detail. People's names. Distinct features. Things I shouldn't have known. Couldn't have known. But that's only half of the issue. I have a much bigger problem."

"Yes." Phil raised his voice again. "You do have a bigger problem. The entire city is looking for you, thinking you are the Valentine Killer. You need to let me help you."

"No. The problem is, I can't stop, Phil. I've tried. I wanted to write a happy ending to this story. And I couldn't. Then I tried *not* to write anything at all, and I couldn't do it either. Do you understand? I'm like an addict hooked on the most powerful drug in the world. I don't want to write this book, but I *have to* finish it, or else it will kill me."

"And what happens when you finish it?"

"I don't know how it ends yet." He shook his head, the flickering lights swaying in his peripheral vision. "But it's going to be awful no matter what I do. I know everybody is focused on the victims now, but this is worse than just a few people dying. Much worse. If he can get his way, we will be in a world of hurt."

"What are you talking about?" Phil was pleading again. "I'm begging you, pal. Tell me where you are. I'll come alone. I won't tell anyone. Not even Kathy. Let me see you, please."

A tear ran down Levy's cheek, tickling his skin, and he wiped it away with the back of his hand. "Thank you, my friend. That means a lot, but I have to stay. It might not be possible anymore, but this is my last chance to try to write a different ending. I will give it my best shot. Phil?"

"Yes, John."

"Can you promise me something?"

"Anything."

"Even if I don't make it, please believe me. I didn't kill anybody." He hung up the phone before his friend could respond and closed his eyes.

A part of him wanted to get in touch with Alex. To explain that she was wrong. That there was still time for her to help him catch Luca. Stop him before he completed his monstrous quest. But it was a fantasy. She sold him out to the police. It stung. Logically, he understood why she did it. But it stung nonetheless.

And more than anything else, he wanted to call Lilly. To hear her voice. To feel her touch. There was some indescribable magic in her presence. She was like a strong wine—made him lightheaded and not quite himself.

And then there was the physical connection. He felt almost ashamed about how much she turned him on. Levy had never been shy, but sex to him was a function of love, not a vessel. A reason to be closer to the person he cared for, like throwing more logs into an already burning fire. It needed to be done from time to time, but not something to obsess over, even with Grace. Their intimate connection was strong, but it was mundane. A part of the routine. Something they did when the mood struck, and then they would move on with their lives, not thinking about it until the next time.

With Lilly, it was different. She was wild and unpredictable, and he couldn't get enough of her. He remembered reading about a rat that had an electrode connected to its pleasure center, which would give it a moment of bliss if the animal pressed on the special lever. Once it discovered the lever, it continued to step on it. Without breaks, forgoing food, water, and everything else until it died from exhaustion. He thought it wasn't a nice analogy, but Levy could understand the rat now. It was addictive. He didn't want to have Lilly from time to time. He wanted to have her *all the time.*

"It doesn't matter," he said out loud and sat up, his spine cracking in protest. He was fairly certain that his romantic prospects ran dry the moment TV stations plastered his face next to a *Valentine Killer prime suspect* headline. Despite the predicament, he smiled at the absurdity of his situation as he envisioned meeting a future blind date. *Hello. It's nice to meet you. My name is John Levy, and you might know me as the guy everybody thought was the Valentine Killer. Oh, you forgot you had an appointment? I understand. Maybe a rain check? No? Wow, you're literally running. You must be really late.*

He stood up and walked across the room to the window, his steps silenced by a shaggy rag under his feet. The view was just as cheerful as his room—a rain-battered parking lot with a handful of cars that had seen better days. A large neon Motel sign, its letter "T" dark, loomed at the farthest side of the large space, pulsating through the rain.

As Levy gazed out the window, he saw two gray sedans pull into the parking lot. One took a spot near the entrance, and the other proceeded through the open space and pulled up not too far from the building itself.

At first, the significance of their arrival eluded him. Still, as he continued to watch, a growing sense of unease settled in the pit of his stomach. He ran back into the room, flipped the lights off, and then returned to the window again, pressing his face to the dirty glass.

Between the lack of light, the heavy rain, and the tinted windows of the cars, he couldn't make out the passengers. But he didn't have to. A moment later, the doors of both vehicles swung open. Four men, all dressed in black, stepped out of the car next to the building. Four people emerged from the vehicle on the other side of the lot as well— three men...and a woman. The men moved about with a sense of urgency, but the woman paused there for a second, staring in his direction. He couldn't see her face, but at that moment, he knew.

"God damn you, Alex." His mind raced, looking for an escape

route, a brilliant idea that could untangle him from the center of the deadly web. But as Levy watched seven men and the woman jog across the parking lot, their arms at the ready, the weight of the inevitable bore down on him, suffocating his hopes. The dance of fate had reached its final stage, and there was nowhere for him to hide.

TWENTY-SIX

John Levy was there. I knew it even though, from where I stood, there was no way to see the man. It was dark, and the window across the parking lot looked like a giant wet mirror, pulsating in unison with the glitchy Motel sign behind my back. But I could sense him there. Lurking behind that glass and staring me in the eye. We were like two duelists who had walked their pre-measured distances away from the midpoint and now were readying their pistols, waiting for the signal to unleash violence.

A terrible feeling settled in my gut. I led the police here, with DD stuffing me in the back of his car as if I were a common perp, without as much as a glance or a word. When he picked me up from Levy's apartment, he stormed through the place, looked around, and just jabbed his finger at the door. I followed it without argument. It wasn't the time to plead my case. That would be later, when it was over. We stayed in the car for almost two hours as DD and his team mapped out Levy's virtual trail. The amount of resources DD had commandeered was staggering, but considering everyone involved was convinced we were after the Valentine Killer himself, not entirely unexpected.

Before long, between the captured video feeds of the city's CCTV cameras and eyewitness accounts, they tracked him down to a cheap motel in East New York. The word motel doesn't exactly conjure up images of opulence and luxury, but the dilapidated place sitting on the corner of Rutledge Lane and Wrenshaw Alley was in a class of its own.

It was a brick building painted in vomit-inducing yellow and, according to one of the cops who shared the back seat with me, was frequented by drug dealers, local working girls, and other citizens of similar caliber. It also took cash payments and never insisted if the client was reluctant to provide their identification. I had no idea how Levy had found this place. Still, for a man just accused of being one of the most dangerous people alive, he was coping remarkably well.

I lost my cool when Sean Gallagher got into our car and watched the man with suspicion. I shouldn't have since I just convinced myself and tried to convince DD that somebody else was responsible for the murders. By definition, Gallagher couldn't be dangerous, but I freaked nonetheless.

But DD's new partner only briefly glanced in my direction, exchanged looks with Dom, and settled in his seat without question. Begrudgingly, I had to admit it was a cool move on Gallagher's part. If he wasn't happy about DD's decision to bring me along, he kept it to himself. That's how partners are supposed to act. Yell at each other in private as much as you want, but it's always a unified front in front of others. DD and I used to be like that, but that was at a different time in a different life.

I didn't want to be here, but I had to. At least, I thought I did. But now, as I stood under the unrelenting rain, cold wind battering me from all sides, doubts started rising to the surface like bile. I hated this case. I'd rather be running away from knife-wielding Franky along with Rico and Lopez than trying to figure out if I was ridding the city of a serial killer or condemning a poor patsy who had trusted me with his hard-to-believe but truthful story to certain doom.

I saw DD ready to move and touched his arm, almost instantly regretting the gesture. He shook my hand off as if touched by something disgusting and turned around to give me one of his intense stares that spelled nothing but trouble.

"I need to talk to him."

"Absolutely not."

"It doesn't have to be long. Just five minutes. Tops."

"No."

He started to move, but I put my hand on his shoulder again, firmer this time. "You wouldn't be here if it wasn't for me."

He turned around again, his eyes burning. "You should have told me what you knew way before tonight."

"I didn't have all the information, Dom. I still don't. You know it's not how it works. We are not even here because I'm convinced he's the guy. We are here because, at the moment, the optics aren't great for John Levy, and I wanted to play it safe."

He stayed silent for a moment and then jabbed his finger at me. "Sixty seconds. That's all you get, you understand?"

I gave him my most obedient smile. "Yes, boss."

When everyone was out of their cars, DD made a sign, and the two groups of cops moved toward the motel in sync, covering the front and the back entrances at once. The motel was a small rectangular building, its front facing the parking lot. One door leading in. One entry in the back. Not a lot of options to choose from. Unless John Levy was about to grow a pair of wings, he had nowhere to go.

We crossed the empty space and filed through the front door, past a disheveled night manager sitting behind the counter, his red eyes flicking about the lobby with great suspicion. Dispatch must have called the hotel before we arrived at the scene, but it didn't seem to have calmed his nerves—the man was as white as a ghost.

"Which way?" DD whispered.

The manager pointed to the right, his fingers visibly shaking. "One twenty-seven."

The group moved down the hallway. They were quiet and efficient, like a pack of wolves on a hunt. My adrenaline spiked for a moment as my body responded to the familiar setting. My hands felt naked without a gun, but DD took mine away back at the apartment, and for now, I wasn't sure I'd get it back when it was all over.

We took positions outside the worn-out door a few seconds later and froze, waiting for a command.

"Breach."

One of the cops swung a battering ram, and the door gave with a thunderous crash. I hung back as the men rushed in, but even from my vantage point, I could see Levy kneeling in the middle of the shabby room, his fingers interlocked behind his head. I wasn't imagining things in the parking lot. He had been waiting for us.

When I walked into the room, they pinned him to the ground and cuffed him. Two large cops brought him to his feet, sat him down on the side of the bed, and then stepped aside.

"Dom?" I came up to DD after he stopped barking orders. "You promised."

He gave me a stare and motioned to his team to leave the room. Then he turned to face me and jabbed that big finger of his in my face again. To be frank, I was starting to get weary of the gesture.

"Sixty seconds," he said.

"Thank you." I turned away from him to face Levy, but DD grabbed my arm with an iron grip. "What?"

"Don't make me regret this." He stormed out of the room, his heavy steps echoing down the dimly lit corridor, the broken door creaking as it swung back and forth on its hinges.

"Alex," Levy said before I could utter a syllable. "Take my laptop. It's in the minibar. I didn't have a chance to hide it properly. Stuff it in the back of your pants under your jacket. Quickly."

Too stunned to argue, I walked to the minibar and opened the door, revealing the laptop behind the row of miniature bottles. I picked it up and tucked it under the belt of my pants, scraping my back in the process and covering it with my leather bomber.

"Listen," I started.

"No. You listen." He leaned forward, his eyes shining with manic conviction under the flicker of the fluorescent lights. "It doesn't matter if you believe me or not. I thought I'd still be able to set things right, but now it's out of my hands. You have to finish the book. Use what's there already if you need to. I've removed the password."

"I saw, but I'm—"

"It doesn't have to be pretty," he interrupted me again. "It doesn't have to match my style or make any sense. But you have to finish the novel in a way that Luca gets caught. He must not complete his quest."

"You surely don't think he'll turn into Lucifer?"

"I don't know. But do you want to chance it and find out? Look." For a moment, the fight went out of his eyes. "I don't care what happens to me. In retrospect, expecting you to buy into this story was stupid. I should have found a better way to tell you."

"John." I reached out and touched his shoulder. "I had to bring you in. Do you understand?"

"I know, and I won't hold a grudge." He chuckled and looked down at his feet. "In my defense, this is the first time I got connected to a man trying to resurrect Lucifer."

"I'm sorry."

Heavy steps were coming back to the door, and Levy fixed me with his stare again. "Keep the laptop in your office. Don't bring it home. You'll be safer this way. And finish it. Please."

I nodded and stepped back just in time to see DD storm through the ruined door again. There was a whirlwind of activity, and then Levy was led away, leaving me alone in the room with my former partner. Awkward.

"Can I have my pistol back, please?"

He stared at me for a few seconds without answering and then yelled into the corridor. "Jenkins!"

A young man's head popped into the room, and DD told him to bring my gun. Jenkins gave us a curt nod and disappeared briefly before returning and handing me my trusty HK.

"Thanks." I stuffed the gun into the holster, trying to keep my face straight—the darned computer had a sharp edge that kept cutting into my skin.

"You're lucky we found him. Otherwise, you'd be spending the night in a holding cell." DD gave Jenkins another nod, and the man disappeared again.

I shrugged. Sometimes, the best argument with DD was silence. Don't poke the bear. Let him get it out of his system.

"What were you thinking, Alex? This is low, even by your standards."

"What the hell is that supposed to mean? What would you do if someone showed up on your doorstep and told you that story?" I shot back. "And don't tell me you'd arrest him on the spot. The guy's loaded. He can hire a team of lawyers and give them more money to play with than your precinct's budget. I doubt you'd even be able to bring him in, but even if you did, he'd waltz right out of there, and you'd get slapped by the captain for doing such frivolous stuff."

"Maybe." DD walked through the room and stood by the window, watching his men load Levy into one of the cars. "I'm going to talk to him, but I wanted to give you an opportunity to come clean first."

I said nothing, wondering why the back of DD's head wasn't smoking under my stare.

"You said he was writing a book. We didn't find anything that looked like a manuscript at his apartment, and here..." He turned back to me and made a sweeping gesture. "Here, it doesn't look like he had a chance to settle down yet."

"You'd have to ask him," I said.

"Okay." He sighed and headed for the door. "Suit yourself."

"Is someone going to drive me home?"

"Nope."

"Asshole," I said under my breath when I was sure DD was out of earshot.

I watched the two police cruisers pull out of the parking lot, put on strobe lights, and get on the road. As they disappeared into the rain, I opened the minibar, pulled out two tiny bottles of vodka, and called a taxi.

The laptop was killing me, its sharp edges scraping my back raw, but I didn't dare pull it out of my pants as I sipped on stolen alcohol in a dingy room.

The vodka was on par with the place—cheap, harsh, and left a nasty taste in my mouth. I wondered if the bottles were bootlegged and filled with paint thinner. It scraped my throat like sandpaper as it went down, but I relished the pain as it calmed the storm that was raging inside me.

My phone rang, and I almost jumped, startled by the loud sound.

"How's my favorite private investigator doing?" Morton's voice purred in my ear. "Any progress retrieving the necklace? My client would love an update."

"Yes." I put a big smile on my face. "The plan is already in motion. Everything's coming together swimmingly."

TWENTY-SEVEN

John Levy didn't know how long he had spent in the interrogation room. It was a bare cube painted in dark green with splotches where the original gray still showed through. There was a one-way mirror on a side wall and two wide-angle video cameras on the opposite sides of the ceiling. It smelled of moldy paper, burnt coffee, and cigarettes. The cop who brought him in cuffed his hands to the metal table in the middle of the room, his feet to the anchor on the floor, and then left without saying a word.

As he sat there, his hands shaking with adrenaline, he expected the door to swing open at any moment and detectives to storm in, peppering him with questions. But nobody came, and as seconds turned into minutes and minutes turned into hours, his anxiety gave way to fear. He tried to tell himself that he knew exactly what they were doing, making him sweat and putting him on edge, but that knowledge did little to calm his frayed nerves.

When the door lock finally clicked behind him, and two detectives walked into his view, Levy could barely contain himself.

"Mr. Levy. My name is Dominic Deluca. I'm the lead detective on your case," the first man said, sitting across from him and setting a folder on the table. He was stocky and square with large, rough hands that would fit on a farmer or a laborer if not for his clean, well-manicured nails. He pointed in the direction of the second cop. "And this is my partner, Detective Sean Gallagher."

Levy nodded and waited as Deluca read him his rights and had him acknowledge that their conversation was being recorded.

"You've got the wrong guy," he said after they went over a series of questions establishing his identity. Somehow, the slow back-and-forth calmed his nerves. It was going to be an ordeal; there was no way around it, and to survive it, he had to stay strong. "I had nothing to do with the murders."

"Mr. Levy," Deluca opened the folder and pulled out what looked like a CCTV print, "is that you?"

Levy leaned over the table, the chain rattling as he shifted his hands to take the photograph. It was him, no doubt. Standing in front of the counter at the rare bookshop, facing the camera. "Yes, it's obviously me."

"Could you please tell me what you were doing at that place?"

"You might be shocked to hear this," Levy said, anger rising in his chest. "But I was looking for a book."

"What kind of book?"

"A rare one."

"Okay," Deluca said patiently and pulled out another photograph. "How about this one? Can you identify this person?"

The picture wasn't of great quality, but as Levy stared at the grainy print of a man running under the long sheets of rain, he found it hard to breathe. A series of images flashed in his mind. The inky void of the graffiti on the brick wall. And the dumpster, streams of rainwater running off its half-closed lid.

He squinted. Hard. Trying to will the images away.

"Mr. Levy," Deluca repeated. "Could you identify this person?"

"Yes. It's me."

"This picture was taken at the end of the block where the bookstore is located but on a different day. Or rather, on a different night. But you know that already, don't you?"

Levy kept his eyes closed, his mind racing. He had to think of something. Of anything. Just not to see the arched foot sticking out of the jaws of the steel monster.

"Tell me, Mr. Levy."

It was a different voice, soft, almost purring like a cat, and Levy opened his eyes with a start as he stared at Gallagher. He'd never heard him speak before, and he sounded nothing like Levy imagined he would.

The man leaned over and tapped his finger on the photograph. "It's pretty clear to me what happened there, but I still can't understand one thing."

"What's that?"

"Was it planned?" Gallagher flicked his finger at the picture, moving it closer to Levy. It spun like a top and then slowly came to rest, almost at a perfect angle. "Or was it spur of the moment? Perhaps you saw the right person, and you just *had to* do it?"

"It wasn't me!" Levy screamed. "I didn't kill those people. Yes, I was at the shop. And it is also me in the back alley. But I didn't put the bodies in that dumpster, I swear. I saw a fucking foot sticking out of the trash bags and panicked, like anyone else would."

"I never said the bodies were in the dumpster."

"Oh, don't give me that *I caught you* tone, Detective. I know my situation sucks, and I have no idea how I got there. One moment I was drinking martinis in a Brooklyn bar. Then I was in the city, accosted by a homeless guy because I was too close to the cardboard box he called home. I didn't want a confrontation and moved away, and that's when I saw the foot. That's when he saw it, too. He kept yelling after me that he had nothing to do with it. I'm sure he can confirm my story. And so can the bartender."

"There was no homeless person at the back alley," Deluca said. "And sure, we will check with the bartender at the Brooklyn joint. But you know who we already spoke with?"

Levy eyed the detective with suspicion. It was a trick question, no doubt, but he couldn't see where it was possibly going. "Alex Watts?"

"No." Deluca gave him a humorless smile, picked up the still from the bookshop, and held it before Levy's face. "We spoke to a very nice lady who owns Secret Scrolls. And she told me that there was this man who came by her shop. What he was looking for was something rather unusual. Apparently, he required a manual of sorts that could be used to communicate with demons. And the tome he was specifically describing had a horned angel on the cover and get this—grooves in bonded leather for sacrificial blood."

Levy said nothing as he stared at the photograph.

"Do you understand my predicament, Mr. Levy? I have a monster running around the city killing people in a," Deluca gave an exaggerated shrug, as if looking for the right word, "what some might say a ritualistic way. And then, I have you looking for instructions on how to ritualistically kill people. To make things worse, you just happened to be at the location where we find not one, but three bodies. Do you understand how this might look suspicious to some people?"

"I'm telling you; this is just a coincidence. One has nothing to do with another."

"I'll tell you a secret, Mr. Levy." Deluca leaned over, his face almost touching Levy's. "I've yet to meet a detective who believes in coincidences. And I am willing to wager my meager city salary that the jury will not believe in that either. It's over."

"Well, if it's over," Levy said, "then I'm going away for the rest of my life. Why are you wasting your breath, then?"

"Today's your lucky day, Mr. Levy. You'll learn so much today that you won't know what to do with all that knowledge. I'll tell you another secret." Deluca threw a glance at his partner. "He probably thinks he has nothing to lose. What do you think, Sean?"

"Oh, he most certainly does," the man said. "Tell him."

"New York is a forgiving state," Deluca said, leaning back in his chair, his posture relaxed. "It doesn't have capital punishment. The last time somebody was executed here was in 1963. Eddie Lee Mays was executed by electrocution for first-degree murder."

"He thinks he's safe," Gallagher chimed in.

"He does. Have you ever watched police shows, Mr. Levy? It's a recurring theme: a nosy federal agent wants to steal a high-profile case from a hard-working, charming detective with the local PD. You know what's funny? There's some truth to that. I, too, have some nosy federal agents who would love nothing more than to take away the first bona fide serial killer case in New York City in decades. Can you imagine what a case of that magnitude could do to a career? You'd get book rights, interviews, and documentaries. If you get really lucky, maybe even a movie. Who wouldn't want that? You'd think we'd fight those pesky feds tooth and nail. Right, Sean?"

"We would, wouldn't we?"

"Unless," Deluca tapped his massive index finger on the tip of his chin and then pointed it at Levy, "we don't mind giving away the fame and the riches. Because once those guys with fancy badges take over, that becomes a federal case. And a federal case will go to trial in a federal court. Do you know what's still on the menu in a federal court, Mr. Levy? He doesn't know, Sean, does he?"

"No, he does not."

Levy's eyes darted back and forth between the two detectives. He didn't know what to expect from the interrogation room, but he certainly hadn't expected this. His throat tightened. No one was even remotely interested in listening to his story. There was no good cop, bad cop routine here. By the looks of it, both detectives had already made up their minds before they even came through the door. Nobody was going to listen to his denials now. They wanted a confession in exchange for keeping the possibility of a death sentence off the table. A *death sentence.*

It was like being trapped in a nightmare where the walls kept closing in on him no matter how hard he tried or which path he took. For a moment, he thought about the fateful evening when Phil came to his place unannounced. He wondered what would have happened if his friend hadn't decided to check in on him that night. Would he have gone through with it? And would all those people who had died a horrible death still be alive?

"I know exactly where you're going with this." He put his head down, studying his cuffed hands. "I thought if I acted in good faith with you, Detective, you'd give me the benefit of the doubt. Listen to my side of the story, at least. But it seems that my expectations might have been misplaced. I want a phone call now and a lawyer."

"I must warn you, Mr. Levy—"

"Save it," he said wearily. He wanted to lift his hand up to stop the detective from speaking, only to have the gesture cut short by the cuffs' chain, yanking his hand back down. "I have no interest in talking to you anymore. Have somebody bring me a phone, and until I speak to my lawyer, this conversation is over."

"Suit yourself." Deluca put the photographs back into the folder and stood up. "When you come crawling to me with or without your lawyer, begging to keep this case in New York, it'll be too late, and I'll happily attend the show when the time comes."

The detective pushed the chair back, its legs scraping on the cement floor like nails on a chalkboard. He walked out of the room without as much as a glance, with Gallagher on his heels.

A few moments later, a police officer came to collect him and walked him to a phone booth. He was told he could make up to three phone calls and that all would be recorded.

Levy hesitated as he stood in a small, cramped space, staring at an old-fashioned rotary phone with faded numbers. He listened to the muffled sounds of the bustling precinct seeping into the booth—a mix of conversations, doors opening and closing, the phones ringing. He should be calling Phil, he thought, who'd, in an instant, assemble the best team of criminal defense attorneys money could buy. Still, as he stared at the scratched and worn-out phone surface, he couldn't bring himself to do it. Something that Alex had told him. What if she had been right? What if he *was* the killer? A real-life Jekyll and Hyde?

He closed his eyes, took a deep breath, and stepped away from the phone. For the first time in his life, John Levy decided to gamble. He needed a sign if the stakes were truly as high as he thought. An undeniable proof that he was on the right path.

He opened his eyes and walked outside the booth to face the officer who'd brought him there.

"Nobody to call?"

"It's complicated," he said, giving the man a tight smile. "If I don't have my own attorney, do I get one assigned?"

"You want a free public defender? You won't qualify for one." The cop tried his best not to show surprise but failed miserably. "Aren't you very... Never mind. If you have the means, the state won't approve it."

"It doesn't have to be free," Levy said as the officer led him back to the interrogation room. "I'll pay for it, but yes, I want a public defender."

He didn't know how long it took before the door opened again, and he started to doze off. It was a long day; adrenaline had worn off, and Levy was beginning to crash. He heard the sound of approaching heels and turned toward the entrance without much interest. He expected to see a young woman. A cheap pantsuit. A pair of sensible flats. Perhaps a recent grad of a city college law school. An idealist with shining bright eyes and a fiery ambition to make a name for themselves against all odds.

The woman who entered the room did wear a pantsuit, but it was tailored to perfection to fit her sculpted physique. Her hair, each strand meticulously styled, cascaded in sleek waves that framed her symmetrical features with an air of understated sophistication and grace.

She crossed the room, the pair of sharp black Manolo Blahnik leather pumps click-clacking on the rough cement floor, and took a chair that was previously occupied by Dominic Deluca.

"Oh, John," Lilly said, giving him a wide smile. "Why don't you ever listen to me?"

TWENTY-EIGHT

"What weather, huh?" The Uber driver tried to make small talk as he picked me up from East New York.

I made a grunting noise and uncomfortably shifted in the back seat—the laptop was pinching my skin, but I was taking no chances even now. In a high-profile case like this, anything was possible. DD was clearly not in the mood to trust me. I wouldn't put it past him to track the taxi and then interview the driver about my behavior. Just because he could. He was anal like that. It's an excellent quality when chasing bad guys together. Not so much being on the receiving end of it.

"You come to this part of town often?"

"No." The guy was clearly not getting the message. "Was here for work."

"Oh wow. What do you do?"

"Try to make people happy," I snapped. "Usually fail at it."

That shut him up. No doubt he would tell people he drove a cheap call girl from East New York back to Brooklyn, and for the whole trip, she was full of self-hatred and remorse.

I didn't care. At least I didn't have to make an effort. And while the guy was wrong about my profession, he wasn't entirely off about the self-hatred and remorse.

Despite Levy's pleas about taking his laptop to my office, I returned to the house first. It was late, and I needed to shower, feed the cat, and get at least a couple of hours of sleep. Some food wouldn't hurt, either.

I got lucky. A plate of two-day-old leftovers was at the bottom of my fridge. It didn't hit the spot, but it at least quieted my rumbling stomach. The first glass of gin and tonic calmed my nerves but didn't quite get me where I wanted to be. The second didn't do the trick either, but I was a lightweight when it comes to drinking, and I wanted to get some sleep, not spend the next few hours hugging my toilet.

Had I gone straight to bed then, I would have fallen asleep right there, but I could still smell the filthy odor of the motel on my skin and decided to get a proper wash first. That was a mistake. The sleep was completely gone when I stepped out of the hot shower.

I wrapped myself in a towel and sat on the bed, stuffing a pillow behind my back for comfort. If sleeping wasn't an option, I could try to be productive.

I wasn't ready to read the manuscript. Not yet. First, I needed to learn everything there was to learn about the next victim in case Levy wasn't the killer. Unlike the others, where there were only hints of the person's identity in the manuscript, Victoria Winslow was a public figure with a large social media footprint. For the first time since John Levy had walked into my life, there was a chance to stop the Valentine Killer before he could claim the next victim. I wanted to take full advantage of that.

As usual, I started with the public information; in Victoria Winslow's case, that was plenty. She wasn't exactly an obscure person. She was only twenty-three years old, but she took the internet by storm in the past two-and-a-half years. Originally from Pennsylvania, she had moved to New York, hoping to make it in the fashion industry.

After securing a job in a boutique store, Winslow started a fashion blog that went unnoticed for a few months, gathering only a handful of followers. But then, by a stroke of luck, a fashion reporter came to the store during Winslow's shift. She chatted her up, telling the woman about the blog. They clicked, and a few weeks later, the reporter looked up her web page, liked the material, and mentioned Victoria in the paper. The rest, as they say, was history.

There was a hurricane of sponsor deals and a few shows in London, Paris, and Dubai. Before long, the blog's following swelled into hundreds of thousands and then into millions.

I pulled up a picture of Victoria meeting one of the royals in London. She was a stunning woman. And she was tall. The internet is an infamously unreliable source of people's height, but I could tell she was at least six feet tall. Perhaps even six foot one, but it didn't make her look awkward; quite the opposite. She had a graceful gait and a catlike quality to her walk. Her face was striking, too. It was thin, with high cheekbones, blonde hair, and pale skin, and yet, she had some of the darkest eyes I'd ever seen. She was like a magic creature you could only find in a forbidden forest.

I'd checked her fashion blog. It was a predictable mix of fashion news and updates, tips, and product reviews, which I assumed were the main drivers of Victoria's revenue. To my surprise, the blog was well-written and engaging, and Victoria came off as genuine and pleasant in her videos. She might have gotten lucky in the beginning, but her success was not without merit.

After scouring the publicly available information, I turned to my tools of the trade and dug deeper. It seemed that fame didn't go into Victoria's head. Without breaking some rules, it would be hard to get an accurate figure for her income, but judging from the brand names she partnered with, it had to be at least in the high six figures. And yet, the woman didn't seem to own any real estate and still occupied a relatively modest two-bedroom apartment in Battery Park in Manhattan.

There was no publicly identifiable boyfriend either. She had been occasionally photographed with a famous sitcom actor in the city, but it didn't look official. There were no sex tapes, drug use, or tax evasion that I could find. In fact, Winslow seemed to be completely scandal-free. I liked that girl. I wanted to ensure she wouldn't become another item on the Valentine Killer's list. Normally, I'd spend a few days watching Winslow from afar before trying to approach her. But these were not normal times. Perhaps I could go to her place first thing in the morning. Warn her.

My phone jumped next to my knee, vibrating.

"Oh boy," I said, looking at DD's number lighting up the screen. "That can't be good."

"Alex?"

"We better not make it into a habit," I said as I answered the call.

"What?"

"This. You calling me."

"It's not funny," he said. "I really need to talk to you."

"You called me," I said, unwilling to stop serving DD his own medicine. "Talk."

"You can save your sarcasm for later." There was not even a trace of surprise in his voice.

It irked me. After all the wonderful things he saw fit to accuse me of just in the course of the last thirty-six hours, he could at least have the decency of being surprised that I was still taking his calls.

"Ever heard of a woman named Victoria Winslow?"

I winced as if he had punched me in the stomach. "Come again? You're breaking up."

He wasn't breaking up. I could hear his gruff, annoying voice coming through my phone's speaker as clearly as if DD was sitting on the bed beside me. Something caught in my chest, choking me, and I jabbed at the mute button with my finger, trying to buy some time.

"Alex?"

I took a few long, deliberate breaths, trying to get my emotions under control, and then unmuted the call again.

"Alex? Can you hear me?"

"Yes," I said, surprised at how level my voice sounded. "I can hear you now."

"Victoria Winslow," he said again. "Have you heard of her?"

"Yes. A fashionista socialite? What about her?"

"She's dead." His voice was flat. Nobody else would pick up on the tension hidden behind the measured tone. Not even his new partner. But I *knew* this voice. It was like looking at a winding trebuchet. The slow turn of the wheel. The taut cables singing with tension. The weights suspended in a giant sling. And then a moment of stillness, a brief pause before the violent fury of a lightning-fast release.

I only heard that voice twice before. The first time was when DD's mother passed away. He grew up without a dad. His father was a beat cop, killed by a stray bullet in a bad neighborhood when Dominic, the middle boy of three, was only five years old.

His mother, Mary, was a school principal and one of the toughest women I'd ever met. It was hardly a surprise she continued to look after the three boys without missing a beat. DD and Marcus, his oldest brother, followed their father's footsteps and joined the NYPD. Peter, the youngest, joined the army and served somewhere in Europe.

When Mary got cancer, she took it just like she did everything else—head-on. She worked for as long as she could and stepped down when she thought her condition would not let her fulfill what she saw as her responsibility to the community.

When the day everybody knew was coming finally arrived, I thought DD would be mentally prepared. But I was wrong. It shook him to the core. On the surface, he was as stable as ever. Collected, organized. But underneath it all, there was a storm brewing. In the next six months, he went after the most dangerous and violent cases he could find. Went undercover. Busted open a drug ring operation nobody wanted to touch. At some point, it got so rough I didn't know if he would become famous or turn up dead. Perhaps both.

To my great relief, he did neither. Just showed up one day at the precinct, and though he looked as rugged as he did during the previous six months, I knew the storm had passed. DD was back.

The second time I heard that tone was... Well. That was when we stopped being partners, and that's entirely a different story.

"Did you hear what I said? She's dead."

"I heard you. The Valentine Killer?" I asked.

"It's a match," he said without elaborating, but he didn't have to.

My mind filled in the blanks and all their gruesome details. The graceful magic creature was no longer roaming the forbidden forest. Feeling guilt for something you couldn't control wasn't the best use of one's time, yet that was precisely how I felt. "When?"

"She was found about an hour ago."

"So, Levy has an alibi, then?"

"No, he does not," he said. "She's been dead for a very long time. A few weeks at least."

"A few weeks?" My mind raced. That didn't make any sense. I was just looking at the woman's blog. She updated it twice a week; the last entry was two days ago.

"There's something else. She wasn't found in the city."

"Oh." That was even more significant. I wasn't quite sure what to even make of that information. If I were to allow the possibility that Levy wasn't the killer, there must have been a reason for a new location. Perhaps the killer was starting to feel the heat of New York's finest. The entire city was on edge, especially after Benjamin French. He could be branching out and trying his luck in other places. Or it could be something else. "Does it really match him?"

"I don't know for sure yet," he said. "Haven't had a chance to see the body or have it examined. But I don't think it's a copycat. I think it's him."

"You sound awfully convinced."

"Just a hunch." He cleared his throat. "But this is not why I called. Levy's got a lawyer and clammed up. And I really need for him to be talking."

"That's hardly surprising," I said. "I told you he was going to get a real team and—"

"He asked for a public defender."

"A what?"

"He doesn't qualify for free representation, so he's still footing the bill, but yes, that's what he picked. Do you think you have any leverage over him? Get him to talk?"

"No," I said. "I don't think so. If anything, he seemed pretty pissed at me last time I saw him."

"Well, it was worth a shot. One more thing. Did he ever mention anything about going to Chester County in Pennsylvania? Something around..." There was a rustling of papers, and he gave me a few dates. "I don't have the exact dates for now. Once my coroner has the chance to do the autopsy and examine Winslow's body, I could give you something more precise."

"Chester County?"

"Yes. Somebody found her in a commercial freezer. It was a large cold storage center, and she wouldn't have been found for a long time if not for the sale of the property. The private equity fund that owned it sold it to an anonymous buyer. When the new owners came to check in on their investments, they found a few things they weren't expecting."

"I see."

"I gotta go. Please call me if you think of anything we could use as leverage to get Levy talking."

He hung up, and I just sat there, clutching the phone in my suddenly sweaty palm. A sickly chill went down my spine. Levy never told me anything about going to Chester County. But it didn't matter. I knew someone else who went on a two-week trip to the farmlands. To spy on a supposedly cheating husband of a wealthy lady with an annoyingly squeaky voice. Me.

And if DD's intuition was telling him she wasn't killed by a copycat but the Valentine Killer himself, my intuition was telling me something else: that once the forensic pathologist in the Manhattan morgue had a chance to look at poor Victoria's body, he was going to tell DD the exact date of her murder. And that date would match my loathsome trip to Pennsylvania up to the minute. Of course, it could have been just a coincidence. A meaningless fluke. The problem was DD didn't believe in coincidences. And neither did I.

TWENTY-NINE

"I don't understand." John Levy watched Lilly sit in front of him, resting her slim, delicate hands on the hard surface of the steel table. A signet ring gleamed on her right pinky, its intricate engravings capturing the flicker of the harsh overhead lights. A large band of smoothly polished gold looked like an alien artifact next to the rough, scratched metal that kept John Levy captive. "What are you doing here?"

"I guess a better question would be," Lilly said, tilting her head slightly as if studying him, "what are *you* doing here?"

He stared at her, numb, a dull pain slowly spreading behind his eyes. He was like a fish thrown onto the beach by a rogue wave. There was a new world around him, but it was different. Alien, hostile. It moved under a different set of rules. The colors, the smells, the shapes. Everything was wrong. Nothing made sense.

Under the unforgiving fluorescent lights, the objects in the room looked lifeless. Flat. But not Lilly's face. It looked like chiaroscuro portraits by Da Vinci and Caravaggio. A striking interplay of light and shadow. He shook his head, and the strange effect subsided but did not entirely disappear.

"So, what are you, a lawyer? It doesn't make any sense. I thought you were an accountant. Remember what you told me when we first met? Was it a lie?"

"No." She shook her head. "It wasn't a lie. In some ways, I am an accountant. And a lawyer. And a lover. I am many different things, John, but all of them are just small pieces of my most important role for you."

"Which would be what, exactly?"

"Your muse, of course." She reached out and traced her finger on his hand, making him shiver. "I am who you need me to be. Always have been. Always will be."

He yanked his hand back, the cuffs painfully cutting into his wrists. "Guards!"

"What are you doing, John?" She took her hand back but didn't stop smiling. "Are you trying to get rid of me? You can't. We are forever bound to each other now. You wanted me here, and so I came to help. Don't you want to get out of this hellhole? See the sunlight again?"

"Do you have anything to do with this?"

"Do with what, John?"

"The murders," he spat. The numbness in his chest started to melt, giving way to fury. "Was it you? Are you the Valentine Killer? Did you gut those poor people?"

"You're disappointing me, John. Do I look anything like Luca? I thought you had a chance to watch me closely a few times." Lilly gave him a mock frown and opened the top button of her jacket and then another. She leaned forward, giving him a glimpse of her bosom. "Perhaps you require a demonstration to refresh your memory?"

"Stop it." His fist crashed onto the table, the bang reverberating through the empty room. "Guards. Guards!"

Lilly pushed the chair away from the table and stood up, the abrupt movement and the screech of the chair legs on the cement floor startling him. She walked around the table and stopped behind Levy, putting her hands on his shoulders. He tried to shake them off, but she held him tight, her fingers digging into his flesh, the nails almost drawing blood. Her head came close to his, and then her lips traced his neck and ear, tickling his skin.

He froze like a wild animal caught in a hunter's trap, his eyes shut in terror, goose bumps running up his arms and legs. A hurricane of emotions ripped through Levy. He was furious and scared. Excited and yet ashamed of his arousal. She smelled of lilac and jasmine, just as he remembered.

But there was something else. Another smell lingering at the periphery of his senses, almost untraceable. A scent of ash. Faint and evocative, it seeped into the air, coiling around him like the tendrils of a shadow monster. It whispered of charred remains, of smoldering destruction, and the harbingers of unspeakable horrors. Fear seeped into Levy. It was primal and raw. He trembled like a caveman in the dark, a pack of hungry beasts howling at the entrance to his shallow shelter, their teeth snapping inches away from his face.

Her lips brushed his neck again, and she bit into his ear. Hard. He yelped, more from surprise than pain, unable to move, a warm trickle of blood running on his neck and down his shirt.

"Stop it," he whispered. "Please."

"Open your eyes, John."

He did.

He was standing on top of a small hill. A desolate expanse of a once-fierce battlefield stretched before him as far as he could see. Charred and dismembered bodies lay strewn across the scarred earth, their forms twisted and broken. Banners that used to fly proudly over the troops were now trampled into the mire, their once vibrant colors smeared with dirt and blood.

Cracked shields, shattered spears, and broken swords—the tokens of the violence unleashed—littered the vast battlefield. An acrid stench of ash, burnt hair, and flesh hung thickly in the air, mixed with the mournful cries of the dying and the screeches of the vultures that descended upon their gruesome feast.

"What are you doing to me? What is this place?" Levy whispered. A fallen steed lying at the foot of the hill, all of its legs broken and a spear sticking out of his bloated belly, neighed pitifully as if to answer his question. The beast turned his head to face him, its large brown eyes filled with pain meeting John's gaze. A vulture circled in the air and then landed on the horse's neck. A single peck followed, quick and merciless, plucking the eye of the animal. The beast shuddered, unable to move, and the vulture struck again, digging into the empty socket.

"Stop it, please," Levy cried out. "Why am I here?"

"Open your eyes, John."

He snapped his eyes open. The dark-green walls with splotches of old color coming through filled his vision, and he cried in relief, grasping at the cold table, his nails scratching the surface.

"Do you understand now?"

"No." He put his head down, sobbing. "I don't understand at all."

"You're the key, John." Lilly's fingers found his chin and gently lifted his head until he faced her. Her mouth still smiled, but her eyes were hard, unmoving. The pupils were so wide there was almost no visible iris left. And they were black. Like the goat graffiti on the weathered wall above the dumpster. An absence of light. A glimpse into the chaos itself.

"Are you..." He struggled to find the right words.

"I am what, John?"

"What do you want from me?"

"You know what I want, John. You've known it all along."

"I thought," he swallowed, "I thought you wanted to be with me."

"Yes." Her hand grabbed his chin harder. "I did. Still do. But that's secondary. What's important is that you finish the book."

He recoiled back as if she struck him, wrestling his head out of her grip. "Guards! Guards, I need help!"

"Stop being a child." This time, she hit him, her hand landing across his face, making his ears ring. She stepped away from him and then walked back to her chair. "You need to get a grip on yourself, John. None of this would have happened if you weren't acting like a fool. You'd never be arrested, and instead of sitting in this dreadful room, you would be rewarded with gifts beyond your imagination."

"Fuck you." His cheeks were still wet with tears, but he sat straight, facing her. "I don't know who the hell you are, but I will not finish this novel. No one will."

"Is that so?"

"Even if I wanted to write it," he scoffed, "how do you think it's going to work? The two detectives who were here before you made it sound like, at this point, I only have two options. If I confess to the murders I haven't committed, they'd get me life in prison. And if I don't, they'd punt me to the feds, and there's a non-zero chance I'd get executed."

"No, you'd—"

"Where do you picture me writing it? During the trial? In front of the jury? 'Excuse me, Your Honor, I'm too busy finishing the book that will spell doom for humanity to answer your silly questions.'" He threw his head back and laughed. A bitter, mournful sound. "Or right before they strap me to the table and pump me full of drugs? You see, you've made a mistake, Lilly. Or whatever your actual name is. I'm done either way."

"Neither is going to happen, darling." She sat down and buttoned up the jacket. "And just so you know, the choices you just presented to me do not exist. Those two detectives deceived you."

"Sure."

"Yes. They did. Your case had been transferred to the feds before you even stepped into this room. Detective Deluca broke some rules when he interviewed you, but he's just that kind of a guy. Wants to get to the bottom of it, no matter what it costs him. But you don't have to take my word for it. What's going to happen in the next," she glanced at her watch, "forty-seven minutes is that two federal agents will come to pick you up. You are famous now, John, you see. And the federal government doesn't want to take any chances."

"What the hell are you talking about?" He didn't want to believe her. But the way she spoke and her confident posture gnawed away at his conviction. He was like a young buck driven by a pack of hounds into the hunter's nest. Unable to stop as he barreled toward his inevitable demise. Waiting for the bullet to strike his chest and spill his blood.

"They want to put you into a secure location, John. I'm sure you've heard of supermax facilities before. There's one in Northern Virginia where they are planning to take you. Not the most cheerful establishment. But it is not meant to be. It's simply meant to keep you safe, if miserable, until you are ready for your trial. And then for your inevitable execution."

"Screw you," Levy said.

"That's rather ungrateful."

He said nothing, watching her with contempt.

"But I'll let it slide. I don't want you to suffer, John, so I've arranged for your escape. When—"

"I'll do no such thing."

"The truck with your guards will get ambushed by my trusted advisors," she continued, unperturbed, "you will escape. There'll be a car waiting for you with cash, documents, and tools you'll use to change your appearance. Then, you will return to Brooklyn, retrieve the manuscript, and do your absolute best to finish it. Are we clear?"

A genuine smile appeared on his face for the first time since John Levy stepped into the interrogation room. "You know, I've almost lost hope. Ever since I'd realized the story in the manuscript could be real, I almost went insane trying to figure out how to stop it. First, I tried to write a different ending, but that was a failure. Then, I tried not to write it at all, but that wasn't possible either. I was so mad that Alex betrayed me. That I got arrested. But now I see it was truly a blessing in disguise."

"How so?"

"Because I won't do any of that crap." He leaned back in his chair and winked at her. "What I will do, however, is tell the guards about you and your plan when they come in. I recently told someone that writing this book was like the most powerful drug known to man.

Impossible to get off of. Sometimes, the only way to make the drug addict quit is to lock him up."

"You're planning to sacrifice yourself?" she said, slight annoyance in her tone. "That is your brilliant plan? Taking the blame for something you didn't do and dying in shame? Cursed by the families of those poor people instead of writing the book? Is that what you want?"

He shrugged and pursed his lips, not bothering to answer.

"Well, that's just pathetic." She stood up and walked to the door, allowing him a moment of triumph. Then, as her hand touched the handle, she stopped and turned back to him with a sly smile.

"Leave already."

"I'm about to," she said. "I just want to give you the last piece of information to consider before I go. You can choose to stay imprisoned, of course. But here's what happens if you do. Alex Watts, her sister Tina Spencer, along with her husband Chad, and their daughter Olivia. Phil Cohen and his lovely wife, Kathy. And their kids, of course. Emily is so bright, and I hear Sarah is a hoot when she picks up her violin."

"What are you talking about?" For a second, Levy was glad he was seated and cuffed to a table as his knees turned into Jell-O. Large drops of perspiration beaded on his forehead, running down his temples. "Don't you fucking dare."

"I've only named a few, John. There will be others who you hold dear. And they will meet the same fate as that girl with a butterfly tattoo. Remember her?"

"Don't you touch them, you psycho." He jumped, grunting, pulling on the restraints with all his might, oblivious to pain, his vision blurred from fury. "I swear, I will kill you with my own hands."

"Goodbye, John. I trust you'll make the right choice. See you on the other side." She gave him a small smile, opened the door, and stepped out of the room.

The overhead lights blinked, plunging him into darkness for a moment, and when they turned back on again, John Levy was alone.

THIRTY

"Alex." DD sounded as if he was running out of patience. "I'm going to hang up now. I can't help you."

He was on speaker, his voice gruff as usual, and I paced my living room like a caged animal, stomping the trail between the window and a couch. Trying my best not to hurl the phone at the wall. Spots thought it was a game and lunged for my toes every time I walked past him. "I was wrong, dammit. He couldn't have possibly been in PA. I was wrong about the whole thing. And while you and Gallagher are giving each other congratulatory hand jobs, the actual killer is still out there. Laughing at us and looking for the next target."

"Alex."

"You gave me so much grief over not coming to you early enough, and maybe you were right, but you have to listen to me now. He is not your guy."

"Alex." He raised his voice enough to get my attention. "Levy doesn't have an alibi. Just because all of a sudden you've got doubts, nobody's going to release him. It's out of my hands. And PA is irrelevant at the moment. There's plenty of evidence against him here in

New York. If something comes up in Chester County, too, that'd just be icing on the cake. Then they can wrap him up with a bow."

It took me a moment to process the importance of what I had heard. "They? Is that what you said? Did the feds take the case off your hands?"

"Yes. We weren't even supposed to interrogate him."

"Wait, didn't you say—"

"Yes, we did."

I grinned, despite being mad as hell. That was the DD I knew. He did what was right, not what the regulations allowed. That was why Deluca was the best detective in the city. Perhaps that was also why he was still out in the cold instead of running the precinct. "I'm sorry."

"Eh." I could picture him shrugging those big shoulders of his. "Nothing you can do."

"What's going to happen now?"

"I've no idea. All I know is that we aren't supposed to talk to him until he gets picked up."

I chewed on my lip. "What did his lawyer say?"

"I don't know if he's gotten one yet. I'm out of the loop. But if he didn't get one already, my guess is they'll assign someone to him once he gets to Northern Virginia."

"Northern Virginia, really? Supermax?"

"Yep."

"Okay. Well, shit."

"I'm sorry, Alex."

There was something in DD's tone I hadn't heard in a long time. Sympathy. Something ached inside of me, and I angrily brushed it away. It wasn't the time. "Can you at least keep me posted if anything comes up?"

"I'll do what I can."

He hung up, and I stopped pacing and looked at my watch. There was another phone call I needed to make.

After our meeting inside the fitting room in a boutique shop, Olga

Ryghenko texted me from a burner phone with instructions on how to get the necklace. Today was the day to put that plan in motion. Still, despite the possibility of the biggest payday in my PI career, I wasn't even remotely excited to see this case through. If anything, when I dialed the number, I hoped the woman got cold feet and wouldn't answer the call. She did.

"Are we still on?" I said when the line connected.

"Yes. Do you remember your instructions?"

"Of course."

"Okay," she said. "I'll see you soon."

I stopped by my office to drop off Levy's laptop and drove to the city, listening to a weather channel. I was too wound up to listen to music and couldn't stomach the news on the off chance they'd announce yet another victim of the Valentine Killer. I thought I'd stay clear of the news channels for a while now. So, the weather station it was. The rumbling baritone of the meteorologist calmed my nerves even when he said that the shit show of the past few weeks wasn't the main event and the big storm would hit the city in the next few days. There was a lot of speculation whether it would outdo Hurricane Sandy. Still, it seemed that the authorities were taking the threat seriously. I took my eyes off the road for a moment and glanced at the dark, apocalyptic skies spitting out buckets of rain. A shudder ran down my spine—as far as I was concerned, it couldn't get much worse.

It only took me forty-five minutes to get to Midtown, which was a miracle, and I had at least twenty minutes to kill. The encounter would take place at the subway station on Fifty-Seventh and Seventh, and I planned to park in an underground garage. But as I approached the intersection, a van pulled away from a parking meter in front of a deli. I slammed on the brakes, hoping no one would rear-end me, and maneuvered the car into the spot.

"Perfect," I said when the car stopped. The entrance to the subway station was only fifty feet away, and the large glass wall of a local bank across the street acted like a mirror, giving me an almost complete coverage of the intersection.

I turned off the ignition, muted the radio, and sat in the dark, listening to the drum of the water on the roof of my car, waiting for Olga's signal. The rain, harsh and intense as I drove to the city, became milder, its pitter-patter almost hypnotic. I stared out the window, checking out passing cars and telling myself I wasn't about to doze off, but when my phone vibrated with Olga's message, it startled me.

I zipped the jacket all the way up, pulled the hood over my head, and stepped out into the rain, the chill in the air snapping me back to reality. I jogged toward the entrance to the station and walked down the stairs, blending into the crowd waiting for the Queens-bound train.

The timing was going to be crucial. Since giving or selling me the necklace wasn't an option, Olga devised a simple but brilliant plan to provide her with an alibi.

I positioned myself where the third train car would stop and checked the schedule app. A shiny star crawled up the Seventh Avenue line, approaching the station. Another moment later, I could hear the screeching and the rumbling. Then, a few seconds later, the head of the train appeared down the tracks, heading in my direction.

I started to walk. Slowly at first, then faster as the train stopped and opened its doors, letting the evening crowd out. I saw Olga and two of her girlfriends step out of the second car just in front of me, heading for the exit. Olga was on the right, walking next to the train, a small Kelly bag on her right shoulder.

I caught up to the woman and brushed her as I passed, the bag sliding off her shoulder and onto mine. Then I peeled off, and as she and her friends went up the stairs, I continued to the end of the platform until I reached the "No Exit" gate. I glanced back, making sure no one was watching, stepped through the gate, and ducked onto a small platform behind the station, facing the tunnel. Dim overhead lights illuminated the tracks stretching ahead, disappearing into the shadowy distance.

Taking care not to drop the bag onto the tracks, I slid the latch on its side and reached inside, my fingers stumbling over a few items before settling on a metal chain. A jolt of anticipation ran through me as I brought the necklace under the dim lights of the tunnel and placed it on my palm.

Perhaps the necklace wasn't expensive—if Mehta and Olga were to be believed—but it would surely fool me. The chain was beautifully crafted, the intricate links of polished metal broken up by small, yellow-green stones. The pendant, cut in a rectangular shape, was large, the size of a Bic lighter. I'd never seen anything like this before. A sizable gem lay in the glimmering heart of polished metal, its hues dancing between gold and amber like a fleeting sunset over a distant horizon. The light seemed to have been trapped inside of the stone, shining and sparkling as I turned the pendant this way and that. It was beautiful.

I moved the necklace into my jacket's pocket and checked the app. There was another Queens-bound train approaching, and I had to be ready.

A few minutes later, as the train stopped, I headed back around onto the main platform and, a few seconds later, worked myself into the crowd. Olga's plan had worked without a hitch.

She told me that before leaving the apartment, she'd make a show to ensure her husband and friends saw her wearing the necklace. Then, during a shopping spree in Midtown, she'd quietly take it off and hide it in a bag.

Then, after convincing her friends to take a train and ditch Tom and Jerry, she'd feign panic after exiting the subway station. She'd claim that someone must have snatched her purse and the necklace on the train or in the crowd. Her husband would be angry, no doubt, but she'd have two unsuspecting witnesses. After admonishing her for not sticking with the guards, he'd have to let it go.

It was a simple plan and not without holes, but who was I to complain? It worked. That's all that mattered.

I ran up the stairs, taking two steps at a time, and burst onto the street, ready to dash for my car. Except it wasn't there.

"What in the world?" I stood there momentarily with my mouth open, icy rain pelting my face. A large white Mercedes SUV was parked where I'd left my Corolla. I looked around wildly, wondering if I'd confused the location, but it was impossible. The deli was right behind me, and I could see the glass wall of the bank on the other side of the street. It was definitely the spot. "Shit."

I crossed the sidewalk, took refuge under the awning of the deli, and dialed Morton.

"How'd it go?"

"I got the necklace," I said, "but it'll take awhile for me to get back."

"Something wrong?" There was a genuine concern in his voice. "Are you in danger?"

"No." I cringed. Explaining operational failures wasn't exactly the proudest of moments. "My car is gone."

"What do you mean, gone?"

"It's not here." I looked up and down the street as I spoke just to make sure I wasn't crazy. "It was either stolen or towed. Either way, returning to Brooklyn in this weather will take me awhile."

"Hang on one second." He put me on hold before I could answer, classical music filling my ear. A moment later, he was back. "Where are you? I can have a limo pick you up. Five, seven minutes tops."

"Fifty-Seventh and Seven," I said. "Northeast side. Are you sure?"

"Of course I'm sure." I could see his plump lips grinning. "I can't leave my favorite PI out in the cold."

"She's paying you double, isn't she?"

"Oh, you're good." He laughed. "But you'll never know. I never said the client was a woman. And maybe I'm doing this pro bono."

"Yeah, right. A lawyer with a big heart. Don't make me laugh."

"I take offense at that kind of talk, but I forgive you since you're bringing gifts. The driver's name is Marsha, and she's the best," Morton chirped. "I'll see you soon."

I hung up and pressed deeper into the wall, hiding from the rain. I stuffed my hands into my jacket pockets, keeping them warm, my fingers brushing against the necklace. The pendant, smooth and frigid against the skin, seemed to pulsate under my touch. I marveled at the fate of the strange item. A fusion of iron and gemstone. It formed somewhere in deep space, in the heart of an asteroid. It traveled billions of miles, lit the skies of a planet that happened to cross its path, and crashed into the ground with great force. And then was found by curious creatures, only to be made into a jewelry piece. It almost seemed unfair—a dull end to an extraordinary story.

A large black Suburban pulled up to the curb, and its window rolled down, revealing a young woman. "Alex Watts? I'm Marsha. Mr. Morton's driver."

"Thank God." I dashed through the rain and dove into the warm belly of the car. The vehicle revved its engine, accelerating through the slush, and I leaned back, savoring the warmth of the heated leather seats. At least something was going right, and in another hour or so, my bank account would feature the biggest single deposit it had ever seen. I still didn't know how to help John Levy or track the Valentine Killer, but as we flew toward Brooklyn, my heart felt lighter in my chest. Perhaps my luck was finally turning.

THIRTY-ONE

John Levy made up his mind long before the door to the interrogation room opened again. It didn't matter what Lilly's threats were or who was potentially on the list for Luca to kill. As long as the killer was at large, no one was safe. But if Levy talked to the federal agents, he could at least try to foil her plan and protect those he cared for. If anything, he was anxious to see the agents when they finally came.

"Finally," he said as the first of the two men, a large, stocky man with red hair cut to a short buzz, stepped through the door. "I need to talk to you, guys. It's urgent."

The red-haired man nodded and lifted a finger, as if asking Levy to wait and let the second man, carrying a large duffel bag, into the room. He was also tall but leaner, with the haggard face of a long-distance runner. A shock of black hair was slicked back and styled neatly with gel.

"Can I talk now?" Levy said when the door closed again. "This is really important. I have some information about—"

"My name's Agent Murphy," the redhead said, "and this is Agent Velasquez."

"It's nice to meet you—"

Murphy moved surprisingly fast for his size. Before Levy could even process what was happening, the man covered the distance between the door and the table. He lifted Levy by the collar of his shirt and buried a giant fist in his stomach.

The sudden impact struck him with the force of a thunderclap, a powerful blow that reverberated through his entire body. He collapsed on the table, thrashing about as his lungs struggled for air, but none came.

The two men worked in tandem without giving him a moment of respite. They unchained his hands from the table and feet from the floor anchor, laying him on his stomach on the cement floor. Velasquez held him down as Murphy cuffed Levy's hands behind his back and flipped him over as the large man unzipped the duffel bag.

"What the fuck." Levy gasped as he saw a thick, padded mask with two holes for the eyes, a bulge for a nose, and a rubber mouthpiece like on snorkeling equipment. "What am I, Hannibal Lecter? What are you doing?"

He tried to fight back, but Murphy punched him in the stomach again and shoved the mask into his face, forcing the mouthpiece between his teeth and breaking his lower lip. The mask smelled of talcum powder and stale rubber. What was worse was that his nose was blocked, and he could only breathe through the mouthpiece. It had a thin membrane at the opening that made a humiliating gurgling sound every time he inhaled or exhaled.

After securing the mask with a buckle at the back of his head, the two men lifted him off the floor and put him upright.

"Now, Mr. Slurpy," Murphy said, looking him up and down and checking his restraints. "You wanted to tell us something?"

Levy stared at him through the mask, wanting to scream, his mouth uncontrollably drooling from the rubber piece pressing down on his tongue, but made no sound. He'd seen people like these before. Murphy and Velasquez were bona fide bullies. They took pleasure in tormenting defenseless people. They'd have no interest in helping him. And with a mask on his face, he couldn't talk even if he wanted to. He'd need to find another way.

"A fast learner, this one," Murphy said, patting him on the shoulder. "But it doesn't matter. There's a special crowd where you're going. They've been there awhile and are hungry, you know what I mean?"

"Let's go, Murph," Velasquez said, checking his watch. "It's a long drive. I don't want to be late."

"Relax. We'll get there when we get there."

They pulled Levy out of the room and marched him down the hallway and into an elevator as fast as his chains would allow him. As the doors started to close, Levy caught a glimpse of Deluca watching him across the hall, but the next moment, the doors slammed shut, and they descended to the ground floor.

He soon found himself in the precinct's loading bay, exposed to the elements, shivering in the cold after the hot interrogation room. The rain whipped at his body as Murphy and Velasquez hustled him at a breakneck speed through the open space toward a massive black armored truck parked near the gate.

Murphy let go of him for a few seconds to swing open the heavy door at the back of the truck, and then the two agents hoisted him up and tossed him inside.

Levy looked around. It was a depressing sight. A small overhead light illuminated two rows of hard, unforgiving benches bolted securely to the floor. There was also a rectangular window on the roof. It was too small for a grown man to climb through and too dark to brighten the grim surroundings. A series of sturdy anchors were placed on the walls at even intervals, their metal loops glistening dangerously in the dark.

After securing Levy to one of them, Velasquez took a seat next to him, and Murphy, after closing the door, took a spot on the opposite bench. A few moments later, the prison on wheels was in motion, the rough bench under Levy jumping up and down.

"Tell me," Murphy said as the truck settled into a steady rhythm after seemingly reaching the highway. "I'm really curious. How does one wake up in the morning and decide his sole purpose in life is to kill other people? And not just kill. This one is a freak, Timmy. A real piece of work."

"I've heard," Velasquez replied without much interest. He was nodding, his eyes glassy.

Levy stared at the man, questioning him as desperation rose in his chest. Perhaps he was a fool for not calling Phil. For taking a gamble on a public defender. From the looks of it, he would be transported to a place from where there was no escape. It truly seemed like the end of the line.

"Nothing to say, bitch?" Murphy leaned toward him and slapped him on the mask. It was a slow slap, almost lazy, but Levy's movements were restricted, and his head jerked back from the impact, hitting the wall. He groaned, stars floating in his vision.

"Oh, you don't like it? I'm sorry, I can't hear what you're saying." The red-haired agent continued and mockingly put his palm next to his ear as if listening. "I know it's hard to talk when your mouth is busy. But you better get some training now. It's always going to be busy where you're going. You're going to love it. Make some friends. It'll be glorious."

Levy watched the scowl on the agent's face as his heart pounded in his chest, sweat streaming down his arms and back. He knew he was losing it, but he couldn't stop himself from falling into the deep well of anguish and despair.

"What?" Murphy gave him a lecherous smile. "I can tell you're getting excited."

Red blinding rage swallowed Levy whole, and he screamed, thrashing in his restraints, his muffled cries bouncing off the hard surfaces of the wagon.

"You little shit." Murphy stood up and grabbed the anchor beside Levy with his left hand. "Let's teach you some manners."

He hit Levy in the chest first, making him gasp for air. Then, taking a wider stance and finding balance, Murphy let go of the wall and rained a series of hard blows all over the prisoner.

John Levy tried to protect himself from the punches, turning this way and that, giving the assailant his shoulders and elbows. Still, the lack of mobility and the unrelenting attack soon rendered his defenses useless. Before long, his vision started to blur, his body hanging listlessly on the chains, blood squirting from his mouth through the mask and onto the steel floor with each breath.

"Enough," Velasquez said. "He needs to walk on his own when we get there. I don't want to write reports like the last time."

"Sure." Murphy stepped back, his eyes scanning Levy as if appreciating his work, his breathing still ragged. "Just wanted him to get a little taste of what's waiting for him at his new home. I'm really doing him a favor."

"Whatever, man. Just chill." Velasquez leaned against the wall and closed his eyes. "And don't make so much noise. I want to take a nap."

John pulled himself up and settled on the bench again. He was in agony—each breath sending electrifying jolts through his entire body.

"Don't you worry." Murphy took a seat and gave him a wink. "Nothing's broken. I'm a pro."

He looked like he was going to say something else, but there was a loud screeching outside, and the truck slammed on the brakes, throwing the agents off the benches. Levy bounced around the bench, his already battered body screaming in protest as it slammed into the wall repeatedly, but the chains kept him in place. A moment later, there was a thunderous clash, and the vehicle abruptly stopped.

"What the fuck was that?" Velasquez got up off his knees and wiped his face with his hand. It came off bloody. "We must've hit something."

There was a strange noise outside, as if someone had walked on the truck's roof, and then the small window shattered, sending a rain of glass shards inside. A moment later, a round object rolled in and fell into the truck with a heavy thud.

"What the—"

There was a loud bang, and Levy watched in horror as a thick plume of smoke came out from the object, engulfing both agents. Velasquez collapsed first, his hands clutching to his chest. Murphy struggled for a second longer, crawling on all fours toward Levy, but then succumbed to the gas as well.

As a thick cloud moved toward Levy, he held his breath, waiting for the poisonous substance to suffocate him. His lungs screamed, begging for oxygen as his panic reached a crescendo. Finally, unable to hold it anymore, he drew in a shaky breath, anticipating the gas burning his mouth and throat.

Nothing happened. The air had a metallic tang and a sour smell, but as far as he could tell, it inflicted no ill effects on his body. He took another cautious breath, deeper this time, and exhaled, the mouthpiece gurgling as the air escaped his lips.

There was another loud bang, and the door swung open, letting the cold air into the truck. It was dark, the rain coming down hard, but once the gas dissipated inside the wagon and Levy's eyes adjusted to the dark, he saw an empty field outside the truck.

He waited for a few minutes, trembling from cold and anticipation, certain that someone would step through the doors at any moment. But as minutes ticked by, the heavy rain remained the only sound coming from the outside. Levy looked at the two agents sprawled on the floor before him. They weren't moving, and as far as he could tell, they weren't breathing either. There was a ring with keys on Murphy's belt.

He gently poked the man's side with his foot, waiting for the agent to jump up and unleash another furious beating, but Murphy remained still.

Levy separated himself as far from the wall as the chains allowed him and grabbed the agent with both feet, pulling the bulky body toward himself. It was slow work, and he had to stop a few times to rest. When Murphy got within Levy's reach, he leaned over, pulled the keys off the man's belt, and unlocked the restraints.

He glanced at the open door that swung in the wind. Levy cautiously approached the edge of the truck, his senses heightened by the pouring rain and the chill that permeated the air.

They seemed to have stopped in the middle of an open field, the relentless downpour turning the vast expanse that stretched as far as he could see into a muddy wasteland. Through the haze of the rain, his gaze fixated on a gray sedan parked not far from the truck.

Levy jumped into the mud, his shoes making a squelching sound, and moved away from the truck. Then he unbuckled the mask and cautiously drew in the air. It smelled of rain and dirt. It was the smell of the countryside.

Satisfied, he headed toward the car. The rain was fierce. Each droplet seemed to amplify his discomfort, seeping through his clothes and sending shivers down his spine.

The vehicle was empty except for a carton box in the front passenger seat, and Levy dove inside and closed the door. There was a key in the ignition, and he turned the car on, cranking up the heat, grateful to be out of the rain.

When he stopped shivering, he turned to the box and slowly lifted the lid, unsure what to expect.

"What the hell?" he said, looking at the odd collection of items in front of him. There was a change of clothes that seemed to be his size, a jacket, and a pair of sneakers. There were also a few wigs, a fake beard, and a thick wad of cash in twenty-dollar bills wrapped with a rubber band. A small note was tucked under the band on one side of the wad, and he pulled it out and opened it. It was written in a hurried cursive with a pencil, small letters of uneven size jumping up and down the yellow paper. Levy turned on the cabin light and started to read.

Dear John,

If you're reading this, perhaps there's still hope for you. These items will help you return to Brooklyn and stay undetected for a while. I'm confident that you know where the laptop with the manuscript is. Find it, and complete your mission. It is bigger than you or me. I've grown to like you in the past few weeks and hope you can finish what you've started. These items won't last you too long, but if you finish the book, it won't matter. Everything will work out then, I promise.

Love,

L.

Levy slowly crushed the note in his hand and threw it into the box, a strange calmness enveloping him like a warm blanket. Lilly was right about two things. One, these items were going to help him get back to Brooklyn. And two, he was going to finish the book. Just not in the way she hoped.

THIRTY-TWO

I must have been more tired than I was willing to admit. Or perhaps it was the combination of heated seats that wrapped around my body like a warm blanket, the dark skies outside, and the relentless rain hitting the car window with a hypnotic rhythm. Regardless of the culprit, I was sound asleep before Marsha reached the West Side Highway. When I opened my eyes, we were in Prospect Park, pulling into an underground garage of a small office building.

"Sorry," I said, wiping the drool off my chin. "It's been a rough couple of days."

"It's all good," the driver said, giving me a quick smile in the rearview mirror. "I'm used to it."

She swung the car around and backed into a tight parking space next to a luxurious Mercedes sedan.

"Now what?"

"Right there." She pointed at the metal door in the corner of the garage. "Mr. Morton's office is on the second floor. You can't miss it. When he bought the building, there were no other tenants, so he was the only one with access to the garage. It's at a premium in this neighborhood."

"Sweet." I licked my lips. "Got any gum? My mouth tastes like a herd of goats spent the night there. Probably smells that way, too."

She dug into the armrest compartment and, a few moments later, emerged with a half-finished roll of Mentos. "That work?"

"I'll take two," I said, popping them into my mouth and savoring the minty flavor. "Much better. Thanks."

I got out of the car, went through the door at the end of the parking lot, and climbed the stairs to the second floor. Marsha was right. There was a short hallway lined with a plush carpet. It ran about fifty yards past a few storage rooms, and at the end of it was a solid mahogany door with a simple bronze plaque that read *Ezekiel Morton, Esq.*

"Hundred grand," I whispered, suddenly embarrassed over the ridiculously expensive Kelly bag in my hand. "Be cool, Alex. Be cool."

I rang the doorbell and waited. There was a sound of approaching footsteps, and then a moment later, the door swung open, revealing a man in the most impeccable business suit of gray herringbone wool I've ever laid my eyes on.

"Ah. My favorite private investigator is finally here."

Ezekiel Morton, Esq. didn't look anything like I pictured him throughout our multiple interactions. He looked like he was in his late forties or early fifties and wasn't fat at all. Morton was tall, fit, and broad-shouldered, his large, muscular figure moving with the grace of a large cat. His hair, the color of burnished gold, was combed back in a somewhat old-fashioned way, as if he was trying to look like Peter O'Toole did in his prime.

"Hello," I said, stretching my hand to meet his. "It's nice to finally put the face to the name."

"Likewise," he said.

I met his eyes. They were calm, deep, and green like the water in the bay I once saw in the Caribbean Sea. And that's when I knew. There was something in them that the words couldn't quite describe. Like a door left ajar in a large house that let the cold air in. You don't know where it is, but it makes you shiver just the same.

I dropped the bag on the floor and reached for my gun, but he was too fast. Too fast and too strong. A baby gazelle fighting a lion in his prime would stand a better chance.

He rushed me, his movements so fast they looked blurry, and I went down hard, the air leaving my lungs with a whimper. His knee crushed into my back between my shoulder blades, and before I could do anything else, I heard the rattling sound of fastening zip ties.

He flipped me on my back after he secured my wrists and feet, my fingers crushed under my torso. I buckled, trying to kick him with both of my legs, but he easily dodged and then, in one swift motion, wrapped another zip tie around my neck.

"You fucking pig—" I managed to say before he pulled on the end of the tie, turning my furious shout into a pitiful gurgle.

"Don't struggle," he said, watching me with those calm, beautiful eyes. "Unless you would like to pass out. This is just tight enough for you to breathe. If you try to fight it, your neck muscles will contract, making them bulge. That will restrict the airflow."

I stopped moving and stared at him, my mind racing, the tie on my neck painfully cutting into my skin.

"I'm going to pick you up now," he said. "It'll get uncomfortable. I suggest you stay as still as you can."

Morton reached out and took my gun and the Kelly purse and opened it, digging inside. Not finding what he was looking for, he patted me down and smiled as his hand stumbled over the necklace in my jacket pocket. He pulled it out and laid the pendant on his palm for a few moments, turning it this way and that, admiring it, and then stuffed it into the front pocket of his suit.

"Let me go," I hissed, instantly regretting it. He wasn't joking when he said I couldn't talk. The mere movement of my vocal cords made breathing almost impossible. I coughed, making it worse, the zip tie strangling me.

"I told you not to move," he said, grabbing the band on my neck and pulling it away from the skin.

I wheezed, grateful for the air entering my lungs again.

"Okay. Let's go now."

He grabbed me by the waist and threw me over his shoulder. I dangled like a rag doll, my bound wrists helplessly swinging behind my back. The zip tie on my neck dug deep into the skin again, cutting the airflow. I tried to stay still, gasping for air, but panic started to set in as Morton trotted down the stairs leisurely. I thrashed in terror, only making it worse, my vision dimming.

"Almost there, Alex," I heard him say, and then he set me down. There was a snapping sound, and the pressure on my neck disappeared. I coughed and wheezed as my lungs reclaimed oxygen, and I took in my surroundings. He brought me back to the garage level and settled me in the back seat of the Suburban. Marsha was nowhere to be seen.

"See." Morton smiled and patted me on the cheek. "Didn't I say you'd be fine?"

"Fuck you," I managed. It sounded raspy and weak.

He shrugged, buckled me in, shut the door, and took the driver's seat. The engine revved, and the car pulled out of the garage.

"Don't try to do anything stupid," he warned as the Suburban climbed onto the street level. "The windows are soundproof. No one will hear you, and you will only make me angry."

I said nothing.

"But we don't have to talk about unpleasant things all the time. First of all," he said, as the Suburban picked up speed, "thank you for finding the necklace. You have no idea how long it took me to track it down, only to be snatched right from under my nose. That bank robbery was most unfortunate. And apologies for not paying you. I realize that must be upsetting."

"Scum."

He glanced at me in the rearview mirror and smiled. "I'm sorry,

Alex, but you won't need money anymore. It would be silly to pay you now."

I watched him silently, moving my hands behind my back. Looking for a weak spot.

"Don't bother with the zip ties," he said, as if reading my mind. "Those are not your regular straps. I invented them myself. You see, Alex, there's so much that went into this. You don't think I'd risk you getting away, do you?"

"Why was Winslow in PA?" He was talkative and boastful. Showing off. I didn't have the opportunity to escape for now, but if I kept him talking, perhaps I could buy some time. Learned what made him tick. I didn't love my odds, but a few extra minutes could be the difference between life and death.

"Oh, you're going to love this. It took me years to put everything in motion. I knew that once I started, it'd make a big splash. And with a high-profile case like this, the police wouldn't rest until they had something concrete. Unchallengeable. Levy taking the fall would be great, but I needed something much more. I wanted a story. And not just any story. Something spectacular."

"Gutting people alive isn't spectacular enough for you?"

"Don't be crass, Alex," he said. "This is for a higher purpose, and you know it. Anyway. I didn't want to settle with John Levy. I needed something bigger. And then it came to me. It was magnificent. A Shakespearean sonnet. A Daliesque painting. One patsy was good, but two would be genius."

"Two?"

"Yes." He gave me one of his creepy smiles. "What if Levy had an alibi for one of the murders? Imagine the horror of the prosecutor. A gaping hole in their entire attack strategy. That could unravel the whole case. And then, as if by magic, we discover that Levy had a helper. A passionate lover, perhaps, willing to plunge to the same depths of depravity as Levy himself. It could be that Levy questioned his partner's dedication to him. Made her furious. She wanted to prove her worth. Show him how much she loved him. How much she cared."

"She?" A cold shiver ran down my spine. "She? And how much did she care, Morton?"

"Oh, she cared plenty, Alex. She even traveled to another state and killed a poor woman to prove it. A young and talented socialite, Victoria Winslow. It was such a tragedy."

"You're a monster," I whispered. "No one would believe you that I had anything to do with it."

"I beg to differ." He shook his head. "If the police look hard enough, and in a case like this, they most certainly will, they'd find the smallest details. Things they might have missed if Levy was alone."

"What things?"

"Things like Levy's partner's hair, for example. Or a small piece of her nail embedded into the victim's skin. And payments she'd received from our good friend John Levy."

"You fucking bastard." I buckled in my seat and tried to kick his chair, but it was too far. It all made sense to me now. The wire transfer from a numbered account. The weird smell I sensed when opening the front door. The hairbrush at an odd angle in my bathroom. "You broke into my house."

"I had to. So many details, Alex. I fed that nasty lady clues for months to make her suspect her poor, loyal husband. And the wretched whore was too busy sleeping around to pay any attention. And then there was the not-so-easy task of ensuring she went to you to track her boring husband down."

I slumped in my chair. The adrenaline was wearing off, and I was crashing. Desperation was starting to settle in. I needed to do something. To throw him off-balance. Make him angry. Anything to force him to make a mistake. "What's the plan? You think by killing me, you'll become Lucifer? Are you that stupid? I can assure you, there's major disappointment waiting for you there. There are no demons,

Morton, or Lucifer. You're just a cruel idiot who had a shitty childhood."

He laughed, startling me. A crisp, contagious, full-throated laugh. He must have been a hit at every social event he'd ever been to.

"You have some high opinions of yourself, Alex," he said when he finally settled down. "You're not one of the special ones. I wish you were, as I'd be one step closer to my final form. But fear not. Things are rather strict with special ones. I have to follow the instructions to the letter. With you, there are no rules. You and I can play together for a long while. I'll learn new things. You'd be surprised how many things there are to learn. Before I hunted for the special ones, I practiced a few times, you know? You have no idea how hard it is. It's always the little things."

I shuddered. He talked with such ease about the killings. There was no trace of humanity in him. No feelings. No compassion. A true sociopath. There would be no reasoning with him. No bargain could be struck.

"There was this woman I had," he continued. "She cut her wrists by accident because the restraints were too rough. It was such a mess. I ordered a special pair after that. Wonderful craftsmanship. And there was another. She died too early because I was moving too fast. Details, Alex. Always details. Think of yourself as a gift to science. You'll help me learn new techniques. Refine old ones. Then, when I'm ready, you'll go the same way as the others. It'll be your final gift to me. To make it look like there was a quarrel between the two lovers. We'll write a story where Levy kills you and then, broken-hearted, kills himself. A modern twist on an old tale. Romeo and Juliet. Othello and Desdemona. No loose ends, no more clues to pursue. Case closed. The play ends. Everyone applauds. Curtain."

THIRTY-THREE

There was a state-wide manhunt for John Levy. His name was everywhere—on muted television sets in gas stations and variable electronic displays along the highway. When he briefly stopped to get gas, buy a sandwich, and use the toilet, his slightly younger and much rounder face stared at him from the front pages of fresh newspapers stacked near the counter in a deli.

"Crazy last few days, huh?" the old lady behind the counter said as she wrapped his sub into a piece of paper and stuffed it into a plastic bag. "First, this serial killer fella gutting people alive, and now the storm."

"Uh-huh," he mumbled into a prosthetic beard, giving her a twenty-dollar bill.

"What I don't understand," the woman continued, waving the sandwich around like a conductor's baton, "is why are they looking for him here, out in the sticks. He's probably one of them rich folks. Snatches poor girls off the street right in front of his house, ya know?"

"Yeah."

"Anyway." She finally pulled the register out, counted change, and dropped it into his hand with the sub. "You stay safe out there, my friend."

"Thanks."

It was a bizarre experience he couldn't quite describe as he drove the car he'd found in the open field next to the prison truck. As he made his way up north, he passed four roadblocks with random car checks, the last one at the entrance of the Goethals Bridge. But thanks to a wig and a very itchy fake beard, he went through all of them unmolested by the police.

The weather seemed to be on his side, too. There was a freak storm coming from the north. Its southernmost edge was now battering the state of New York around Buffalo and Albany and getting stronger still as it slowly continued its unrelenting roll toward the Big Apple. And while it hadn't quite made its way down to the city just yet, the wind gusts hitting the car occasionally were so strong he had to compensate to keep the vehicle sliding off the road. But the cold rain and punishing winds kept the police inside their patrol cars longer, making them unwilling to look at every vehicle that rolled through the checkpoints.

As Levy drove, the chatter on the radio went from the occasional updates about the approaching storm to almost nonstop coverage. And predictions gradually shifted from *it won't be as bad as Sandy* to *this is looking downright apocalyptic*. When Levy crossed the Verrazzano Bridge, it was almost six in the morning, and yet, there was not even a hint of light in the sky, as if the sun itself had been swallowed by the impending storm.

As he entered Bay Ridge, the ominous absence of dawn's light cast an eerie pall over the once-familiar neighborhood, imbuing the streets with unsettling tension. Levy's heart clenched, his grip on the steering wheel tightening as he glanced over the manically flapping windshield wipers at the foreboding, unyielding clouds illuminated by occasional flashes of hidden lightning.

He drove down Third Avenue, unable to resist stealing a glimpse of his apartment building. The mere thought of a hot shower, a decent breakfast, and clean clothes sent goose bumps up and down his arms. He'd pay a fortune now for the unassuming view out of his kitchen window at the magnolia tree in his backyard, illuminated by four blue lights.

But it was a fool's dream. Two gray sedans were double-parked at both ends of his block, and a large van was idling at a hydrant near the intersection. At this hour, they couldn't be anyone else but cops watching his old place. Ready to swoop in and take him down. Or, if luck would have it, shoot him first and ask questions later. He couldn't blame them. Between the terror imposed by the Valentine Killer and the apocalyptic storm ready to slam the city in the next twenty-four hours, everyone's nerves were frayed.

Levy swore under his breath and drove on, leaving the fantasy behind. A few minutes later, he parked near a flimsy flashing neon sign: *Alex Watts, PI*.

He watched the rain-slicked street for a few minutes. Like everywhere in this neighborhood, the cars lined every inch of the side of the road, but between old junkers and a convertible Beetle, he didn't see anything that could pass for an undercover car. Levy took a deep breath and stepped out into the storm.

Concealed by the cacophony of howling winds and pounding rain, he quickly crossed the sidewalk and positioned himself near the door of Alex's office. With careful precision, he aimed his elbow at a small section of the window near the doorframe and struck, the roaring gusts of wind masking the sound of shattering glass.

He cleared a few remaining jagged pieces that threatened to tear at his flesh and then reached through the gap, deftly manipulating the latch. The door opened with a nearly inaudible click, and a moment later, Levy was inside Watts's private sanctum, the fury of the storm subsiding behind the closed door.

He locked it again and went about the place looking for the laptop, relying on the meager light provided by the streetlamps. As Levy searched the bookshelves, the shrill wail of a siren pierced the air, cutting the night like a blade.

"Shit!" he exclaimed in panic, looking around like a spooked animal, and darted toward the nearest cover, taking refuge behind Alex's desk.

He squatted there, holding his breath and praying that his intrusion had not set off a hidden alarm as the siren grew louder by the moment. But then, as if mocking his terror, the siren's pitch shifted, and an ambulance, its strobe lights slicing through cascading rain, barreled past the office. Soon, the echoes of the horn faded into the distance, swallowed by the storm.

Relief flooded his veins, his trembling hands brushing against the cool surface of the desk. Cautiously, Levy emerged from his hiding place and pulled on the drawer in front of him. A grin tugged on the corner of his lips as his eyes locked on the familiar shape of the laptop.

"And now we are in business," he whispered.

He moved the laptop to the small bathroom in the back to ensure the monitor's glow wouldn't be seen from the street and opened the lid.

"Oh, Alex," he said as he recognized the last few sentences on the screen. The manuscript ended precisely where he had left off. It seemed that Alex didn't add anything to the story.

Levy sat on the floor, leaning against an unforgiving wall, and placed the computer on his lap. He paused for a few seconds, listening to the howling wind outside, and gently lowered his fingers on the keyboard.

"It doesn't have to be perfect," he reminded himself as he wrote down the first sentence and then another.

Slow at first, the story started to flow, his fingers flying over the keys. He may not have been looking for perfection, but he needed the story to make sense. To be logical. It had to be consistent enough that it could play out in real life.

He started with Luca on the hunt for his next victim. Victoria Winslow. She wasn't like the others, he remembered. She was famous. That was something he could use.

His imagination flew untethered. A dinner party and a ball filled with celebrities to the brim. Perhaps Victoria would be invited to cover the red carpet. He pictured her standing in front of the glitzy steps, microphone in hand, talking to an A-list movie star. Asking them what they were wearing that evening. He could see her tall, statuesque figure confidently striding up the stairs into the giant ballroom with golden chandeliers. Waitstaff in white dinner jackets shuttled champaign flutes and hors d'oeuvres between distinguished guests.

"Paparazzi," he exclaimed. Excitement built in his chest. That was going to be his loose link. He typed as fast as he could, his fingers aching. "Oh, this is perfect."

Luca had been planning to try to snatch Victoria after the ball. He'd break into her car and patiently wait for her to get in. Then, he would put her to sleep and drive her back to his lair. Except...he wasn't. A naughty young paparazzi would fall for the tall fashion blogger with the face of a goddess and the figure of a supermodel.

Perhaps he was new to the job and didn't care much for taking celebrity upskirt pictures and hoping for wardrobe malfunctions. Instead of chasing the famous geezers and hoping one of them got into a car with someone other than their wife, he'd sneak into the underground parking lot and wait for Victoria to arrive. Hoping that his charm and wit could get him a view of the underpants after all.

But then, as he entered the dimly lit parking lot, he saw a tall, hulking figure breaking into Winslow's car. He'd call the police and tip them off, getting the arrest on camera. Saving the goddess and getting the exclusive of a lifetime. Surely, he'd get a chance at her underpants once she found out who saved her.

"I got you, fucker." Levy chuckled. With each keystroke, he crafted a conclusion leading to Luca's capture. He wrote a furious standoff in the parking lot. Luca charging at the officers, only to be tased and shackled like an animal. The trial. The epilogue told from the perspective of a doctor on death row. It was perfect.

It was almost noon when Levy typed the last sentence.

. . .

As the doctor watched, the line on the monitor stayed flat—the Valentine Killer was no more.

He exhaled and put the laptop next to him on the ground. Exhaustion tugged at his every fiber. He lay down on the cold bathroom floor, the laptop screen still casting its glow upon him. John Levy closed his eyes, the chaos of the storm outside fading with each passing second. He slept without dreams.

THIRTY-FOUR

My road trip with Morton was coming to an end. You'd think the guy with a kidnapped woman in the back of the car would go on the back roads to avoid attention. But you'd be wrong. Morton took Prospect Park Southwest and then followed the busy Linden Boulevard all the way to East New York with the confidence of a man driving home from a grocery store.

I thought I'd have a fighting chance when Morton was unloading me from the car. There was no zip tie around my throat, I was relatively free to move, and he'd be standing in an awkward position to pull me out of the Suburban. My plan was to get slack and low, making myself as heavy as possible. To force him to overextend himself into the cabin. If I timed it right, when his body was off-balance, leaning over my lap, I could go for his jugular. A well-placed bite and Morton would bleed to death in seconds. That wouldn't solve the issue of supposedly indestructible zip ties on my hands and feet, but I could deal with that problem later without a maniac actively trying to murder me. One thing at a time.

As the Suburban pulled through the automatic gates of a large private house, I braced myself, readying for the fight of my life.

It didn't quite work out how I had planned. After we stopped, Morton rolled down the windows, got out of the car, and approached it from the side, a spray bottle in his hand.

"Night night," he said, pulling the trigger a few times.

"You little shit." I buckled, trying to get as far away from the window as fine, sweet-smelling mist clung to my face and body. It had a sickly sweet scent, not entirely unpleasant, but it was fooling no one. It was the fragrance of malevolence, of twisted intentions veiled behind an aromatic façade. The last thing I remembered was an equally noxious smile playing on Morton's lips as he watched me fade to black.

Strange sounds woke me up. There was a ticking somewhere behind me, like a clock, but somehow, I knew that wasn't it. For every four clicks, there was a quiet, almost at the edge of my ability to hear, mechanical hiss, pneumatic breathing of a machine. Then, a moment later, after the clicking stopped, I could sense a light draft on my thighs and buttocks. Click, click, click, click, and then a gentle blow of air. After that, the cycle would start over again. An air filter of some kind, not that this information did me any good.

My head hurt, the base of my skull hot and tender, my temples tight, as if squeezed by a vise, but when I blinked my crusty eyes open, the headache seemed to be the least of my problems.

The room around me was the stuff of nightmares. It was a large cube, its walls wrapped in layers of cushioned fabric. A surgeon's table was built into one of the walls, and a harsh fluorescent glow reflected off the rows of sharp, gleaming instruments. A shelf next to it was stocked with vials and retorts. A huge assortment of bottles of different sizes with color-coded labels, signed in neat cursive, lined a few shelves below it.

But the worst part of the room was in its center, where a system of mechanical pulleys was built. I dangled in it like a fly caught in a spiderweb, my naked body suspended upside down by my ankles, my wrists anchored to the floor below. The cocktail of a hangover from whatever chemical Morton had used on me and blood pooling in my head because of my inverted position must have been the reason for the massive headache. I craned my neck, looking at the custom-built padded cuffs that gripped my limbs, a primal terror ripping through my mind. There was no escaping this. I pulled on the chains with all my might, making them rattle, the fear blinding me, but it was all in vain.

Throughout my career in law enforcement and then as a free-lancing PI, I'd been in more hairy situations than I could count. I'd been ambushed, cut, beaten, shot at...you name it. I might not have subscribed to DD's morbid ideology, but fear was an old friend, and I knew how to deal with it. But nothing in my entire life had quite prepared me for the situation I was in. To be displayed like a bug for the person who'd feel nothing as he slowly dissected my living, breathing body. A lepidopterist's new toy.

The door swung open without a sound, and Morton stepped in, wheeling an IV drip on a platform, a busy look on his face. He'd changed from the business suit and now wore a white lab coat over ironed-out, navy-blue scrubs. He wouldn't be out of place as an extra on the *Grey's Anatomy* set. At least until the cast members started disappearing without a trace.

"And now she awakens," he said. His voice sounded different, muffled by the padding on the walls. Soft, almost purring. Like a large cat. But there was more to that change than just the room's acoustics. His cadence, tone, everything was different, as if Ezekiel Morton had entirely transformed into another person. The one who had met me at his office was the hunter. Deadly and efficient, but still somehow more human than whatever the monster standing in front of me was now.

Despite my circumstances, the irony of the situation did not escape me. I had accused John Levy of a split personality. A Dr. Jekyll and Mr. Hyde persona. Instead, it was Morton who had two different shells. Just in his case, it was more like Mr. Hyde and Mr. Hyde on steroids.

"I'm looking forward to learning new things," he said. "And, while you might not see it this way, I want you to know that I am grateful for your help."

"Fuck you," I said. "Go to hell."

He ignored me, walked to the base of the pulleys, and pressed a button on a small rectangular control box I hadn't noticed before. The chains rattled, and the bonds pulled on me hard. I wanted to scream, but only a whimper left my lips as my lungs struggled for breath and my body stretched to the limit in four directions.

"This is so much better," he said. "I would enjoy talking to you, but people tend to scream when I work. And I don't like all the screaming."

He rolled the IV drip next to me and adjusted the dials. "It's an adrenaline cocktail, in case you were wondering what it was. And don't you worry about the dosage. It won't kill you." He gave me a reassuring smile. "Quite the opposite. It'll make you more alive than you have ever been. I used to work as a chemist for many years. This is one of the best mixtures I've ever made. Details, Alex, remember? Do you know why you're upside down?"

I wanted to curse him out, say something venomous and biting, but could only produce a pitiful wheezing sound.

"A pure accident. Like penicillin," Morton said, visibly pleased with himself, as he readied the needle. "On one of my practice runs, I put the cuffs backward and didn't feel like redoing them. Imagine my surprise when I found out it was so much easier to keep my subject alive with all that blood flowing to their head, and then—"

Morton stopped mid-sentence, leaving the needle hanging off the IV station. He pulled out a phone from his lab coat and watched the screen for a few seconds, a frown creasing his forehead. Then, without warning, he stormed out of the room, closing the door behind him.

I stared at the door for some time, fighting for breath, convinced it was a cruel joke. A way for him to screw with my head. To make me think I might be out of the danger zone, only for him to come back and inflict the most devastating pain known to man. But as the minutes ticked by and the door remained closed, I wondered if something happened that might have derailed Morton's plans.

And then, after what seemed an eternity, the door swung open again, and before I had a chance to lose my mind, there was the face I had never expected to see in a million years—DD.

"Holy shit, Alex," was all he said when he saw me. He rushed toward me, frantically going between the pulleys and the remote control. Soon the chains rattled in reverse, lowering my naked ass down on the floor as at least half a dozen police officers filed into the room. And then I was free, shivering like a leaf in the wind, catching my breath, and hugging DD for dear life as he shielded me from the rest of the crew with his bulk.

"Don't just stand there, you idiots. Somebody, get her a damn blanket and some shoes," DD roared, and the underlings spilled out of the room like scared chickens. Two minutes later, Jenkins, who I remembered from the motel operation, returned with a Mylar sheet and a pair of slippers. I gratefully wrapped myself in a silvery cocoon, and DD took his jacket off and put it around my shoulders.

"How?" That was all I managed.

"You're gonna be pissed." He smiled. "I told you I would get a subpoena to track your phone."

I smiled back. "Never been happier being tracked."

"I saw you travel to East New York out of the blue and wanted to know what was up. We followed you here."

"How did you end up in the house, though?"

"It's a poor neighborhood, and the house seemed abandoned," he said as he escorted me outside to a police cruiser. The Suburban was still there, all of its doors open. The yard looked like a beehive, with cops going over every inch of the property. The rain had stopped, but the temperatures seemed to have dropped below zero, and I shivered under the flimsy blanket. "But then, we get here, and it looks like a CIA compound. Motion sensors, proximity lasers, and video cameras watching the backyard from every angle possible. That didn't smell right, and I didn't see you anywhere. I had to make a judgment call."

"Sounds like someone broke protocol."

"You mind?"

"Not in the slightest." I pressed myself deeper into the warm seat of the car, pulling DD's jacket all the way up to my ears. "What about Morton?"

"Who?"

"Ezekiel Morton? The guy who kidnapped me? He's the attorney who hired me to find the missing jewelry. But apparently, he also moonlights as a serial killer."

"Wait." DD stared at me. "Are you telling me it wasn't John Levy who brought you here?"

I gave him a hard look. "You don't think I'd remember? And how would he bring me here if he's on his way to the supermax?"

"I don't know what to tell you, Alex. I've never heard of Ezekiel Morton until now. I'll have my guys look into it, but get this—we pulled up property records, and not only this house but also the one on the other side of the street is registered under a corporation. I'll give you three guesses to tell me who owns the corp."

"I don't think I'm in the mood."

"John Levy."

"No way. I am telling you. This is Morton's doing. He's trying to make it look like John and I worked together. He confessed to breaking into my house. Planted evidence to implicate me. He was planning on killing me first, making it look like Levy did it. And then he'd make John commit suicide. This is all him. He's the Valentine Killer."

"I have a hard time believing this," DD said. He gave me a look I couldn't quite understand.

"What?"

"Levy's escaped."

I stared at him, unsure I'd heard it right. "What do you mean, escaped? How?"

"His prison transport was ambushed. The driver and both guards are dead. Looks like a poisonous gas, but we won't know for sure until we get the results."

Jenkins returned, pulling DD aside and urgently whispering something into his ear. My former partner nodded and then came back to me.

"They found a tunnel," he said. "Between this house and the one across the street. I'm sure there's more security equipment we haven't found yet. That's how Levy escaped."

"Damn it, DD," I said. "It wasn't John. What part of that do you not understand?"

"Look." He closed the car's door and leaned against the window. "I'm sorry, but there's no record of Ezekiel Morton on these two properties. Jenkins is going to take you home and take your statement. Give him Morton's description. But my suspicion is that those two are working together. Everything is under Levy. It doesn't look good for him. And, frankly, it doesn't look good for you, either. And unless something else turns up that contradicts the evidence, you might be in real trouble, Alex."

"What the fuck, DD?" My throat still hurt, each word leaving my vocal cords sorer than before, but I was boiling over with fury. "Do you think I strung myself up, naked, in that house? Do you, for one second—"

"Alex." He put his shovel of a palm on my forearm.

That shut me up. DD wasn't exactly a gentle type, but there was nothing but compassion on his big bulldog face at that moment.

"Alex. Of course, I believe you. You've been to hell and back. And I will do everything in my power to get to the bottom of this. But this isn't just about you and me anymore. You understand that, right? Look, like I said, Jenkins will drive you home. He's found your clothes and your gun, by the way. Give him your statement and take it easy for a while. Take a few days off. Watch some TV. Or better yet, stay away from the TV. Read some books, instead. Knit, or whatever the hell you do, to take your mind off things. Let me do my job. Okay?"

I sighed, deflated, and leaned back into the seat, my eyes fixed on his. "Find him, DD. For the love of all that's holy. Find Ezekiel Morton."

THIRTY-FIVE

The rain returned with a vengeance as Jenkins drove us back to my house. It started as a pesky drizzle, teasingly tapping the windshield, but it soon turned dark. The heavens erupted, and the sky unleashed a torrential downpour upon the miserable souls trudging along the highway. In the blink of an eye, what was once a mild mist turned into a deluge, challenging the limits of the cruiser's windshield wipers.

The temperature remained precariously around the freezing point, dancing on the edge where water and ice played a dangerous game of coexistence. In minutes, the road transformed into an ice rink, slick with a sheen of black ice.

Our journey to Bay Ridge was brief, but the ruthless weather had already taken its toll. Along the way, I spotted the aftermath of Mother Nature's fury—five cars had lost control and found themselves hopelessly stuck in roadside ditches. Two of them lay overturned, their wheels spinning helplessly in the air like beetles on their backs.

"I'll check the house for you," Jenkins said after he parked the cruiser next to my porch steps.

"No, that won't be necessary."

"I'm sorry, but I have to insist." Jenkins offered me a hand as I stepped out of the car, shivering in the cold rain. "Dominic will eat me alive if I don't."

"Fine. Just watch the steps."

Hand in hand, we climbed the porch, holding onto each other for dear life, the black ice underfoot testing our balance. Then I waited for him in the hallway, the stuffy but familiar smell of the house calming me down.

"All clear," Jenkins said, coming down the stairs and holstering his weapon. "But make sure all your doors and windows are secure before you retire."

"Will do. Thanks for the ride." I took off DD's jacket and handed it to Jenkins, holding onto the edge of the Mylar blanket to make sure it stayed in place.

He nodded and stepped outside into the rain. I locked the door and turned around when my doorbell rang. I frowned and checked the peephole, but seeing Jenkins on my steps, I opened the door again.

"Everything okay?"

"Sorry, I almost forgot. Here." He handed me a business card. "This is my direct line. Calls to this number get priority, so it'll go through even in bad reception areas. If anything happens, call it immediately, and we'll have the cavalry here in no time."

"Thanks."

I took the card and turned around, only to find myself staring at a pair of bright green eyes.

"Spots. You scared the bejesus out of me."

The cat yawned, stretched, and fell on his side, sticking his belly out.

"Oh, I see how it is." I squatted next to him and rubbed his soft, warm belly. "Are you hungry? Come on."

I refilled the cat's bowl, and while he munched away, I drew a hot bath and threw away the clothes Jenkins had found at Morton's house. The underwear, the jeans, the shirt, and, painfully, my favorite leather jacket: they all went into the garbage bag. I guess I could have washed them, but the mere idea of Morton's fingers touching them was so repulsive I knew I'd never be able to put them on again.

After disposing of the tainted clothing, I waited for the cat to finish his meal. When he was done, I picked him up by his soft belly and went into the bathroom, setting my gun on a small table next to the tub. Spots gracefully settled on a rug beside it, his eyes never leaving me, as if he understood the turmoil that raged within. He was good company. Probably better than most of my ex-boyfriends.

I stepped into the hot water and settled in as the warmth of the bath penetrated my skin, soothing my muscles and slowly erasing the chill from my bones. But despite the comfort, I couldn't escape the images of Morton's house, haunting my mind like malevolent ghosts. The padded room, the surgeon's table. Long rows of carefully labeled bottles. The glistening of the clear liquid on the needle's tip as he readied to puncture my vein.

I closed my eyes, attempting to find solace in the darkness. To block out the ghosts. But like an unending nightmare, the scenes played relentlessly in my mind, tormenting me with Morton's icy, calculating eyes and grotesque grin. The pain and horrors he had subjected his victims to was all too vivid.

I shuddered, contemplating how close I came to sharing the same fate as the poor souls who had visited the padded room before me. The endless agony under the watchful, unwavering eye of a psychopath.

I took a shaky breath. I needed to get over it. There'd be time to deal with the PTSD. There'd be an opportunity to heal the invisible scars and mourn those who had fallen. But that would come later, after Morton was caught. Or killed. For now, I needed to focus on the task at hand. To strategize and plan my next move.

I had no intention of taking a break and resting, as DD had suggested. Did he really say I should read and knit? Despite my shitty mood, I chuckled out loud.

Knit.

I was certain I'd know how to stab somebody with a knitting needle. Knitting? Not so much.

I glanced at Spots. The cat was wrapped around one of my slippers, his eyes half-lidded, his whiskers twitching in contentment.

"I'm sleepy too, Spots, but there's no time. I'll go to the office after this," I said, looking at the cat. He flicked his left ear, as if giving me a sign that he was paying attention. "I need to write the ending of this stupid book. And if John is in the city, maybe he'll find a way to contact me. He knows where my office is. Maybe we could catch Morton if we work together."

Spots yawned, and I yawned back and rubbed my face. I needed to get out of the bath, or else I'd fall asleep right there and then. I closed my eyes, took a deep breath, and put my head under the water, letting the darkness envelop me. Savoring the stillness of the moment.

When I emerged, there was a slight shift in the air. I couldn't tell exactly what it was, but when I glanced at Spots, I knew he felt it, too. His ears perked up, and his eyes were now wide open, staring into the depths of the house, his nose twitching as if he smelled something unfamiliar.

I grabbed the gun off the small table and stepped out of the tub, the soapy water sloshing softly around me. I flicked the lights off and listened while my eyes got used to the darkness.

At first, I heard nothing, but then there was a subtle movement. A creaking of the wooden floor. A rustling of someone's breath. Then, there was silence again. And then another stealthy movement.

I flicked the safety off and, leaving wet footprints on the tile floor, moved out of the bathroom, the barrel of my trusty HK leading the way. My heart was pounding with such force that I was sure it could be heard on the street. Morton must've come back for me, to finish what he'd started.

But as I traversed the darkened house, I shed my fears like a snake losing its old skin. This was my house. It was my fortress, my castle. Pink stucco, old leaky windows, and all. This time, he'd pay.

I crept into the living room, my finger twitching near the trigger, to find a man's silhouette. A black cutout in front of the window, frozen in the iron sights of my pistol.

"Ah!" the man yelled as I entered, lifting something rectangular to his face in a protective gesture. "Alex, don't shoot."

I froze, recognizing the voice, my finger trembling at the tip of the trigger. I stepped back and switched the light on. "John?"

He peeked over the edge of the laptop, squinting against the bright light. "Don't shoot me, please. I'm unarmed."

"Are you out of your mind? What the fuck are you doing in my house?"

"I need your help." He lowered the laptop, giving me a better look, and immediately averted his eyes. "You might want to put something on."

I kept the gun trained on him. "I heard you'd ran. Killed the driver and both guards who were transporting you. And you didn't answer my question."

"I didn't kill anybody. And I didn't run, exactly. Well, I guess I did, but I had no other options." This time, he looked me straight in the eye, and I saw something there I'd never seen before. "Somebody broke me out of the prison car because they needed me to complete the manuscript. Wanted me to write Luca successfully completing his quest. I didn't know how to fight it. How could I? That's why I came to you in the first place, remember?"

I said nothing. He had every right to be passive-aggressive, I supposed. He did come to me when only one person was dead, and a woman named Naomi with a butterfly tattoo was supposed to be next. But he was in my house, uninvited, and I was wet, cold, and squatting naked in the middle of my living room with a gun. If he had any grievances, he would have to get over them.

"But I figured, fine," he continued. "This might be my only opportunity to make things right. They were transporting me to the supermax facility, Alex. A place for the worst of the worst. And from what I've heard, there was a good chance from there, I'd be sent to death row. I'd be helpless there. Completely powerless to change anything. And now the guards were dead, too. No matter what I told the jury, I'd be responsible for their deaths. Nobody would believe me at that point."

"So, you ran."

"I did. I thought perhaps I'll finish the damned book if that's what they want me to do. Just not in the way they want me to. Give it my best shot. And I thought I did."

"You thought?"

"Yes." He averted his eyes again. "I got back to Brooklyn and broke into your office. Sorry about that, by the way. Had to smash your window. But I found the laptop and worked on it until it was done. I was exhausted, and after I finished it, I fell asleep. But then I woke up, and I don't know how, but the story was different. Luca doesn't get captured. He kills the last two victims instead. It doesn't say exactly what happens after he does, but I'm guessing the implication is that he becomes what he wanted to become. The Lightbringer. The prince of demons. Lucifer himself."

I lowered the gun an inch. "You still haven't told me how you got into my house."

"They gave me your car."

"Who?"

He shrugged. "The same people who broke me out of the prison. I had no idea it was yours. After I woke up and realized the book had a different ending, I went back into the car, not quite knowing what to do or where to go, to be honest. And then, I saw a piece of paper sticking out from under the passenger seat. It was your car registration. That's how I learned where you lived, I swear."

"How did you get *in here?*"

"Oh. The door was opened." He pointed behind him with the laptop. "I was about to ring the bell and saw it wasn't locked. I snuck in, thinking you might be in trouble and could use some help."

"Shit. Jenkins," I said, remembering the business card. "I must've forgotten to lock it."

"Who's Jenkins?"

"A cop. Doesn't matter." I pointed the gun down. "Shit, John, I thought you were Morton. I almost shot you."

He gave me a confused look. "Who's Morton?"

"Morton is your Luca." I shuddered. "In the flesh. He kidnapped me and strapped me in his padded room upside down, but luckily, I was on a watch list, and my former partner found me."

"Dominic?"

"Yep. But let's not waste any time. Do we have any idea who the victims are?"

He shuffled his feet. "Yes. I know those two people well. I have a childhood friend. Phil. I just saw him and his wife a couple of weeks ago."

"Are they the targets?"

"No." He looked at me again, and this time, I recognized the emotion behind his eyes. Pain. "No, not them. Their kids."

THIRTY-SIX

The wait was over. That much was obvious. The storm that the weatherman with a sexy baritone had been promising on the radio for the past few weeks was finally arriving to the city. The rain was now so heavy that I could barely see past the hood of the Corolla, the wipers helplessly struggling against the unyielding stream of water.

As the car crawled well below the city speed limit up Fourth Avenue, it got pummeled by the brutal gusts of wind whenever we crossed an intersection or passed an open space not protected by tall buildings. It skidded and drifted, the wheels squealing in protest, and I prayed to every god I knew we didn't hit something and break down before getting to Sunset Park. The few remaining motorists crazy enough to still be out on the road honked and silently cursed behind their windshields as we swerved from lane to lane, avoiding a collision.

"Please go faster, Alex," Levy begged me for what seemed to be the hundredth time. "We have to hurry."

"I'm going as fast as I can," I shot back, crushing the steering wheel under my fingers, squinting at the shapeless gray outside the windshield. We were flying blind, the swimming lights of lampposts as my only navigational markers. Even the GPS refused to work, defeated by the unfolding storm above us. According to the infotainment screen, we weren't driving up Fourth Avenue but were floating somewhere smack in the middle of the Narrows Straight, drifting toward the Atlantic, at least a mile off the shore. And judging by what I saw through the windows, perhaps the GPS wasn't wrong.

"Turn here," he said, his voice cutting through the relentless howl of the wind, the shape of a two-story townhouse looming in the dark before us. "Oh, God."

"What now?"

"The gate." He pointed. "The gate is open."

I could see it now, too. The waist-height wrought-iron gate was wide open, shaking and swinging in the wind. The post on one side had been ripped out of the ground by a colossal force and thrown a few feet away, lodging into a rosebush. Judging by the deep tracks in the mud that ran from the road into the tiny front yard, someone must have driven a large car straight through the gate, skidding to a sudden stop right next to the steps of the brick porch.

I saw Levy tense and reach for the door handle, and grabbed his shoulder before he could get out of the car. "Don't be stupid."

"He must be here," he hissed at me, trying to shake off my hand, his face white with terror and fury. "I can feel it."

"I doubt it. It looks like he's been here, but he's already gone. Or worse. This could be a trap. And if he is still inside, he will kill both of us if you rush in there like an idiot. You have to follow me, do you understand? We've only got one shot at it."

He took a few shaky breaths, trying to calm down, and finally gave me a nod.

I parked the car in front of the house, pulled out the gun, gritted my teeth, and stepped out into the storm.

The icy wind clawed at me like a hungry beast, tearing at my clothes and threatening to snatch me away. Raindrops the size of marbles pelted my skin, frigid water forcing its way into every nook and cranny of my clothing. I was drenched to the bone before I could take two steps, shivering like a leaf in a hurricane. In the darkness, the flashes of lightning cut through the sky, illuminating the world around me like fleeting snapshots of a camera. Each burst of light exposed the landscape in stark, frozen frames.

I leaned into the wind and rushed toward the house, the barrel of my gun swinging back and forth in a deadly arc, ready for any surprises. Levy was on my heels, relentlessly nudging me forward.

The lock on the door to the house was smashed in, and the wood around the keyhole splintered into a thousand pieces. As we stepped through the threshold and closed the door behind us, blocking out the raging storm outside, I saw what I feared the most. We were too late. Morton had already come and gone, leaving a trail of destruction behind him.

The house had been ransacked. The table in the dining room was on its side, the broken dishes scattered on the floor, their remnants like shuttered memories of happier times. A large TV on top of a walnut stand near the wall was still on, gray snow of static playing on its cracked surface in an endless loop. And in the farthest corner of the room, curled into a fetal position, there was a man. His face was pale, eyes closed. His right arm, stuffed under his rigid body, was bent at an unnatural angle. The man moaned softly at the sounds of our arrival, his gray lips moving as if whispering a prayer.

"Phil," Levy shouted. He rushed to his friend and kneeled beside him, turning him on his back and getting the broken arm from under his body.

Phil cried out softly and opened his eyes. He looked around, confusion on his face quickly replaced by a mask of terror. "The girls," he said weakly. "Check on the girls."

"Where?"

"Upstairs."

"Stay here," I barked at John, his wide eyes meeting mine for a moment before I turned and ran up the steps, gripping the pistol with both hands. The house shook and moaned as hurricane-strength winds buffeted its sides, the windows trembling hard as if straining against the very fabric of the storm.

I knew we were too late the moment I set foot on the second floor. The air hung heavy with the stench of fear and desperation. There was less destruction, but I could clearly see Morton's trail as he climbed the stairs before me. The faintest scuff marks on the wooden steps were like breadcrumbs leading me further into the heart of darkness. A woman, Phil's wife Kathy, I presumed, was lying on her side next to the kids' room, her eyes closed.

I checked the rooms first and, not finding anyone, came back to her side. She was alive, her breathing soft and steady. There were no visible wounds or broken bones as far as I could tell, but there was a large bump, the size of a golf ball, on the side of her head.

I left the woman undisturbed and went back down the stairs. Phil was sitting on the floor now, leaning against the wall and cradling his broken arm. Now that I could see him better, one side of his face was black and blue, a deep cut on his cheekbone still bleeding.

"The kids?"

"Taken, I'm afraid." I did my best to keep myself in check. Not to scream in horror and frustration.

"Oh God," he breathed, tears streaming down his face. "Kathy?"

"Your wife's alive and seems stable, but I'm certain she has a concussion, so do not try to move her. That can make things worse. Wait until the ambulance is here."

"I've tried calling 911," John said. "But nothing's going through. The lines are jammed. All I get is a busy signal. It must be the storm."

"Shit. Phil," I turned to the man, "do you have cameras around the property?"

"Yes. We have a security system," Phil said, pointing toward the back of the house with his good hand. "It's in my office. The code is 3447."

"Keep trying the phones. I'll be right back."

I rushed to the office, my heart pounding like a war drum, and opened the monitoring station. Four cameras watched over the house, two in the front and two in the back. I quickly scrolled through the list of video files until I found what I was looking for—a large white Mercedes SUV driving off the road and slamming its front grill into the gate.

A moment later, Morton emerged from the driver's seat, his tall, ominous figure silhouetted against the dark sky. He paused momentarily, his eyes scanning the area like a predator searching for prey. Then, he rushed toward the house and kicked the front door in, the sharp crack of splintering wood reverberating like a gunshot.

I leaned closer to the screen, my jaw clenching, as Morton disappeared into the house.

I fast-forwarded the video until he reappeared again a few minutes later, ushering two girls in front of him and into the SUV. I gritted my teeth as I watched his hands, almost gently, squeezing the shoulders of the kids as he guided them toward the vehicle.

The lights over me flickered, and then a moment later, the house plunged into the darkness, startling me. I stared at the black monitor before me, stood up, and rushed back to the living room.

"John? You okay?"

"Yes. Seems like the lights are out."

"Damn it." I took a shaky breath. "For a second, I thought Morton was back. Any luck with the phones?"

"No." John Levy stood up and walked to the window, peering outside. "And it looks like a rolling blackout."

"It's not just us?"

"I don't think so." He turned to me. "It's dark as far as I can see."

"Wait a second," I said, frantically digging into my pocket. I pulled out Jenkins's business card and dialed the direct number. It rang six times and clicked right when I was ready to give up.

"Hello?"

"Oh, thank God. Jenkins, this is Alex. I need you to trace a license plate for me," I said, not wasting any time on explanations. "A white Mercedes SUV."

"Shoot."

I gave him the numbers and held my breath as Jenkins checked the system.

"Okay," he said as he returned a few moments later. "I got it. The car is registered to Lucas Rimmon. He lives on a large property on Shore Road. The house was purchased at the end of last year."

"You got the address?"

"Yep." He gave me the location. "What are you—"

"Jenkins?" I pulled the phone away from my face and stared at the screen. "Fuck."

"Call dropped?" Levy said.

"Yeah." I tried calling Jenkins back, but the line didn't even ring this time. "Nothing. But I got the address. A mansion in Bay Ridge."

Levy checked his own cell phone. "I don't even have a signal. What do we do now?"

I looked at the two men. "Phil. Do you have any firearms?"

He shook his head. "No. I used to have a rifle but sold it last year."

"Okay, John. You'll have to stay here and help out. Keep an eye on Kathy. And keep trying the phones. Maybe you'll get lucky. I'm going to check on the address that Jenkins gave me. It's the only lead I've got."

"No." Levy stood up, a look of determination on his face. "I'm going with you. I have to."

"He's right," Phil said, forcing himself off the floor. "I'm useless with a broken arm, but John is pretty strong despite his frail appearance. He can be of help."

"Morton is a beast," I protested. "Without a weapon, you'll just be in my way. I can't worry about anyone else when I'm there. We'll both get killed if I'm distracted."

"Okay." Levy looked around and then marched to the kitchen counter, returning a moment later with a large chef's knife and stuffed it down his belt. "See? I got a weapon. Let's go."

"Well, shit." I watched Levy's stubborn face, weighing my options.

"Come on."

"Okay." I fixed him with a stare. "Under one condition. You're not running off on an impulse. No bullshit heroics. You follow my lead. You do what I say, how I say it, the moment I say it. Is that clear?"

"I got it." Levy gave me a nod. "I won't be a liability."

"Fine." I holstered the gun and headed for the door. "Let's do it."

THIRTY-SEVEN

"Holy hell," I yelled, swerving the car in surprise as a piece of ice the size of a cue ball struck the windshield. The glass cracked, concentric circles spreading away from the point of impact like ripples from a pebble hitting a pond's surface. A moment later, there was a massive blow on the roof, and another.

"Belt Parkway," John shouted over the cacophony of the raging storm and violent hail claps on the car's hood.

I nodded, taking a sharp right turn and gunning down the street as fast as I dared. We shot across the intersection a moment later, miraculously missing a dump truck heading north. The car jumped the curb and came to an abrupt stop under the overhead highway.

"That was close," I said, watching as hail pounded the street a few feet away, ripping through the awnings and shattering the windows in the building on the other side of the street. Large pieces of ice struck the road and the sidewalk, leaving pockmarks. The ice chunks disintegrated on impact, shards spraying the street like shrapnel.

"What in the world are we going to do?"

"There's nothing we can do," I said, watching the roofs of a few cars parked along the road cave in. "We just have to wait it out."

A few minutes later, the hail finally stopped, and I pulled out from our temporary refuge, speeding south again. But the storm only picked up in intensity, the wind howling like a wild demon as it pummeled our car. The rain subsided, but as we entered Bay Ridge, it started to snow—large, wet flakes sticking to the broken windshield. The wipers made an awful scraping sound as they dragged over the broken glass.

"You've got to be shitting me," I said, marveling at the view. The temperature continued to drop, and the snow danced, swirling and twisting in sinuous arcs as if a horde of ethereal white snakes had taken flight just above the surface of the road.

"Makes you wonder," Levy mumbled under his nose.

I said nothing, keeping my eyes peeled on the road. I knew exactly what he meant, though. The storm engulfing the city seemed apocalyptic. The entire city was out of power, and the darkness was nearly absolute. The blizzard choked the streets in an icy grip of death as if Lucifer himself was about to pay a visit. I shook my head. Contemplating if Morton had supernatural powers wasn't going to help us. The rational part of my brain rebelled against the mere notion of such an idea. Morton was no Lucifer. He was just a crazed man on a killing rampage, ready to hurt two of the most innocent souls of them all. The storm was just a coincidence. It would not stop me from getting to the house on Shore Road and, if I had to, putting a bullet in Morton's head.

And then a blinding brilliance shattered the darkness. A lightning bolt struck with a vengeance, its incandescent fingers reaching down from the boiling clouds above us to touch a towering tree just ahead. My ears popped as the shock wave hit the vehicle.

"Watch out!" Levy's voice pierced through the chaos, urgent and raw with fear.

Time seemed to slow down to a crawl as my foot slammed on the gas pedal, the engine roaring in response. The car surged forward, narrowly escaping the path of the falling tree, now a blazing inferno of jagged wood. I could feel the searing heat and smell the acrid scent of burning timber as we flew under it, the blazing branches slapping the trunk of the Corolla like the claws of a fire demon grasping at its escaping prey.

But then we were through, my heart thumping in my chest, and just a minute later, we were near Shore Road. Instead of turning, I forced the car over the curb and parked it on the sidewalk, the tall wall of a large estate partially blocking the wind.

"The entrance is on the other side," Levy said.

"I know. But we can't waltz through the front door," I said, unbuckling and stepping out into the blizzard. The cold stole my breath as the wind hit my face, my skin going numb within seconds. I walked to the wall and eyeballed its height. "Give me a boost."

Levy squatted, his back against the wall, and clasped his hands together, interlocking his fingers to make a stirrup. I stepped into his palms, and he grunted, catapulting me into the air. My fingers grabbed at the cold stone of the edge of the wall, and I pulled myself up, making non-lady-like noises as I went.

The wall was about two feet wide, and on the inner side of the garden, it was less than six feet above the ground.

The backyard sprawled below me like a meticulously crafted masterpiece. An ornate labyrinth of hedges, now covered by an inch of snow, was sculpted with a precision that almost didn't seem human. The winding paths led to the heart of the garden, where an imposing marble fountain stood tall, its water now frozen. Half a dozen statues surrounded the fountain's wide oval basin.

But my eyes were drawn to the other side of the yard, where a large house sat on the top of the hill. The hulking silhouette was dark, the curtains drawn everywhere, except one window on the second floor facing the ocean. I peered through the blizzard, and my heart skipped a bit as I saw two small figures sitting on the chairs beside each other. A large candle was set on the table behind the two girls, throwing wild shadows around the room, its flame unsteady.

"Alex," I heard the voice from below and glanced back at Levy. "Let's go. Help me up."

"Come on." I lay flat on the span of the wall and reached as far down as I could. John took a few steps back and ran up the wall, grabbing my hands. He was heavier than he looked. I groaned, pulling him up with all my might until he threw himself over the wall, and we lost balance, tumbling into the garden below.

The hedges softened the initial blow, but then John fell on top of me, both of us going through the soft branches of a bush and into an unforgiving embrace of the hard ground. The impact knocked the air out of my lungs, making me gasp in pain as I struggled to get my bearings.

He recovered first, pulling me up and dusting me off.

"It's a miracle I didn't cut my leg," he said, pulling the knife from his belt.

"I saw the kids," I said, leaning closer to his face. "They are in the study upstairs. I think they are still okay."

"Good. Let's keep them that way."

I pulled the gun from my holster and headed toward the house, the wind swatting me in the back, my fingers burning from the cold. We crossed the large patio, leaving prints in the snow, and a moment later, I stood in front of a sliding door leading to the kitchen. It was dark inside, but I could see the outlines of the furniture and, in the opening at the far side of the room, the stairs to the second floor.

"Come on," I whispered, more to myself than to Levy, and tried the door. It wasn't locked. I pulled on it with my left hand as slowly and quietly as possible until there was a gap wide enough for me to squeeze through, and I stepped into the kitchen.

It was quiet, the warm air infused with the scent of jasmine and burning wood, making my skin tingle. I went deeper into the kitchen and turned back momentarily, trying to see where Levy was. And that's when something large and heavy smashed into my side.

It catapulted me through the air, my ribs catching the side of the kitchen island. I slid on the slick marble, the gun roaring in my hands, and crashed on the other side of the platform. My trusty HK, knocked out from my grip by the impact, clattered deeper into the kitchen. I turned, getting on all fours, and that's when I saw Morton emerge from the darkness and rush toward me.

It seemed that my bullet had found its mark. His left shoulder was bleeding, but it didn't slow him down. Before I could move, he was on me, throwing me back to the ground, his hands swatting mine aside and going for my throat.

His fingers crushed my neck with such force, for a second, I thought he was going to rip my head off. My vision started to dim, but then I saw Levy jump on Morton's back, the knife slashing wildly. The pressure from my neck disappeared as Morton roared in agony and rose to his feet, trying to shake Levy off.

I flipped on my stomach and lunged toward the gun when I heard a yelp of pain followed by a crashing sound. I didn't stop to look, but before I could reach my pistol, two hands grabbed my ankles and pulled me away, flipping me over. My ribs met the kitchen island again, something cracking inside me as a hot flash of pain went down my torso. I could see Levy's feet sticking out from behind the island. They weren't moving.

Morton, his face twisted with rage and his crisp white shirt soaked in blood, pulled me closer and straddled me, pinning me to the ground. I struck him in the face, but he only shook his head like a bull annoyed by a fly. Then his hand struck out with lightning speed, hitting me across the face. I wheezed, blood gushing out of my eyebrow and nose, and then his fingers were on my throat again, no doubt planning to finish the job.

I buckled and pushed with all my might, but there was no use. Bright specks of light appeared in my vision, and then I saw nothing, thrashing in darkness as his fingers continued to bear down on my neck.

But then the pressure disappeared, and my blurry vision returned a moment later. Morton was still straddling me, but his eyes were dazed, and I could see John Levy collapsing behind him, the remnants of a broken kitchen stool in his hands.

I thrashed under Morton as his eyes started to refocus and pulled my legs out, kicking him in the chest as hard as I could. Free now, I scrambled away from him on my back and buttocks, trying to gain distance. He shook his head, recovering, and lunged for me again just as my fingers wrapped around the pistol handle. I leveled it and squeezed the trigger.

The bullet hit him on the side of the lower jaw, almost completely taking it off. Morton rose off his knees, a gurgling sound coming out of his ruined mouth, his eyes wild with pain and confusion. I shot again, this time hitting him square in the head, and he went down like a puppet whose strings had been cut off. I lowered the gun, propped myself on my elbows, and leaned on the side of the kitchen island, breathless.

I tried to call for Levy but only managed a pitiful croak at first. I swallowed, doing my best not to pass out from the pain in my throat, and tried again. "John."

"I'm here," he said, his voice thick with pain. "I think I might have broken my foot. And my ribs. And probably something else."

"Okay." I forced myself off the floor and stood up, swaying on my feet. "Stay here. I'll get the girls."

I walked up the stairs, heading for the light, keeping my pistol ready for any surprises. The house was quiet, and as I made it to the landing, it dawned on me—it was quiet outside, too. The storm was abating, and the wind was dying down.

I crept through the hallway and then, a few moments later, stood in front of a large mahogany door leading to the study.

"Emily? Sarah? Are you there? My name's Alex, and I'm here with Uncle John."

There was silence at first and then, a moment later, a whisper-quiet response. "We are here."

I stepped into the room, squinting my eyes against the light of a large candle. Two girls, their faces pale, sat by the window in plush, old-fashioned rocking chairs, holding each other's hands. "Anyone else is in here?"

They shook their heads in unison without making a sound, clearly not sure what to make of a woman with a gun whose face was covered in bruises and blood.

"Don't be afraid of me," I said, putting the gun down and getting on one knee. More to preserve my strength than to get on their level. "Your parents sent me, and John is here with me. He's waiting downstairs."

"Are they okay?" one of the twins asked.

"Yes," I said. It wasn't the right time to explain the intricacies of Phil's and Kathy's conditions.

"What about Uncle John?" the girl said. "We heard fighting. And gunshots."

"He's fine," I said. "Bruised up like me, but he'll live. He will be brand new in a couple of weeks. Are you okay? Can you walk?"

They glanced at each other as if confirming that it was okay to trust me and nodded.

"Great," I said, doing my best not to groan as I stood up again. "Come on. Let's get you the hell out of here."

THIRTY-EIGHT

"I'll be right back," I said after getting the girls in my beat-up Corolla's back seat. It took us a long time to bring John down the winding steps. He couldn't quite put his weight on his left foot, and his right shoulder was dislocated, rendering his arm useless. Considering that at least three of my ribs had been broken, I didn't quite enjoy the walk either, especially with John leaning on me for support, but it wasn't the right time to complain.

"Where the hell are you going?" John asked, his face contorted in pain. "We need to bring the girls back."

"I forgot my gun in the house," I lied. "Just give me a minute and we'll get on the road."

I walked away from the car before he could say anything else. My trusty firearm was just where it was supposed to be, tucked securely into its holster, but there was still some business in the mansion I couldn't leave unfinished.

I went around the giant wall and, cursing under my breath, climbed the stone steps again, this time entering the house from the front door. The kitchen, still shrouded in shadows, loomed to my right. I averted my eyes from the crumpled figure on the floor and a pool of dark liquid surrounding Morton's head. It wasn't the first time I took a life, but it's never easy. Even if the life you took belonged to a psychopath like Morton.

The people you kill... They always come back to haunt you when you expect them the least. In nightmares. In daydreams. The mind is creative to remind you of what you've done. It could be a passage in a book or a phrase you hear on the TV. But before you know it, you're back to where it happened. When you are forced to relive the violence and ask yourself if you could do something different to avoid that. Because no matter whose life you take, you always pay for it with a piece of your soul.

I walked through the enormous foyer with tacky Roman columns adorned at the top with golden bas-reliefs and an even tackier white grand piano at the base of the stairs, its white keys looming in the darkness like the fangs of a strange monster. As I climbed the steps to the second floor, the wooden planks creaked under my feet. The creepy, lonely sound echoed throughout the house. I passed the study where I had found the girls and walked to the end of the hallway.

A large, thick steel door stood in front of me. I'd seen it when I climbed the stairs for the first time, the hulking silhouette in the distance, like a portal to another dimension. At that moment, I'd chosen to ignore it. Convinced myself that I had other, more urgent things to take care of—save the girls, look after John, bring everyone back. But as we hobbled down the steps, John's good arm wrapped around my shoulders for support, I knew I'd made a mistake. It didn't even matter what I believed. But if there was even a remote, one-in-a-billion chance that Morton's bloodthirsty quest wasn't a giant string of coincidences wrapped in a fever dream of a sick individual, I had to do something about it. To make sure no one ever got access to what started it all—the ancient book of evil. The guide that broke Morton's fragile mind and sent him on a killing spree.

And here I was, standing in a dark hallway before the door, my courage suddenly gone. What if it wasn't just the book that awaited me there? After all, Morton usually took his victims straight to the place where he tortured them. Yet, I found Emily and Sarah sitting peacefully in the study as if they had been waiting for something.

I assumed we just happened to come in time, but what if I was wrong? What if the spot in the middle of that wretched place was taken by someone else? Perhaps I was about to walk into a crime scene—a naked body stretched to its limit, disemboweled before the poor soul was allowed to expire. The way I would have died if DD hadn't found me in time.

I drew a sharp breath and let it out slowly, bile rising in my throat. The last thing I needed was to throw up in Morton's house.

I looked at the door. It was slightly ajar, a line of bright incandescent light streaming from the gap. It seemed the room had its own power supply as the lights in the house were still off. There was a ticking sound coming from inside, like a clock. Four clicks and a hiss, and then four clicks again. I shuddered, cold sweat running down my back. I needed to open that door, yet I couldn't bring myself to do it.

"Come on, Alex," I whispered, touching the round handle. It was cold and smooth, like ice. I was hyperventilating now, unable to control my breathing. "Just fucking do it."

I pulled on the handle and swung the door open, staring at another padded room.

"Thank God," I whispered as I looked at the empty space. It was larger and brighter than the one Morton had been so kind to introduce me to. Instead of a pulley system in the middle, there was a large table. It had no legs or drawers and seemed to have been machined from a solid piece of polished steel. Strange symbols were carved on the sides of the table, and a set of restraints had been attached to its surface with welded anchors. Thick leather bonds would have secured the victim's legs, arms, and neck. I suppressed a shudder, thinking of what he had planned to do on that table.

And there was something else—a simple wooden podium installed a few feet away from the sacrificial table.

A closed leather book, somewhat smaller than I had imagined, lay on top of it. My eyes were immediately drawn to the thick cover, etched with deep grooves resembling pulsing veins, as though waiting to be infused with the essence of life itself.

As I traced the intricate design with my gaze, my pulse quickened —a horned and winged angel adorned the cover, exquisitely detailed, radiating grace and power. Its inhuman eyes seemed to follow me. Observing. Judging. The pendant from the necklace, the missing piece of the puzzle, was neatly embedded in the angel's body, like a key, its olivine pallasite glowing. Ready to reveal the secrets hidden within the book.

I reached for the tome and hesitated, my hand trembling above the cover. A part of me wanted to open it and leaf through the pages. Try to figure out the book's provenance. To finally put to rest the question of whether anything that had happened to me and others over the past few weeks had been more than the work of Morton's sick imagination.

I lowered my hand, the tips of my fingers resting on tanned leather. The surface was smooth except for the rough edges of the grooves.

The book was cool to the touch. Ordinary. The sensation seemed to have broken the spell. It was like touching a leather purse. I picked up the tome, stuffed it into my pants, next to the holster, and headed out of the room.

"It took you awhile," Levy said when I returned to the car. "Found it?"

"Yep," I said, without elaborating. The engine revved, and I maneuvered the car off the sidewalk and onto the rain-slicked road, the tires hissing as they struggled for purchase. The drizzle still persisted, but the storm had already passed, leaving in its wake a trail of black, heavy clouds rolling toward the ocean like a routed army. The wipers intermittently swept across the damaged windshield as I drove, leaving a better view of the world awakening from the storm's grip.

Before long, the first rays of the sun peeked through the parting clouds, and the soft glow spilled across the landscape, casting the wet streets in a warm, golden hue.

"I feel like I haven't seen the sun in months," Levy said, cradling his arm.

I smiled and nodded. I knew exactly how he felt.

Phil had been sitting on the porch steps when we pulled up. Emily and Sarah stormed out of the car and into their father's embrace the moment the car stopped. He grimaced as they disturbed his broken arm but didn't let go.

"Kathy?" I mouthed to him.

"She's fine," he said. "Came to about ten minutes after you'd left. Resting now."

As if on cue, the door to the house swung open, and Kathy came outside. Her face was pale, and she didn't seem steady on her feet, but she rushed down the stairs and joined the rest of her family in a fierce hug.

"What happened to that man?" Phil asked.

"He won't be a problem anymore."

"Thank you," he said. "My family owes you a debt we'll never be able to repay. If you ever need anything, just ask."

I nodded, embarrassed. As if sensing it, my phone vibrated, and I pulled it out of my pocket, multiple voicemail and text messages appearing on its screen one after the other. "It looks like I've got service. I'm going to call DD. John, call the ambulance for Phil and Kathy. And for yourself, too."

"Are you okay?" Deluca blurted as soon as the line connected.

"It's hard to overstate how nice it is when DD cares," I said, smiling.

"I always care." He tried to sound gruff, but I could hear the softness in his voice. "Where are you? Jenkins said you called asking to track a license plate, but the call dropped. We sent someone to the address just in case, but the car got disabled during the hailstorm. Are you still there?"

"No. Morton is...was there," I said, steeling myself for what was about to come. "He's dead now. I shot him in self-defense. He kidnapped two girls and was planning to kill them. Luckily, I got there soon enough."

"Where are the kids now?"

"They are with their parents." I gave him the address. "I'm happy to give you a statement, too. I just was hoping I could go home first. I'm sure tons of people need to talk to me, and I'm exhausted."

"Of course." There was some noisy breathing on the other side of the line, as if he was deliberating whether to say anything else. "I'm truly sorry, Alex. This must've been hell."

"Thanks. I'll see you in a couple of hours. In the meantime, it'd be great if you could have somebody come over here."

I stuffed the phone in the back pocket of my jeans and turned around to see Levy staring at me. "You didn't tell him about me. Why?"

I shrugged. "Technically, you're still a fugitive. You probably should turn yourself in, considering we got Morton, but I didn't want to make that decision for you. I think I owe you that much."

"Thanks." He gave me an awkward smile. "I'll stick around until the police come. It's time to surrender. I'm fairly confident I'll be acquitted of the charges. Though this time, I'll probably opt for a good lawyer."

"I think so, too." I watched him closely. "I'd give you a hug, but I don't think your shoulder would appreciate it. Or my ribs."

"That's okay." His smile grew wider. "Maybe next time."

"Next time?"

"I still need to pay you for your services. Especially," he made a vague gesture with his good hand, "since it looks like Morton stiffed you on a payment. Perhaps over dinner?"

"Sure," I said and headed toward the Corolla. My car was a sorry sight—a busted windshield and ruined paintwork. My left mirror was hanging by a wire.

"Saturday?" he called after me. "I'll pick you up since your car is, well, you know."

"Sure," I said. "As long as DD doesn't change his mind and put me away. You never know with this guy."

"I think my chances of being locked up are much higher than yours."

"Touché," I said. "Didn't think about that. Good luck."

I got in the car and started down the road. As I was halfway down the block, I caught a glimpse of the house in my rearview mirror. Two girls hugging their parents. John was standing aloof, leaning on a broken gate, and clearly in pain, but with a huge smile on his face.

I turned on Fourth Avenue, heading south, and they disappeared, replaced by the view of fluffy clouds. I turned on the radio, and the sexy baritone came on, telling the city that the worst was over and that the storm had ended. Somewhere in the distance, I could hear the sounds of an approaching siren. Then, a few moments later, an ambulance with a police cruiser in tow roared past me as they headed north.

I smiled. My cheeks were getting wet, and I wiped them clean with the back of my hand. I hated crying, but at that moment, I didn't care. No one could see me now, and I was heading home.

THIRTY-NINE

I came to the cafe on time, but DD was already there, sipping on a large cup of black coffee, his face splitting into a wide grin as he stood up to greet me.

"Your shiner is almost gone. A few more days and you might be able to pass for a respectable lady."

"Don't you worry. No one will ever confuse me with anything even remotely respectable." I gingerly touched my eyebrow with my fingertips. "It wasn't too terrible. Only four stitches. The doc said I got lucky, and it shouldn't leave a scar. Nothing like your back."

DD cringed and instinctively moved his shoulders up and down. On our second day as partners, we went in to check on a domestic dispute call in one of the projects in Alphabet City. Instead of finding an arguing couple, we were ambushed by the members of a radical anti-police organization.

We were able to fall back and barricade ourselves inside an office in the lobby of the building. But not before my arm was grazed by a bullet, and DD was shot through his triceps and got a nasty stab under his right shoulder blade. He got lucky as the blade missed his lung and other vital organs. Still, it took the doctors twenty-five stitches, and DD spent a week in a hospital before he was allowed to be discharged. He still sported a large, faint scar that he said ached every time the air pressure would drop. It was an ongoing joke at the precinct that Deluca knew better than any weatherman when the rain was coming.

"Coffee?" he asked, changing the subject. "It's almost as shitty as at the station."

"I'm good. What's the latest?"

"Quite a few things. You're no longer a person of interest. Your statement had more eyeballs on it than I'd ever seen in my career. Us, the feds, journos. We even had somebody drop by from the White House."

"The White House?"

"You know how it is." He smiled. "With a story that big, everybody wants a slice of the pie. I suspect there will be a lot of chest-thumping and big speeches for as long as the public cares. After that, they'll move on to something else."

"Are you getting a promotion?"

"You're funny." DD chuckled and took a sip of his coffee. "Nah. I don't need a promotion. As long as they approve my OT, I'm good."

"What's up with John?"

"It's a bit complicated because he was deeply entangled in this. But from what I've heard, they are almost done putting the pieces of the puzzle together. My guess is they'll release him by Friday morning. It doesn't hurt that he's got the best defense lawyer money can buy."

"So I've heard." I didn't tell DD, but I spoke to Phil after I'd given statements to the NYPD and the feds. Phil told me he was hiring a white-shoe law firm to represent Levy. Though John, being his stubborn self, of course, insisted on paying the bills. "Did anyone figure out why Morton targeted Levy in the first place?"

"I don't think so." DD shook his head. "That's something I'm afraid we might never find out. Morton was pretty wealthy himself. Apparently, he was a brilliant chemist. There were some psychotropic formulas he'd patented over the years that paid him handsome royalties. I guess he came across Levy in social circles when he was still at the helm of that financial firm. Or, perhaps, read about him in the papers after his wife's accident and considered him a good target. One thing's for sure."

"What?"

"If he hadn't confessed to you about him being a chemist, we would have had a hard time clearing Levy. The scope of the network he'd built was truly staggering. Multiple corporate shells. Trusts. Numbered banking account. And all of them were connected to Levy in a way that was just far enough removed to raise suspicion and lead a good investigator toward John but not too far where it'd be lost. Levy owes you his freedom."

"And I owe him my life," I said. "And you, too. It seems like I'm in debt all around."

An awkward silence settled over our table, neither of us willing to break it.

"You saved mine once," DD finally said, fidgeting in his chair. "I guess I'm just paying you back. So, we're even now."

"I thought we were already even," I blurted out before I could stop myself. "Ah, shit. Sorry, I couldn't help it. Look—"

"It's okay, Alex." He fixed me with a stare. "We both fucked up that day."

"How so? I thought I was the only one." I shook my head. "I'm just going to shut up now."

He gave me a soft smile. "Your mistake was bigger, yes. But I should have listened to you. Because if I had, you wouldn't have been in that situation to begin with. Wouldn't have to make that call."

My eyes burned a little, but if DD was hoping to see me tear up, he was going to be disappointed. "So, now that we got that out of the way, what's next for you?"

"Same shit." He shrugged. "Catching bad guys, getting shot at, drinking burnt coffee. How about you? You didn't leave on the best terms, but after this, you'd have some serious political capital at the precinct."

"Meaning what exactly?"

"Have you considered coming back?"

"Well," I said, "the benefits are certainly better with the city. The pay is probably better, too. I'm not sure you've heard, but instead of paying his bill, the last client tried to kill me."

"There were rumors."

"Yeah. Didn't like that guy. But..." I trailed off.

"But what?" DD leaned closer to me, his face turning serious. "I mean it, Alex. If you ever wanted to try it, this would be the moment. I'm sure some people would grovel and whine behind the scenes. But I think we could make it happen if I pulled some strings. You're a great detective. Always have been. You're reckless sometimes, but your instincts are second to none. The cap would be on board."

"And you know that, how exactly?"

"Because he told me." DD leaned back again. "Not in that many words, but yes."

"I appreciate it." I looked at my former partner and placed my hand over his. He stiffened but didn't move. "I really do. Especially coming from you. And I know what I'm about to say will sound corny, but I feel like I've found my purpose for the first time in my life. I like the independence. I like that I can pick and choose what to work on, even if the choices sometimes are less than glorious."

"I see."

"Maybe you got it backward, DD."

"What?"

"Maybe it's not me who should be considering going back to the NYPD. Maybe it's you who should consider coming to the dark side."

"Like what, becoming a PI? Working for myself?"

"Not for yourself. For me. As a junior partner."

"A *junior* partner, you say?"

"Still a partner," I said. "And I was there first. Also, I caught the infamous Valentine Killer. You see, we can't possibly be on equal footing. But I promise to give you a long leash."

"Very funny."

"You know, we'd make a good team," I said, smiling. "And I'm only half joking. We could open a bigger office and hire a few people. Watts and Deluca. Has a nice ring to it."

"It does." DD returned a smile, his eyes crinkling at the corners. "But as much as I'd enjoy that, I think we're better off as friends."

"It works for me."

I stood up, and DD followed suit. I offered him a hand, and he looked at it for some time as if considering whether shaking it was a good idea. Then he took a step closer and gently pulled me into a hug. I tensed first but then leaned back into him, breathing in the familiar scent of his cheap cologne and burnt coffee. It smelled like home.

"Take care, Alex. Be careful out there."

"You too." I watched him leave the cafe and back into the cruiser, the crowd parting in front of his broad shoulders like the sea before Moses. A smile played on my lips. The past few weeks might have been hell, but at least I got my best friend back. That surely was worth something.

FORTY

Saturday was bright and hot. A proper summer day. A few clouds lazily floated in the sky. They were brilliantly white and puffy, as if they jumped straight out of a Pixar movie. I could hear the traffic on the Verrazzano Bridge somewhere behind me—the impatient honking and revving of the engines. I'm sure an out-of-towner, not accustomed to that noise, might have found it annoying. But for me, it was soothing. Comforting. Like a steady rhythm of a giant heart.

I was sitting on the front steps of my house, looking at the cracks between the weather-worn bricks of my porch and wondering where on earth I would find a mason. Surely my sister, Tina, would know one, and surely if I used him, I'd have to sell the house to pay the bill. I think that's what they call a conundrum.

I saw a gray Toyota Corolla pull up in front of the house, and then the window rolled down, revealing John Levy's face.

"Is it new? I didn't know you had a Corolla," I said, inspecting the vehicle. "It's exactly like mine. And how are you driving, anyway? Don't you have a broken foot? And a messed-up shoulder?"

"Hello to you too, Alex. And that's a lot of questions." He smiled through the window. "It's not exactly like your Corolla because it has better options. It is also not my car. It's yours."

I stared at him. "I know how my car looks, and that's not it. My car is still in the shop."

"I'm afraid the title says otherwise."

"Wait." I shook my head, feeling extremely stupid. "Did you buy me a car?"

He made a face. "It's part of my payment. Consider it a bonus."

"A part of the payment? Are you crazy? I can't possibly take a car from you."

"Why not? Didn't you say you were expecting to get paid fifty grand for finding the amulet?"

I made a face. "It was supposed to be one hundred."

"Oh well. I guess when you don't plan on paying, it's easy to throw up numbers. But your car is toast, and I think fifty grand is a fair price for services rendered." He tilted his head. "Are we still going for a meal or what?"

I looked at him, considering. "Give me a minute to powder my nose and put on my shoes."

"Sure," he said. "And to answer your second question—apparently, I've only sprained my ankle, and my shoulder is now fixed. But I have to wear a boot, and my arm still hurts like a mother, so I'd rather you drive if that's okay with you. And, well, it's your car."

I sighed. "Sounds like I don't have a choice. Be right back."

"That is a nice car," I said, getting behind the wheel a few minutes later.

"That's a nice bag." He nodded at the Kelly bag on my lap.

"Funny story," I said, pulling into the street. "The wife of a drug cartel boss gave it to me. I lost it when Morton ambushed me, but when the police swept his place, they found my prints on the bag. They didn't know what to do with it, so they returned it to me. I guess I'm keeping it."

"It sounds very much like an Alex Watts story."

I laughed out loud and winced as my ribs crackled with pain. "It does, doesn't it?"

I thought we'd stay local, but after much bickering, he made me drive to a French brasserie in Lower Manhattan. There, we were ushered in past the long line of people and seated at the best table in the restaurant.

"You've been here a few times, it seems."

"An astute observation." He nodded. "If I didn't know any better, I would think you were a detective."

It seemed Levy, indeed, had been there a few times as two waiters hovered around us the entire time. The manager came to check on *Mr. Levy,* and, at the end of the meal, the chef himself dropped by to see if everything was to *Mr. Levy's* satisfaction.

"Here's the rest of the pay," he said, passing me an envelope as we sipped coffee over a shared creme brûlée.

"All right." I pocketed it. "I'll file it under *I like you, but not enough to work for free.*"

"Oh, so you do like me?"

I smiled and tilted my head, watching the man. He was joking, but he wasn't entirely off the mark. There was something about him that I liked. He was a good man in that old-fashioned way that was almost impossible to find anymore. For a moment, I wished I had met him before he inadvertently introduced me to Morton. But I knew myself—I'd only screw it up. John Levy was better off without me complicating his life. I changed the subject instead. "What's next for you?"

"I have a job interview next week."

"You don't say?"

"Yes. It's nothing very fancy, but it's better than my previous mind-numbing gig. Besides," he rapped his fingers on the table, "it seems like writing won't pan out as a career."

"No." I chuckled. "Please, no more novels."

"I promise. There is one mystery that still remains about this whole affair."

"Just one?" I said. "You never told me what happened to you in your apartment."

"There was this woman." His gaze wandered, as if he recalled something important. "I'd met her on the subway, and there was this instant connection. We had a fling, although I don't know if that's the right name for it. But it was on and off, and I confided in her about the book at some point."

"Did it freak her out?"

"No." He shook his head. "Quite the contrary. She encouraged me to finish it. I didn't think much of it at first. I just thought she was being supportive. But then it almost felt like she was pushing me to do it."

"Morton's driver who took me to him was a woman. And the police couldn't find any leads. She just disappeared into thin air."

"What did she look like?"

"Nothing special." I focused. "Short-ish. Perhaps five foot one. Plain face, button nose, brown eyes. Brown hair with a touch of red."

"That's not her."

"To be fair, maybe she was just being supportive."

He shook his head. "When I opted for a public defender, she showed up in the interrogation room. And she...showed me things."

"What?" I leaned closer. "What kind of things?"

"It's hard to describe. We were outside, looking at some kind of an ancient battlefield. Dead soldiers everywhere. Dead horses. She said Luca would kill my friends if I didn't finish the book." He paused. "And yours."

"That's..." I trailed off.

"Hard to believe. But so was the entire case. But now that I'm hearing Morton was a talented chemist, perhaps it was psychotropics. I have no idea what to think."

"What do you think happened to the woman?"

"I don't know." He shrugged. "I just hope I won't ever see her again."

"That's a twist. Did you tell the police about her?"

"Yes. But Deluca said there was nothing on the cameras in the precinct and they couldn't find anything at Morton's house that would lead them to her. I didn't have much to give them to go on either. And having a name and a physical description isn't enough to find a person in a city of eight million souls, as someone wise once told me."

"True." I hesitated. "How are the girls?"

He grimaced. "They seem fine. Phil has arranged for therapy, and it looks like it's going pretty well so far. The doctor says they should have no lasting effects if they stick to the schedule. Young minds are incredibly resilient. But only time will tell for sure. I'm glad we got there when we did."

We sat in silence for a few moments, the untouched creme brûlée getting cold on the table between us.

"Do you have any hobbies?" he asked, trying to break the ice.

"I used to play the violin when I was little."

"How appropriate." He smiled. "A detective who plays the violin. Are you any good?"

"I used to be. But it seems like I never find the time to do it anymore." I sighed. "Or, as my sis put it, I was never disciplined enough to keep my butt in the chair long enough. What about you?"

"Now that writing is off the list, I'm thinking about doing some family history research. I heard some cool anecdotes when I was growing up. Would be nice to dig in and find out if any of them were true."

"Tell me some."

"My great-great-grandfather allegedly had a button factory in Germany before the war."

"A button factory?"

"Yeah." He smiled. "It sounds weird, doesn't it? It'd be interesting to learn what happened to it. Another one was that when my grandmother was born, he bought her a necklace that supposedly had a very rare meteorite in its pendant."

"Interesting." I kept my voice as level as I could. "What kind of a meteorite?"

"I've no idea." He shrugged. "I think it was lost during the war. I doubt it's something I'd be able to find after so many years."

We drove back to Brooklyn in comfortable silence. If there was some ambiguity before dinner about which way our relationship was leaning, it was gone now. We were firmly entrenched within the friend zone and fully aware of it.

I dropped Levy at his place and, after watching him hobble up the stairs in his orthopedic boot, drove home.

But I was not ready to retire for the evening yet. I stopped by the house and, after picking up a few things, got back on the Belt Parkway, heading east.

About forty minutes later, I drove off the main road in Far Rockaway, followed a dirt path toward the ocean, and parked the Corolla next to a dune.

As I stepped out of the car, the wind whipped at me, filling my lungs with the salty ocean scent. I'd been here many times before. A public beach was just half a mile to my left, and a boardwalk a quarter mile to my right. But here, squeezed between two dunes, I was alone. A lonely speck at the edge of the world.

I walked around the car and opened the trunk, looking at the strange ensemble of items on the floor. A leather-bound book, a hammer. And a small canister of gasoline.

I glanced around, ensuring nobody was watching, and took out the book, placing it a few yards away from the car. Then, pressing on it with my knee, I reached for the hammer, my fingers tightly gripping the wooden handle. Carefully, I maneuvered the claw, feeling it make contact with the smooth surface of the stone. I leaned into it, prying the pendant free.

It rolled off the book, coming to rest on top of the sand, its multifaceted sides throwing amber-colored glares around it.

I picked it up, placed it on a small rock nearby, and then smashed it with the hammer, not giving myself time to reconsider. It burst into a million pieces like a delicate champagne flute falling from a great height, its sparkling shards burying into the sand.

"And now the main attraction," I said, thoroughly dousing the book with gasoline and stepping back before throwing a match. The fire whooshed, fed by the wind, blue flames dancing on the leather cover as the pages curled and blackened as if in agony. I glanced at what looked like pencil drawings on one of the pages, reminiscent of the Vitruvian Man, but they soon disappeared, consumed by the insatiable fire demon.

I watched the fire fizzle and finally die down, the wind ripping apart the ash carcass of the tome and scattering it over the dune. When it was done, I picked at the bonfire with a stick, ensuring no pages remained, and, satisfied, walked back to the Corolla. My mission here was done, and it was time to go home.

I opened the car door, pulled out my phone, and threw it into a cupholder, ready to sit down. The phone buzzed as if protesting such rough handling. I picked it up again, a lone email message notification blinking on the screen. The subject line read:

HELP

"Oh, it better be good," I muttered. "Last time the word HELP was in my inbox, the world almost ended."

I settled into the seat, watching the ocean for a few moments. The sun was already below the horizon, but the sky was still bright, with red and yellow hues coloring the water into a color resembling the pallasite—the rock that had traveled billions of miles before crashing into this world. There was a pang of regret in my stomach for smashing it with the hammer. It felt like I was betraying John Levy and his family. But I couldn't take the risk. Not after everything that had happened. The lives lost. The stone had to be destroyed, and the book burned. There was no going back now. He'd understand. Perhaps one day, many years from now, I'd come clean, and hopefully, he'd forgive me for what I'd done.

I started the engine and returned my attention to the phone, clicking the message open.

"Ms. Watts. I hope this finds you well. My name is Simon Blackwood, and I have a rather peculiar case I was hoping you could help me with."

JOIN THE STORY

Thank you for reading MADNESS. I hope you enjoyed it.

If you liked this book, please take a moment and leave an honest review. Reviews are important for authors and help us sell more books and thus spend more time writing new stories you can enjoy.

And, of course, don't forget to join the newsletter to learn about upcoming releases, exclusive free content, and more. You can do it right here:

wesleycross.com

Thanks again for reading, and I hope to see you soon!